MURDER UNEARTHED

KAT AND MOUSE BOOK 3

ANITA WALLER

BLOODHOUND
— BOOKS —

Print ISBN: -978-1-912986-42-2

For Janet and Peter Stubbs,
long-time friends who have
supported my work from day one.

It's frightening how easy it is to commit murder in America. Just a drink too much. I can see myself doing it. In England, one feels all the social restraints holding one back. But here, anything can happen.

W H Auden

CHAPTER ONE

Rain lashed down, turning the ground of Eyam churchyard into a quagmire. His wellingtons sank in the mud beyond ankle depth, and lifting the spade was an effort with the weight of the heavy mud on it.

He could see little; a moonless night, although hampering his own vision, was also hampering the vision of the rest of the residents around the area, and that, coupled with it being the iciest night of the winter so far, was keeping everyone indoors. His fingers were numb with cold, but when he went out at the beginning of the evening he had no idea he would end up digging the earth out of a grave to put in a new body to join the current incumbent. He hadn't brought any gloves. And he'd never killed anyone before, so didn't know the routine of murder. If he'd known it meant doing this sort of thing, he'd maybe have reconsidered his actions. All she'd had to do was say yes.

He dug until every limb ached and his eyes were stinging with rainwater. He judged he had gone down about three feet and he cautiously peered into the hole. What if he could see parts of a skeleton sticking out of the soil?

Silly sod, he thought. *It's too fucking dark to see owt.* But he decided enough was enough, no more excavating in case he found bones. That would proper freak him out.

Her body was lying to the side of where he had been digging, and he tugged on her feet to drag her towards the hole. Her boot came off as he pulled and he dropped her in fright. He wasn't cut out for this. He picked up her legs once again and slid her across the piled-up mud, balancing her somewhat precariously before giving her the final push that sent her toppling into the grave already sodden with water in the bottom. He shovelled the earth back in.

He could hear his dad's words echoing around his brain. *Always carry a shovel and your wellies in your car boot between October and April, lad. You never know when you'll need it living out here in t'Peaks.* It had been the only advice his dad had given him when he'd rushed home with his driving test pass certificate; perhaps his dad should have told him that if a lass says no, you don't kill her because of it. He was exhausted.

He flattened the mound as much as he could, then walked up and down on it to compact it further before stepping back and staring at it. 'Silly cow,' he growled. 'You made me do this.' He spotted the boot that had fallen off. Picking it up he shoved it inside his jacket. He would throw it in somebody's dustbin when he reached home.

The area looked a mess, mud evident everywhere on the surrounding grassed parts, and he wearily trudged back down to the car, his shovel over his shoulder. He opened the car boot, threw in the heavy spade and decided against changing back into his shoes. He'd have to make sure he cleaned out the footwell before his dad saw it. He'd go mad at the muck in all the nooks and crannies.

He hoped Eyam was far enough away from where he lived in Calver to put the cops off thinking he'd had owt to do with it; he'd have to lie low for a bit, no more drinking, no more going out at night, until the mud had cleared and no one would guess there was a new body in the graveyard.

He didn't look back as he drove away. He'd not got to know her: a first date. She hadn't talked much, a quiet lass, said she lived with her mum in Castleton.

He peered into the gloomy night as he drove, wishing he'd done something about the headlight that no longer worked. Good job it was gone midnight and there wasn't much on the road. He undid his seatbelt so that he could lean forward. He could see naff all. He negotiated his way carefully; his windscreen wipers were nearly useless and that, combined with the missing headlight, was proving to be a pain. He put his foot down and headed towards Stoney Middleton.

He didn't see the man with the huge Alsatian until the last minute and he swerved to avoid them. He aquaplaned on the surface water pouring down from the hills and smashed into a stone wall. His car stopped without the use of brakes, and his head went through the windscreen. He came to rest atop the wall, with smoke puthering from the engine.

The man with the dog dialled 999, explained where he was, and ran across the road. He dragged what he could see was a youngish chap from the wall and tried to get him away from the car. He didn't like the look of the smoke.

By the time the ambulance arrived they found him sitting on the kerbside, his dog by his side, and a dead young man held in his arms.

'Aye,' he murmured, 'he's gone.'

CHAPTER TWO

Doris Lester looked around the cottage and smiled. Finally she had found the place she had been looking to buy ever since selling her home in Sheffield and moving in with her granddaughter, Mouse.

The death of Alice Small had seen this beautiful little cottage come onto the market and it seemed so simple; Alice's will stated that it must be sold, the contents auctioned, and the profits split between cancer research and her church, St. Barnabas in Bradwell. Doris had been a cash buyer, and had said take it off the market and I'll pay your asking price today. The executors of the will had agreed immediately.

And here she was, standing in her new lounge, the keys clutched in her hand.

'Nan,' Mouse called from the front door, 'if I find the box with all the kettle stuff, will you put it on?'

'I most certainly will.' She took one more look around the lounge and headed towards the hallway. The items she had put into storage when she left Sheffield wouldn't be arriving until the following day, but the bits and pieces she had been collecting were split between their three cars, and Kat and Mouse had said they would unload everything. She was to take it easy.

They had made her "take it easy" for several weeks after a fall that had caused some damage to her shoulder, and she couldn't wait for the time when "take it easy" was no longer the order of the day.

She wandered upstairs. The front bedroom overlooked the village, and despite the rain, the view was spectacular. She understood why Alice had loved it so much. Doris stood at the window for a moment watching as Kat and Mouse collapsed into gales of laughter. She decided it might be better not to ask what had tickled them so much. The rain didn't seem quite so torrential, and she felt grateful. Her cardboard boxes might get inside without being soaked through.

Going into the back bedroom gave her the most pleasure. This room was for Martha. She didn't intend losing any of the pleasure she gained from looking after Kat's six-month old baby. Martha would be able to stay over occasionally, and have her own room at Nanny Doris's house for as long as she needed one.

Alice had used the room for her craftwork; Doris had seen it when she came to view the house, but everything in the cottage had been removed; the rare antiques, collectibles and beautiful items that Alice herself had made, sold under the terms of the will. Mouse had attended the auction and wiped out any opposition when buying the Robert Thompson breadboard; she never admitted how much she had paid for it, simply saying "the right amount".

It had pride of place in Mouse's kitchen at the flat.

Doris decided the back bedroom needed to be white, with pretty floral accessories in keeping with the cottage feel of the place, but still sweet enough to be for a tiny baby. She rather thought her own bedroom would end up like that one day, but for the time being it would remain as Alice had decorated it, peach and cream.

· · ·

'Kettle's in the kitchen, Nan,' Mouse called up the stairs, then headed out the door to bring in some more boxes. There was a small second reception room, and everything was being stacked in there.

Nothing could take the smile from Doris's face. This felt so right, this move. She hadn't known Bradwell and the surrounding area before going to look at the cottage; it had really only been a name on the map. She had enjoyed exploring the different parts of it, and it was indeed lovely. She had delved a little into the history via the Internet, and she knew she was going to be happy here.

She filled the kettle and boiled it, then poured the water away and refilled it. That would have to do for getting rid of any manufacturing dust inside the new appliance, her girls would be thirsty. She made the tea and carried the drinks through to the lounge. Kat had brought her a folding garden chair from her home, giving a nod to Doris's age, but Kat and Mouse were sitting on the floor, their backs against the wall for support.

'Right, Nan, it's all in,' Kat said. 'You're to leave everything as it is. We want you to take it easy.'

'I can't take it easy forever, you know,' Doris said mildly. 'At some point I shall stop taking it easy and start to give you two a run for your money again.'

There was a knock at the door and everyone looked startled. Mouse scrambled up, placed her cup on the windowsill and leaned around to see the front door. 'It's Tessa,' she said, and went to let her in.

DI Tessa Marsden's normally bouncy brown hair was flattened by the rain. She ran her fingers through it and then shook it. Drops flew everywhere.

'Thanks, Tessa,' Kat said. 'It's like having a dog.'

'I'm dripping.'

'We can see.'

'Why?' Doris asked, suddenly realising this wasn't wetness from coming from a car, this was proper wetness from being out in the rain for some considerable time.

'I've been to a scene.'

'A crime scene?'

Tessa hesitated. 'I don't know. It's why I went. There was an RTA on the Stoney Middleton road as you head out to Calver, in the early hours of this morning. Young lad crashed his car into a stone wall, no seatbelt on. Must have died instantly. There was a witness who tried to help, but the lad went straight through the windscreen, and he was travelling pretty fast. The witness said he was dead when he pulled him from the wall. He thought the car might go up in flames, there was a lot of smoke, and he wanted to get him out of the way of that. But he said it was obvious he was dead. When first responders got there, the witness was sat on the kerb holding him. It seemed straightforward. Accidental death, bad weather, speed too high, young driver, and the witness said only one headlight was working.'

They waited. There was obviously something else.

'I wasn't involved at this point, RTAs don't come to me, but then I got a call from the coroner. He's not done the full PM yet but there were a couple of things giving him cause for concern, hence my galloping over to the scene to have a look around. I didn't expect to find anything there, obviously, but I needed to see it.'

Kat stood up. 'Tessa, hang on a bit with the rest of it, and let me get you something to dry your hair, and a hot drink. You'll feel more civilised then.'

Doris laughed. 'We've only got tea towels, no proper towels yet.'

Tessa took the tea towel Kat handed to her and towelled her hair, then wiped her face. She once more ran her fingers through her hair in an effort to bounce it back into shape, then gratefully took the cup of tea from Kat.

'Delicious,' she said. 'But will somebody remind me to keep an umbrella in my car, it would definitely have helped.'

Doris held up a hand. 'Let me tell you a little bit of history I've gleaned about Bradwell. Samuel Fox was born here. He invented the steel-framed umbrella mechanism, used silk at first but then when nylon became available he used that. He eventually moved to Stocksbridge to open up a much larger factory, and that's still there today.'

'I'll think about him when I get an umbrella, I promise.' Tessa gave a short burst of laughter.

'So... back to your coroner chap.'

'Yeah, he was concerned. The victim, one Jacob Thorne, was covered almost head to toe in mud. He was dripping wet through from the rain, so whatever he'd been doing it was an outdoor activity, and when they cut off his coat they found, tucked inside it, a ladie's boot. Size four. Obviously not a large lady. The coroner sent me a picture of the boot, and it's not one that any elderly ladies would wear.'

She paused, as if gathering her thoughts.

'He was wearing wellingtons, and when they opened the car boot there was a shovel, thick with mud and wet through, claggy clay mud.'

'You think he'd been digging last night, presumably?' Kat asked.

'Sure of it. But doing what? Where? And where is the person who owns that boot? It would have been a cold wet walk without that boot on their left foot. And Jacob Thorne definitely wasn't gardening in that weather. His parents knew he was out, apparently, but they didn't know where or what he'd been doing.'

'Nobody's been reported missing?' Doris looked concerned.

'Not so far.'

'Then fingers crossed nobody is.'

Tessa cast her eyes around the room. 'You've not got much furniture, Doris.'

'I've got a chair,' she said and patted the arms of the garden chair.

'When do you get the rest?'

'Tomorrow. It should be here for nine, and then I can start to have a home again.'

'So that's why Carl has booked a couple of days off, is it?'

'We need his arms for carrying sofas and suchlike,' Kat grinned. She had been seeing Carl for a little over four months, and they had quickly become an item.

Mouse and Doris had called a "round the desk" chat with Kat once they'd let her know they knew she had a new love in her life, and suggested they move out of her home where they had been living since before Martha's birth.

The meeting had ended with gales of laughter, and Kat realised her life was moving into a new phase. Doris and Mouse did make stipulations before they moved out; they were to be considered first in any babysitting requirements, and they would take charge of Martha's future IT skills. They couldn't leave important stuff like that to her mother.

And now, sitting on a wooden floor in an almost empty house, the trio had become three separate individuals once again, as it had been before Leon Rowe, Kat's late husband, had created havoc in their lives.

But it was a trio united by Connection, their thriving private investigation business. And it was with her Connection head on that Kat raised the next question. 'And supposing you do get a missing person's report in? Where, in the whole of Derbyshire, do you start to look for a small place where digging has been happening?'

'Oh, Kat, don't depress me even more. The short answer to that is I have absolutely no idea.'

The missing person report came in as Tessa Marsden was carrying her cup into the kitchen, prior to heading off back to Chesterfield. She answered the call with trepidation, after seeing it was from the station; they wouldn't have contacted her unless it was concerning the current job.

She listened for a minute, then said, 'Hang on.' Taking her notebook and pen from her pocket, she placed them on the kitchen work surface.

'Okay, go ahead.' She wrote down the details being dictated over the phone, then confirmed that she would go and see the mother immediately. She was within a five-minute drive.

'A misper, newly in,' she said as she joined the others.

'Oh no!'

'Afraid so. Look, I still might be reading more into this than I should be, but you know when you get that... tingle, that feeling that something's wrong?' Tessa shook her head. 'She's an eighteen-year-old from Castleton, so I really hope it's me that's wrong. I'm off to see her mother, find out exactly what we know, get a photo, that sort of thing.' She turned to Doris. 'It's a lovely cottage, lovely atmosphere, Doris. Good luck with the move tomorrow, and please send Carl back to us undamaged.' She grinned and walked out of the door.

CHAPTER THREE

The detached house in Castleton was surprisingly small, and as Marsden walked up the front path, she could see a woman standing in the window. She waved and held up her warrant card, then waited at the door until it was opened.

'Come in,' the woman said, 'out of the rain.' She didn't check Tessa's identity, simply ushered her through the front door.

Tessa followed her to the lounge, the room the woman had been standing in as Tessa had arrived.

'Please sit down.'

Tessa nodded. 'Thank you. I'm DI Tessa Marsden. You're Mrs Harrison?'

'I am. Marnie Harrison. My husband, Andy, is at work but on his way home. He works in Manchester.' The woman was nervous and babbling. She was a tall lady, and kept pushing her dark brown curly hair back from her forehead, as if it gave her comfort, but her brown eyes reflected the pain and worry inside her. 'Would you like a drink?'

'Mrs Harrison, please sit down. I'm fine, thank you. Tell me about your daughter.'

Marnie Harrison sat on the armchair, unspeaking for a moment.

Then she stood and removed a photo frame from the mantelpiece. 'This is Orla. This was taken last year. In Rhodes. In the old town.'

The young girl was beautiful. Slim, long blonde hair worn straight, her face tanned by the Greek sun with a trace of pink lipstick, definitely beautiful.

Marsden studied the photo, then asked if she could keep it. 'I promise I'll bring it back to you, I need to get some copies made. What colour are her eyes? I can't really tell from this.'

'Brown. Her eyes are brown. Of course. Do what you need to do.' Marnie twisted her hands together. 'Please... find her and bring her home.'

Tessa smiled. 'Tell me about Orla.'

Marnie gathered her thoughts. 'She's called Orla French. I was married previously, but my husband was killed in Afghanistan ten years ago. Hence the different surname. I met Andy three years ago and we married last year. That picture of Orla was taken on our honeymoon.'

'You took your daughter on your honeymoon?' Marsden's surprise showed.

Marnie gave a small laugh. 'I know it sounds unusual, but we booked the holiday, then decided to get married and use it as a honeymoon. Orla was already booked to go with us and it didn't occur to us not to take her. Andy's a lovely dad to her – it's why he's on his way back here. I rang to tell him Orla hadn't come home, and he wound up the meeting straight away.'

'So, when did you realise your daughter was missing?'

'I last saw her about one yesterday afternoon. She works in one of the tea shops in the village and I called in for a drink. At this time of year, they close around four. She said she was going to her friend's house to stay overnight, and would see me this afternoon.'

'And her friend is?'

'Emily Carr. I'll have to check her address for you, it's in Hope. Orla said she was going to walk there after finishing work – it's only the next village – but I asked her to come home first and wait for Andy, he would have run her across to Emily's, it was raining so heavily. She said she'd be fine, and I came back home. Got in about two.'

'And she didn't ring to say she had arrived safely?'

'No, and that in itself is quite strange. We're close, like sisters really, and she always keeps me informed of whatever she's doing, even if she's going to be half an hour late home from work if they're really busy, she'll make sure to ring so that I don't worry.'

'And you didn't ring her?'

'No. I try not to do that. It's almost like checking up on her and she's eighteen now. At some point you have to let them go, and keep your concerns inside you. Andy got home around seven, we had our meal and then had an early night.' There was a slight smile, but then the smile disappeared. 'Where can she be?'

'I don't know, Mrs Harrison. So what made you realise she was missing? And I need to know what she was wearing when she left work to walk to Hope.'

'I rang her about one today to see if she wanted to go shopping. It's her day off, hence the sleepover at Emily's place. She didn't answer. I tried three times, then rang Emily.'

Marnie Harrison's face clouded over. 'That was when I knew something was wrong. Emily works in a solicitor's office in Baslow and she answered in a whisper, saying she was at work. I said sorry, and disconnected, then texted her and asked if Orla was still at hers.'

Marnie handed her mobile to Tessa. 'This is the reply.'

Orla not with me. Not seen her since Sunday. She okay?

Marsden took out her own phone and photographed the text. 'And then you rang us?'

'I did. There's something wrong, I know there is. I rang you, then I rang Andy. Oh, and when she left for work yesterday morning, she was wearing a red full-length coat, a padded one, waterproof. She had a Nike backpack, and she probably would have had her headphones in and connected to her mobile phone. She definitely had black knee-high boots on, because she borrowed mine. I remember her saying...' there was a slight choking sound as her memory kicked into gear, 'she said her boots leaked in heavy rain, so could she take mine. Find her for me, please, DI Marsden.'

'We'll try our best, as you know, Mrs Harrison. Do you know where she met with Emily on Sunday?'

'Yes, they go to church, have done ever since they were about twelve or thirteen. They were at school together, used to go one week to Hope church, then the next to St Edmunds across the road, but decided they preferred this one so made this their regular Sunday service.'

There was a bang as the front door opened and Marnie Harrison stood, her face rigid. 'Orla...?'

'It's me, sweetheart,' came the deep tones of the person Tessa presumed was the husband.

He walked into the lounge still carrying his briefcase, and shook Tessa's hand. 'Andrew Harrison,' he said. 'Any news?'

CHAPTER FOUR

Tessa lifted her head to meet his eyes. 'Not yet, Mr Harrison. We've only recently taken the report. Luckily I was in Bradwell so managed to get here quickly. This is out of character for Orla? She doesn't normally take time out and disappear?'

Andy Harrison shook his head. 'No, she never has in the three or so years that I've known her. She's a remarkably level-headed young lady, the kind that's mature and not mature. I mean... she would never answer back, or show off, never be a typical teenager, and yet she was a little bit naïve. For instance, walking into Hope in that heavy rain, in the dark.' His brow creased as he thought about it. The more he spoke, talked through the issues, the more the worry was showing. He ran his fingers through his short grey hair; his blue eyes clouded over as the reality and severity of the situation seemed to suddenly hit him.

'Does she have a boyfriend?'

'No,' was the sharp answer from Andy.

'Kind of,' was the more telling response from his wife.

'Tell me more,' Tessa said.

'I think it's something and nothing,' Marnie said. 'He lives locally, she said, but wouldn't tell me his name. She said there was time enough for that if it progressed. I've no idea who he is, but maybe she would have confided in Emily.'

Marnie crossed the room and stood by Andy's side. She slipped her arm around his waist, and hugged him. 'Let's put our walking gear on and go look for her,' she said softly. 'Let's go find our Orla.' Marnie rubbed her eyes, eyes that were threatening to spill tears once again.

'No, Mrs Harrison. Is it okay if you're Marnie and Andy?'

They nodded in unison, and Andy said, 'Of course.'

'I need one of you to stay here, and I think it should be you, Marnie. If she's hurt, or in trouble, and manages to get back home, she'll want her mum.' Tessa glanced outside. 'It's quite dark because of the weather, but I'll get a team out here and we'll make a preliminary search. If she hasn't arrived home by tomorrow morning then we can start at first light with dogs and a large team. You'll also be allocated an FLO, a family liaison officer. Whoever it is will be here if you need them. They don't intrude but they will keep you informed of any activities. Marnie, go and put the kettle on, I'll nip out to the car and make the arrangements.'

The rain had almost stopped, and Tessa sank into her car seat, took her phone out of her bag and sat for a moment, wondering how to proceed. It really was turning ever darker by the minute; the clouds hadn't lifted during the day and she was certain the deluge of earlier hadn't stopped permanently.

Her ringtone pealed out and she glanced at the screen. The station at Chesterfield – that had saved her ringing them.

'DI Marsden.'

'Tessa, it's Harry.' The desk sergeant's voice was unusually subdued.

'Hi, Harry. I was about to ring you. I need a medium-level search party out in Castleton. Can you organise it, please?'

'I can, but we've some more news about that neck of the woods. We've another misper come in, in the last few minutes.'

'What?' Tessa felt a cold shiver run through her.

'Another young lass from Castleton. She's nineteen. Didn't come home last night. Out of character. Pretty much like the one you're at currently.'

'Hang on, give me the details.'

'Amanda Williamson, her mum calls her Mandy. She's small, dark brown long hair, brown eyes, normally would be at Manchester Uni but she's had pneumonia so is back home with Mum to recuperate. Supposed to be going back to Manchester next Monday.' He read out the address and Tessa quickly jotted it down in her notebook. 'Her mother sounds pretty distraught,' he warned her, 'there's no father, only the two of them. Right, can I make a note you're off to see her? In the meantime, I'll get this search organised. Let's get these lassies found. I'll send the search team to Orla French's address, but I'll tell Hannah to coordinate, you might still be with Mandy Williamson's mum.'

'Thank you, Harry. Tell Hannah to ring me when she gets here. Make everything happen two hours ago, Harry, can you? It's bloody awful weather, and if either of these girls are injured or something, I don't want them out in it for a second night.'

'Understood, Tessa, I'll stay on a bit tonight, just in case.'

Just in case? Just in case what? A third call with another missing girl comes in? Tessa shivered again. She got out of the car and returned to Marnie and Andy. It was starting to look much more sinister, especially if the two girls knew each other, or had some other connection.

Marnie met her in the hallway. 'I've made tea.'

'Thank you. Can you come through to the lounge? I need to ask you two a couple of questions.'

Marnie's face went blank, but she followed Tessa, waiting until they were seated before whispering, 'What's wrong?'

'Firstly, there is a search team on its way. My sergeant, DS Hannah Granger, will be coordinating everything.'

'You won't be here?' Andy queried. It sounded more like a reproof than a question.

'Possibly later. That's the other thing I need to tell you. We have a second missing girl, also from this village.' She paused to let that sink in.

Marnie and Andy turned to each other and clutched hands.

'Who? Do we know her?'

'Her name is Mandy Williamson...'

'Zoe's girl? Oh no!' Marnie Harrison's eyes were huge. 'What's going on? Where are our girls?'

'There'll be a team of searchers here shortly. Andy, I'm going to ask you to stay with your wife. It's dark, and the team know what they're doing. You could possibly hamper them. I have to leave you, to go and speak to Mrs Williamson. Nobody has been to see her yet, she rang through to Chesterfield to report Mandy as missing. When DS Granger arrives, she will probably want to run an eye over Orla's bedroom. Please allow that, won't you. There may be something there that could be a lead as to where she is.'

She stood and walked to the front door. 'I'll be back later.'

She met Hannah on the driveway, so returned to the front door and introduced her to the parents, then left to visit the Williamson household.

Zoe Williamson went out to stand on her front path as soon as she saw Tessa's car pull up outside. She didn't speak, simply held the door open for Tessa to go in.

Tessa and Zoe faced each other in armchairs, and Tessa took out her notebook. 'Give me some details about your daughter, please, Mrs Williamson.'

'It's Zoe,' she said. 'Call me Zoe.' Her short dark hair was flat to her head, wet with rain. She had clearly been outside for some time waiting for her daughter to walk up the street, arrive home in a taxi, get off the bus – anything, as long as she did arrive home. Zoe's green eyes were filled with tears.

Marsden nodded and waited.

'She's a lovely girl, never given me a minute's worry until now, which is why I'm panicking. She rarely goes out other than to church, but last night she said she was meeting someone. I asked her who it was, but she gave me that smile that she has, and said I'll tell you who he is if I decide I like him.' Zoe pushed a photograph across to Tessa. 'This is Mandy.'

A pretty, rather serious-looking girl, stared back at Tessa. Her hair was dark brown and pulled up into a ponytail, high on the back of her head. Her brown eyes stared straight ahead at the camera.

'May I borrow this?' Tessa asked. 'I'd like to get some copies made.'

'You can keep it. I had a larger one made, so have had that smaller one in a drawer. Please... find her for me.'

'We'll do our best, Zoe. Does Mandy know another girl in the village called Orla French?'

'They know each other from church, I believe, but I think that's the extent of it. Why?'

'Orla is also missing. We're keeping an open mind in these early stages, but is there any possibility they could be together?'

'I wouldn't have thought so.' Zoe frowned. 'She's never mentioned Orla.'

Tessa waited, but there was nothing else. She closed her notebook.

'If you can think of any friends Mandy might have had, you need to be ringing around them to see if she's there. We already have a search team in Castleton, but the weather and darkness is hampering us. Tomorrow morning, at first light, there will be a much bigger contingent here. And a family liaison officer will be with you, keeping you up to date on everything. Sit tight. Don't go out looking yourself. If Mandy comes home, she will want someone here, and that must be you. I have to go, to check on everything, but I'll be back.'

As Tessa pulled away, she could see Zoe Williamson at the window staring out into the dark, and Tessa couldn't even begin to imagine how she must be feeling.

CHAPTER FIVE

The carpet fitters were already waiting when Doris arrived at the cottage. She felt thankful that the rain had finally stopped, but the air still felt damp, and everything seemed grey.

She waved at the two men in the van, and unlocked the front door. It was cold, but she knew she couldn't put any heating on; the men wouldn't thank her for it. She had chosen a plain light grey for fitting in both bedrooms, hallway, stairs and landing, and the primary lounge downstairs. She had made a special arrangement with them that they would come back within a week to complete the smaller second reception room, once she had moved everything out of it that was being stored there.

They began work immediately, refusing her offer of a drink, saying that they needed to crack on if they were to be finished before the delivery men arrived with her furniture. As each room was completed, she covered the carpet with old sheets – it was definitely the wrong sort of weather to have furniture removal men trampling on brand new carpets!

As they drove away a much larger van pulled up with her entire life in the back of it. Kat, Mouse and Carl had arrived; Martha had headed off for a playday with Nanny Enid and Granddad Victor.

Carl organised everything, and it seemed to be only a short space of time before the van disappeared, the men replete with tea and scones.

Doris had her cottage.

The search team found a body at eleven o'clock.

Nadine Bond, the family liaison officer allocated to the Harrisons, held her breath when she saw Marsden head up the path to the front door. She had been in this situation too many times not to recognise the expression on the DI's face and she moved to sit by Marnie.

'Marnie, Andy, I'm sorry. It's bad news. We've found Orla's body in the Peakshole Water, quite close to Peak Cavern.'

Marnie crumpled and fell against her husband. He tried to sit her upright, but his wife was unconscious, in a deep faint.

In Bradwell, life felt good. The furniture miraculously fitted, the dust sheets had been removed from the carpets and it was starting to look like the home Doris had known it would become.

Carl stood by her side and looked around the cosy little lounge. 'Okay, Nan, is there anything else you want putting in a different place? I don't want you moving anything on your own. Kat says you're to take it easy.'

'Humph. Take it easy... I'm sick of hearing that.'

He grinned. 'Don't blame me, I'm repeating what I've been told. If you promise not to move anything on your own, I'll go upstairs and help Kat put that cot together.'

'Of course I won't move anything. As if I'd dare,' Doris said, keeping her fingers firmly crossed.

Carl took the stairs two at a time, and found Kat and Mouse

sitting on the floor in the small bedroom trying to make sense of the instructions.

'Thought you'd have this done by now, and Martha asleep in it,' he joked.

Both pairs of eyes turned towards him. There was an absence of smiles.

'It makes no sense at all,' Kat said. 'I put her other one together on my own, but this seems to have a lot more parts than mine.'

'Okay,' Carl said. 'Let's do a trade. I'll put the cot together, if you'll make us a cup of tea. I think Nan could do with one, to stop her from moving her suite into the other reception room. If that carpet was down, I reckon she would be doing it as we speak. She's fancying a more cottage style of suite in the main room, I fear.'

'She's supposed to be taking it easy.' Kat jumped up and moved towards the stairs.

'Kat, a word of advice,' Carl said. 'Don't mention taking it easy to Nan. It wouldn't be a good idea.' He took the Allen key from her and picked up the instruction leaflet.

'Women,' he muttered. 'Useless.' Mouse hit him with the large box the cot had been in and he grinned at her. 'Did you notice I didn't say that while Kat was in the room?'

Marnie buried herself in Andy's arms. She felt so dizzy and ill, and it showed in her face. Andy pulled her as close as he could get her, and they looked at Tessa, then Nadine, willing them to say it had been some horrible mistake and it wasn't Orla.

The quietness in the room, the feeling of hopelessness, told them it was true, and nothing would bring Orla back to them.

Siân Dawson, the Williamsons' FLO, opened their front door, and ushered Tessa through to the lounge. 'She's bearing up,' she said. 'I've said nothing yet about Orla French having been found. Zoe's going to fall apart when she hears that.'

Tessa nodded, and lightly touched the FLO on her arm. 'I know but I have to tell her before anyone else does.'

Tessa stood in the doorway and looked at Zoe. Her eyes were closed but she wasn't asleep. She was intertwining her fingers, obviously deep in thought.

'Zoe?' Tessa said gently.

Zoe's eyes shot open. 'You have news?'

'Of a kind,' Tessa said, 'although not of Mandy. Orla French has been found.'

Zoe stood. 'Is she okay?'

'I'm afraid not. The search team found her body in the Peakshole Water.'

'Oh my God, no. And Mandy...?'

'No sign. The search team have continued with their planned operation, covering a lot of ground. Don't give up hope, Zoe.'

'And how are her mum and dad?'

'Stepdad. They're devastated. And angry.'

Siân came through from the kitchen carrying three mugs of tea. 'I'd already made us a pot. You look as though you need one, boss.'

Tessa smiled her thanks. 'I do. It's not been a good day, as you can imagine.'

All three sat down, but Zoe simply held her cup, as if seeking comfort in its warmth on her hands.

'How did she die?' Zoe asked.

'We don't know yet. She has been taken to the morgue, waiting for the post-mortem to be done. Nobody is speculating, not even the pathologist. Orla was found in the river, which was, and still is, running really fast. We've had a lot of rain. She could so easily have slipped.'

Tessa Marsden didn't believe a word of what she was saying. She felt they should be looking for a second body, that maybe a serial killer had descended on Castleton and taken two young women, but her job at the moment was to keep Zoe Williamson from thinking along those lines.

CHAPTER SIX

'Yes of course. I'll look forward to seeing you in the morning, Mr Barker. I'll initially put you in with Katerina, but eventually we will need to bring our IT colleague, Bethan, into the mix. See you at ten o'clock, tomorrow.'

Doris put down her receiver with a smile. Having business calls transferred to her home telephone number for the duration of the move had been inspirational, but it was time to reopen the office. She had half-expected the call to be from Tessa Marsden, who had learned to trust that anything she said to Connection colleagues remained with them, and she knew Tessa would eventually arrive to talk things through, confirm what she was thinking.

But instead it had been from someone called Ewan Barker, who had lost touch with his son and wanted them to find the missing man. Mouse was embroiled in checking out backgrounds for applicants for senior job opportunities with one of the UK's major employers, so Kat was the logical one to start the ball rolling with Mr Barker.

Doris sank down onto her sofa, reclined it and laid back her head. This cottage was perfect; no wonder the late Alice Small had loved it so much. Doris idly reached to one side to pick up the mail delivered that day and that she had dumped on the side table, and sifted through it. There were four items of junk mail, each addressed to Alice Small at Little Mouse Cottage.

Little Mouse Cottage, clearly a name Alice had stopped using, preferring to use its number rather than its name, and a name that would be resurrected with due haste, as far as Doris was concerned. It was perfect. She pulled her laptop towards her and five minutes later had ordered a plaque for the outside wall, with a hand painted little mouse at the side of the name.

'The icing on my cake,' she murmured to herself, and then changed websites to look at cottage furniture. This room, she knew, needed a cottage style suite. The current one would be fine in the second reception room. She smiled, and picked up the small glass of sherry. 'To me and my little mouse,' she said, and raised the glass.

The morning saw the final carpet laid by eight o'clock. Doris left for the office. She knew the carpet fitters hadn't particularly wanted to start work at seven in the morning, but a promise of bacon sandwiches had swung the deal. Finally her cottage felt her own, and she could get on with doing the things she wanted to do in it.

It was a cold icy morning, and she switched on the heating and the coffee, getting her priorities straight. She would have it nice and warm for when her girls arrived – and the new client, Mr Ewan Barker.

Kat arrived first. 'Mum's picked up Martha this morning. I didn't have to go to their house. They're apparently going on an adventure, so I left Carl loading the dishwasher and came in early. Do we know anything about Mr Barker?'

'Not much. He lives in Grindleford and he's looking for a son he's lost contact with. When he rang I took his name, address and phone number, so get him to fill out a client form, will you?'

Kat nodded. 'I will. No sign of Mouse?'

'No, she was really snuffly with that damn cold yesterday, and she's no appointments today so I'm leaving her to sleep. If she's not down here for ten, I'll pop up when you're in your office with Ewan Barker, and check she's okay.'

'You want a coffee, Nan?'

'I didn't, until I started smelling the coffee I've put on, so I will.' She smiled. 'I'm already full with coffee and bacon sandwiches. I persuaded my carpet men to fit the carpet in the second reception, hereinafter known as the snug, by bribing them with bacon sandwiches. Everything's done, also the furniture can be moved to where it belongs. I'm putting the television in the snug, so the lounge will be a TV-free zone, but my books will be in the lounge. I'm having a cottage suite in there, and the old comfy suite is going in the snug. Oh, and did you know the cottage had a name? Alice must have used it when she first moved there, because it's on her mail, but there's nothing on the outside wall to show she carried on using it. I've ordered a new plaque. It's called Little Mouse Cottage. I loved it, so it's staying.'

'That's lovely. And Mouse will be dead chuffed.'

'Well, one day she'll inherit the place, so it will become even more relevant.'

Kat laughed. 'She's hardly Little Mouse. What is she? Five foot nine, ten?'

The shop bell tinkled and Mouse walked in to the laughter. 'Hey, I hope you're not laughing at me,' she said, and sneezed.

'As if,' Kat chuckled. 'Ask your nan what the name of her cottage is, and you'll realise why we're laughing.'

'Thanks, Kat,' Doris said. 'Drop me in it, why don't you? The cottage was called Little Mouse Cottage. It seems Alice stopped using the name, but I'm resurrecting it.'

'Aw, that's lovely,' Mouse said. 'Really sweet.'

'Hope you feel like that when you inherit the place,' Doris responded, smiling at Mouse as she sneezed again. 'And do you think you should be here? Why not go back to bed with some medication, and stay there until you feel better.'

'I'll be fine,' Mouse said. 'I've had a hot lemon thing, disgusting taste. It had better work. Is there any more of that coffee going?'

'There is.' Nan poured her one and handed it to her. 'Are you working on the recruitment things?'

'I am. But give me a shout if I'm needed for your feller, Kat. Nan, you don't need to stay here if you've things to sort at home, you know. It's not as though we pay you.' She laughed.

'I'm staying. You'll both be in your offices, so I'll man the reception area. I've some work to do on that course I'm taking, and I'm nearly done, so hopefully after today I can forget about it and wait for the results to say I've passed.'

'You said last week you'd failed abysmally.' Kat grinned. 'What changed?'

'I read through what I'd done and decided it wasn't as bad as I'd thought. It's time you two started it. We've a fine collection of certificates on the wall, but we're heading towards the more upmarket ones.'

Kat and Mouse groaned in unison. 'Kill me now,' Kat said. She took her coffee and headed for her office. 'Send Mr Barker in when he arrives, and I promise to remember to get him to fill in the client sheet.'

'Before you disappear,' Mouse said, 'have either of you heard anything from Tessa?'

'Not a thing. I'm guessing that means there are developments. I hope they found the missing girl alive.'

'DI Marsden? I've made this young lass a priority. She was dead before she went into the water, and she died by strangulation. Her hyoid bone was fractured. No water in her lungs. There's a massive contusion on her head, so she was probably knocked unconscious before being strangled. And time of death was between four and six in the afternoon.'

'Shit,' Tessa breathed into her phone. 'I was hoping you could tell me it was accidental. That she'd slipped on mud or something.' She hesitated. 'Right, I'd best go and tell her parents, and officially turn this into a murder enquiry.'

'I've not finished.' There was hesitation at the other end of the phone this time. 'She was approximately fourteen weeks pregnant. I've taken DNA from the foetus.'

'Oh no.' Tessa's head spun. The whole situation was getting worse by the second. 'Is that everything?'

'For the moment. Until we get results in anyway.'

'Thanks. Do me a favour and check that foetus DNA against that RTA victim, Jacob Thorne, will you? Speak soon.' And she slipped her phone into her bag.

Telling Marnie and Andy Harrison was difficult. Neither of them could speak. Like Tessa, they had expected it to be an accident caused by the bad weather. To be told it was murder was, to them, unthinkable. Marnie had held it together until Tessa had told her of the pregnancy, and then she had simply dissolved.

Andy pulled his wife into his arms, and she sobbed inconsolably. Andy looked at Tessa, his face haggard. 'Can we do anything?'

'No, you need to be together. Nadine will remain with you, and she will pass on anything we discover. She's here to help you through this awful time, and I'm so sorry I had to bring you the worst of news.'

Nadine nodded. 'Would you like a drink of water, Marnie? It'll help calm you. It won't make things any better, but you need to be strong.'

'Thank you,' Marnie whispered. 'What happens next?'

'I'm going to see Emily Carr, to try to find this boyfriend.'

. . .

Tessa made no advance phone call. Emily's face reflected shock when Marsden showed her ID, but she quietly asked another member of staff if they could cover on reception for a few minutes.

Emily led her down a corridor to an empty room, and they sat facing each other across a desk.

'This is about Orla?' Emily asked.

'It is. As you know, her body has been found, fairly near Peaks Cavern, which is definitely not on the route to Hope from her house, it's in the opposite direction. However, things have come to our attention that means we have to dig much deeper. It wasn't accidental death; Orla died by strangulation.'

Emily went visibly paler. 'But...'

'But what, Emily? Is there something you know?'

'No. I was going to say but she was simply coming to stay the night at mine. What's gone so wrong that she's dead?' She brushed away a tear. 'I can't believe this is happening. She's my best friend.'

'And as your best friend, did she tell you which lad she was seeing?'

'She didn't need to tell me. She'd been out for a few coffees with my brother. They were starting to get a little serious, but nothing too heavy. She was coming that night to spend some time with Paul and me. We were going to watch a film, have a beer, and then she was going to stay the night with me. Not with Paul.'

Emily sounded angry, as if daring Marsden to suggest there was anything untoward about the relationship between Paul and Orla.

'They hadn't slept together?'

'Definitely not. They'd only seen each other about three times, and the first was accidental. They bumped into each other in Bakewell, and Paul bought her a coffee. They got on really well, and Paul asked if I knew how Orla would feel if he asked her out. I said find out for yourself, and the result of that was a couple more coffees. It was in the early stages, I can assure you. Even Mum didn't know about it. Orla has spent a lot of time at our house, and it wouldn't occur to Mum that the reason was changing.'

Marsden lowered her eyes. 'And there was definitely no one else in Orla's life?'

For a moment, Emily looked troubled. 'N...no.'

'You sound unsure.'

'That's because Orla changed. She was always the confident one, the one who never let things get to her. She was our youth organiser at church, would help anybody. But then she began to change. One day she burst into tears, blamed it on period pains making her feel a bit down, but I'd never heard her complain about them before. I couldn't get anything else out of her, and she asked if she could stay at ours that night. This was way before she started meeting up with Paul.'

'You think she was seeing someone?'

'I don't know, honestly. But one thing I can tell you is that Paul and I, and Mum, were at home that awful horrible wet evening when Orla went missing. Paul was upset, he'd been looking forward to it, because he wanted to kind of formalise things by asking her if she would be his girlfriend.'

'And you didn't ring Marnie to find out where Orla was, when she didn't turn up?'

'No, because I'd done that once before and Orla had a go at me. She said they kept her on such a tight leash, she didn't want them knowing anything. I did ring Orla's phone, but it was dead. No voicemail, nothing. When Marnie texted me the day after, I knew I had to come clean and say she hadn't been to our house, because I'd sat here at work worrying throughout the morning what had happened to her and why she wasn't responding to her phone.'

Marsden nodded. 'So you didn't know she was pregnant?'

This time the shock was obvious. There was utter silence from the young girl.

'Emily?'

'Pregnant? But... who?'

'We don't know yet. She was about fourteen weeks. Would that be before she started seeing Paul?'

'I'm sure of it. The first time he met her in Bakewell was about five, maybe six weeks ago.'

'Then Paul has nothing to worry about. We will need a DNA sample from him, but it will be for elimination purposes. You're sure you can't think of anyone else she might have had sex with? Either intentional or forced?'

'Forced?' Emily's eyes were open wide, as if she tried to assimilate everything Marsden was saying. 'You mean rape?'

'Or someone off limits, maybe a married man, who she had sex with because she wanted to.'

'But this is Orla we're talking about.' Emily sounded anguished. 'She was a Christian, she wouldn't do that. Oh, God,' she said and dropped her head onto her arms on the desk, 'help me.'

Paul Carr was at work at a tyre depot not far from the solicitor's office Tessa had recently left. He was cooperative, polite, and slightly angry that Marsden had interviewed his sister, causing her to become upset.

He confirmed everything Emily had said, and agreed to visit a local police station the next day to give a DNA sample.

Tessa didn't see him thump the wall and wipe away tears. She was already driving away to the next part of the investigation.

CHAPTER SEVEN

Doris was reading through her coursework when the shop bell pinged. She looked up to see a man of medium height, with white hair and a thick jacket which proclaimed The North Face on the front of it. It was blue, and matched his eyes exactly.

'Hello,' he said. 'I'm Ewan Barker. I have an appointment...'

'Welcome, Mr Barker. My name is Doris Lester. I spoke to you on the telephone.'

'Doris, I'm delighted to meet you. And please call me Ewan.'

Doris smiled. 'And it's good to meet you, Ewan. I've booked you in with Katerina, although she prefers to be called Kat. Would you like a coffee?'

'Thank you, I would. It's freezing out there.'

'Then let me take you through to Kat's office, and I'll get you one from her machine.' She moved towards Kat's office door, and Ewan followed her. She knocked and waited until she heard Kat call to come in, then opened the door. Kat stood with a smile.

'Please come in, Mr Barker. Coffee?'

'I'll get it, Kat,' Doris said, and moved to the side table. She quickly poured it, and handed it to the client who had removed his coat.

'It may be freezing out there,' he said, 'but it's certainly too toasty for this jacket in here.'

'Enjoy,' Doris said, and left him to Kat's ministrations.

'Okay, Mr Barker, I need to take some details before we get to the nitty-gritty of everything else.' She pushed a form across the desk to him, along with a pen, and asked him to complete it.

Two minutes later, he gave it back to her with a smile. 'All done,' he said. 'And it's Ewan, please.'

'Thank you, Ewan.' She opened her top drawer. 'Do you mind if we record our conversation? It's so much easier than taking notes, and it ensures I don't miss anything.'

'Not at all.'

'Thank you.' She switched on the tiny machine and placed it between them. 'So, start at the beginning, and tell me how we can help. We will require a retainer before we start any work, as you saw on the form, but we don't stretch anything out, we get on with it and complete as quickly as possible.'

'I know,' he said, turning his blue eyes towards her. 'You come highly recommended.'

He took a moment to think before he started speaking. 'My son, or so I was told many years ago, is called Michael, and it was mooted during the pregnancy that if it was a boy, he would be Michael Ewan. His mother was Helen Fairfax. Helen was reluctant to discuss getting married, and was pretty upset that it looked as though she would be forced into that situation because of the pregnancy, but I always reassured her we could have the baby, and then decide our futures. She eventually came to accept that. The baby was due November 1968, and in September she left. She was seven months pregnant and simply disappeared. We lived on the outskirts of Sheffield at the time, and she had lots of friends. She worked in one of the department stores, Atkinsons, and there was quite a crowd of them who socialised. When I thought about it later, after she'd gone, I realised it wasn't the marriage she didn't want, I think it was the baby. It stopped what she saw as her life.'

He hesitated, gathering his thoughts.

'How did you find out she'd had him?'

'I bumped into one of her friends in a pub one night, and she said she wouldn't tell me where Helen was, but she'd seen the baby and his name was Michael. Carla, the friend, gave me her own name, address and phone number, and I rang her fairly regularly over about a year, but I sensed she was getting a bit fed up with me ringing, so I stopped. I've never seen Michael, but I know Carla had a photo of him because she'd held the baby when she went to see Helen. She said he looked like me. Recently I had a triple heart bypass. It focusses your mind when something like that happens, and I really would like to see him. I did marry eventually, but Jean and I never had children. She died five years ago, so I thought it was time I sorted out my life. I'm hoping you can help me, Kat, because I don't have any sort of idea where to start.'

'Then let's start with what we do know. Do you by any chance still have the name of the friend you used to ring?'

He took out his wallet. 'I do,' he said and handed over a small piece of card that had clearly started life as a beer mat. 'But I do need to make it clear it's not Helen I'm looking for. It's Michael. Helen is the same age as me, seventy, born in 1948 on the 10th October – we shared a birthday. We actually met on our eighteenth birthdays – we celebrated them in the same pub. We were pretty inseparable until the day she disappeared. She left me a note, which I screwed up and threw away, so I'm sorry I don't have that to show you. It said something along the lines of she didn't want commitment, and she would be in touch when the baby was born. That, of course, never happened.' He delved further into his wallet. 'This is the only photo I have of Helen. Please take care of it.'

'I'll photocopy it, and you can put it back where it belongs in your wallet. I can give no guarantees, Ewan, that we will find him. Sometimes, when people want to disappear, they do it effectively. She may have left the country, taking her son with her, and although we could probably track that, once someone is in a different country they simply vanish well under the radar.'

'I understand, really I do. But I have to try. I'm not a rich man, Kat, but neither am I poor. Michael should inherit what is rightfully his, but it's not even about that. I simply want to see him, find out what kind of a man he is. I see him in my head as not too tall – both parents are only average height, and with fair hair. Helen and I were both blonde.'

Kat smiled. 'Ewan, I promise we'll give this our best shot. We'll use Twitter and Facebook to help, if that's okay with you, but if you say no to social media, we'll use other means. We won't use your name, only Helen's and Michael's. How do you feel about that?'

'Kat, I can't come to you for help with finding Michael, and then put restrictions on it. Do whatever you need to do, I'm confident you'll be working with my best interests at heart.'

'We'll keep you fully informed every step of the way, so if ever you want to call a halt to something, get back to us quickly. This is our business card with the three mobile numbers on it, so that you can reach us any time.' She slid the small card across the table to him. 'We will be starting work on this immediately, so please check your emails every day in case we have queries. For anything urgent, we will of course ring you. Will you be paying your retainer by card or cheque?'

'By card. That okay?'

'It's absolutely fine. You'll need to sort that out with Doris before you go. She keeps us in line with the finances.' Kat stood. 'Thank you for your trust in us, Ewan. I hope we can solve this for you, I really do.' She held out her hand and he stood and shook it.

'Thank you, Kat. I'll go and see that lovely lady on reception. She has a beautiful smile.'

Kat laughed. 'You should see her when she's doing her karate training. The smile disappears then. But you're right, she is lovely. And before you go I need to introduce you to Beth, my business partner and Doris's granddaughter, because she will be working on this case as well, and if she has to ring you, you need to know who she is. Beth and Doris are our technology experts. I'm the thinker, so they say.'

She picked up her phone and spoke to Beth.

Seconds later, Beth and her red nose came through the adjoining door, and shook hands with their new client. 'Pleased to meet you, Ewan, but don't come any closer. I was considering going home to bed and staying there for a week until this has passed.'

'Whisky and lemon,' Ewan said. 'Go on, get off home.'

'Good Lord,' Beth said. 'He sounds like my nan.'

'Beth, go home,' Kat said. 'You can't possibly be working. I'll bet anything you're laid back in your chair with your eyes closed, feeling sorry for yourself.'

'Haven't done a thing since I arrived,' she confessed. 'I'll be in bed if anybody needs me.' She turned and went back into her own office.

Kat photocopied the small picture of Helen Fairfax, and handed the original back to Ewan. She took him through to reception, and left him with Doris to pay his retainer.

Doris keyed the relevant information into the machine, and handed it to Ewan to insert his card. With the transaction completed, he smiled at her.

'I don't suppose there's another cup of coffee going, is there?'

'Of course. And a biscuit,' she responded with a laugh. She pulled out a chair tucked under her desk at the back of reception, and closed the laptop lid, before pushing the computer to the edge of the table.

'Please, sit down, Ewan. I'll get our drinks. Presumably Kat was able to offer you some hope?'

Ewan sat. 'She offered me an opportunity, which I've never felt I had before. It's the fact that somebody is trying to find my son, it's a massive thing to me. Even if Helen, the boy's mother, managed to spirit him away completely, at least I'll know I tried.'

Doris nodded. She handed him the coffee, and opened up her biscuit box. 'Help yourself,' she said, and sat on the other chair. 'You live in Grindleford, I understand.'

'I do. Love it there. I used to live in Bradwell, but I found I needed a bigger garden. This was prior to my triple heart bypass,' he said with a grin. 'Now I need a smaller one.'

'I live in Bradwell,' Doris said.

'I left in 2000, when my wife was still alive. She didn't want to leave, she loved our house there, but did recognise its limitations. How long have you lived there? I don't remember you.'

'Two days,' Doris said with another laugh. 'I've bought a little cottage up near the Bowling Green Inn. One small front garden, but a much bigger back one.'

Mouse came out of her office and walked over to Doris's desk. She bent down and kissed her nan on the top of her head. 'I'm going to bed. This damn cold is settled in my head, and it needs to be on a pillow. Please don't disturb me unless there's a dead body or something exciting.'

Doris stood and hugged her granddaughter. 'I'll pop up and see you before I go home. I'll not wake you if you're asleep.'

Mouse walked out of the shop, and Ewan stood. 'Does she need a lift? She looks dreadful.'

'No, she's fine. She lives above here. The white door at the side of this shop is her front door. She'll be in bed in thirty seconds.'

'Dead body? I assume she's joking.'

Doris thought for a moment. 'Not really. We've had one or two to deal with as part of past investigations. And Mouse... Beth... was almost one herself.'

'Mouse? You call her Mouse?' His smile was infectious.

'We do. When she was born she was tiny, like a little mouse, and the name has stuck with her throughout her life. Kat has known her a couple of years, and she calls her Mouse too. It suits her.'

'You're close?'

'Very. She lost her parents when she was sixteen and I stepped in. But we're friends more than anything. I keep her on the straight and narrow, or try to anyway, and she says *Oh Nan,* repeatedly. It's a good relationship. And we have Kat. She too calls me Nan, so this business partnership is a lot more than simply that.'

'How wonderful,' Ewan said, and reached across for a second garibaldi. 'I can't resist these damn biscuits. It's why I don't buy them.'

They chatted for a further five minutes and then Ewan stood and put on his coat. 'Thank you for this, Doris. It's been lovely spending time with you. Could I take you out for a drink sometime? Maybe the Bowling Green?'

Doris felt her cheeks redden. 'Oh... erm... yes. Yes, that would be lovely.'

'Tomorrow night? I can either collect you, or we can meet in the pub.'

Doris felt flustered. 'We can meet in the pub. It's only two minutes away. Eight o'clock?'

'That will be great. I'll look forward to it. And if anything crops up to prevent it, we have each other's contact details. I do understand you have an unusual occupation, so plans may have to change. Thank you for today, Doris. This has turned out so much better than I could possibly have imagined.'

CHAPTER EIGHT

Marsden was sitting at her desk in Chesterfield when her email pinged. She read through it and then leaned back with a sigh. So there was no connection between the foetus from Orla French's womb and the accident victim Jacob Thorne.

She spun her chair round to look out of the window, and pushed her hair back. She knew something was wrong about the whole thing with Jacob Thorne; two missing persons, yet only one body had been found. Gut instinct told her that the mud-covered Jacob had been involved in the second one, but no further bodies had shown up in Castleton.

She was aware that her colleagues were already considering it to be two deaths by the same hand, but she wasn't convinced. If she could place a bet on it, she would say that Orla French's tragic death was linked to her pregnancy; the second missing person Tessa would say was linked to Jacob Thorne. She hoped that one was a missing person and not a death.

She stood abruptly, deciding it was time to head back out to Castleton. 'Hannah,' she called, and DS Granger popped her head around the open door of Marsden's office.

'Boss?'

'Come on, we're going out. I need to be back in Castleton, and soon. I don't want Zoe Williamson thinking we've given up. And bring some DNA kits. We need to eliminate people from suspicion about this baby.'

Nadine Bond opened the door to Tessa and Hannah, and spoke quietly. 'They're both still in bed. They hadn't gone to bed at three this morning, so I'm leaving them to catch up on some sleep. I think they both need it. Do you want me to wake them?'

Tessa shook her head. 'No, we'll go to Zoe Williamson's first, see how she's doing. And I don't think for one minute she'll be sleeping.'

Zoe felt as though she hadn't slept for months. Her hair, unbrushed, was hanging loosely around her face, and her eyes were red-rimmed from a combination of constant tears and lack of sleep.

She looked up as Siân Dawson led Tessa and Hannah into the kitchen. She was sitting at the table, her hands wrapped around a mug of tea. She looked at them without hope, as if her mind had already accepted that she wouldn't see her daughter again.

'We have no news,' Marsden said, keeping her voice gentle. 'I wanted to check in with you, to let you know the search hasn't slowed down, we've simply had to widen it. We have had groups of officers all over Castleton, and have spread out towards the Hope area, and up into the hills around Winnat's Pass.'

She watched as Zoe's bottom lip trembled. 'You think you'll find her alive?'

'I don't know.' Again Marsden spoke quietly. 'It's been so cold during the nights, and she has been missing for two of them...'

She watched as Zoe dipped her head in acknowledgment.

'You've had no further thoughts on who the man was? The one she was meeting?'

'No, I'm sorry. I've been backwards and forwards on this, but Mandy was... is... such a private girl. She wouldn't have told me until they were practically engaged. She wasn't the sort to bring friends home from school, or even to talk about anything that had happened at school. She went through her life quietly, organising it to suit her. She wasn't ambitious, was quite happy to be in Castleton, never yearning for the bright lights of cities, she was a contented child and an accepting adult.'

Zoe stood and walked to the window, as if expecting to see Mandy walking up the back garden path. 'I miss her, I miss her quietness. It feels so wrong here without her.' She fished out a tissue that had been tucked up her sleeve, and dabbed at her eyes. She turned.

'Is it the same man who's killed Orla? Has he taken my Mandy as well?'

The Williamsons and the Harrisons lived a mere three streets away from each other; grief was palpable in both homes. Marsden drove from Zoe's home around to Andy and Marnie's, feeling as if the weight of the universe was on her shoulders.

Andy and Marnie were sitting in the lounge, neither speaking, both staring at the mound of mail that had been sent by caring people wanting to express their sympathy. Their small front garden, edged by a stone wall, was covered in sprays of flowers, with candles flickering gamely in the wind for minutes before being extinguished by a stronger gust of wind.

Andy looked up at Tessa, bleakness etched into the lines on his face.

'DI Marsden,' he said. 'Any news?'

'Nothing as yet, Andy.' Tessa turned to Hannah, who handed

her a sealed tube. 'I need a sample of DNA, for exclusion purposes, Andy, please.'

He looked shocked. 'To exclude me from what? I was in Manchester when Orla... when she was...' He stopped, as if unable to say the words.

'I know.' Again the gentleness was evident in Marsden's voice. 'We're taking samples from as many men in the village as we can get around, or track. Somebody fathered your stepdaughter's baby, and it's quite possible that whoever did that, killed her because he didn't want that pregnancy to progress. Taking DNA samples is always more about exclusion than inclusion. So, if you can open your mouth, sir, we'll cross you off our list of male residents.'

She gave him no choice, no chance to argue against what they were doing. He opened his mouth, and she scraped cells off the insides of his cheeks before putting the sample stick back into the tube. Hannah wrote his name on the label.

'Thank you, Andy. That's much appreciated. We've taken over that prefab building in the schoolyard as a control room, and leafleted Castleton and all surrounding villages, asking males to voluntarily take DNA tests. We've had a steady stream all day. Anybody who doesn't volunteer will be visited.'

Marnie took hold of Andy's hand as if to reassure him, comfort him, but said nothing. It was as if she had lost her voice, her sense, along with her daughter.

'You don't hang around, do you?' Andy's voice reflected sorrow and pain.

'We can't, Andy. We still have another missing girl, and you need closure.' Her phone stopped any further conversation, and she moved into the lounge to take the call. She listened, made the simple response of *thank you very much* and closed down the call.

'Hannah, we have to go. Marnie, Andy, if anything, and I mean anything, comes to mind, please call me or tell Nadine. She's here to be the contact between us.'

They left half-drunk mugs of tea and walked out the door.

They sat in the car before speaking further, Hannah going first. 'Boss?'

Tessa sighed. 'I hate to be proved right when it's not a good right. Know what I mean?'

Hannah turned to her. 'What's wrong?'

'SOCOs removed a glass from Mandy's bedside table for DNA and fingerprint samples. They got both. The fingerprints have also been found inside that car that crashed with Jacob Thorne driving. Mandy Williamson was out with him that night, I'll bet my pension on it.'

Hannah stared out of the windscreen, her hands resting on the steering wheel. The cogs in her brain felt as if they were revolving at speed.

'She may not be dead.'

Tessa's face was grim as she nodded. 'We have to assume she's alive anyway, until a body turns up. You're thinking he could have tied her up somewhere? Kept her for later? Where the bloody hell do we start looking?'

'Is my beautiful woman in, Nan?' Carl's voice accompanied the ping of the doorbell.

'She certainly is. You're lucky you've caught us, we were about to close up. Kat wants to take some flowers across to the cemetery and I need to check on Mouse before I go home.'

'She's no better?'

'No, we sent her to bed. I'll go and make sure she's well medicated.'

'You get off,' he said. 'We'll lock up. Who's she taking flowers for?'

'The young lad who was Leon's first murder victim. She looks after his grave, takes him flowers every so often. His mum lives in Bakewell, so Kat said she would look after things for her.'

'Special lady, isn't she, our Kat,' he mused.

'Very special. And don't ever underestimate her. She has the mental strength of ten men.'

He held up his hands with a laugh. 'Trust me, I wouldn't ever underestimate any of the three of you, let alone Kat! You all scare me.'

'Good. That's as it should be.' Doris tried to keep her face straight but failed miserably. 'Kat's in her office. Go and get her. I'll grab my stuff and head upstairs to Mouse. Tell her I'll see her tomorrow.'

Carl dropped a kiss onto the top of her head as he went by her chair, and opened the door to Kat's office. She was putting on her coat.

'Nan's off to medicate Mouse. She says she'll see you tomorrow. So we're going to visit a grave?'

'Craig Adams. He was Leon's first murder victim, or at least the first one we knew about. I look after his grave because his mum doesn't live in the village, and because... because I want to.' She sounded defiant.

'Hey.' Carl pulled her into his arms. 'I wouldn't expect anything less of my Kat. And I'm happy to go where you lead. I'll even carry the flowers.'

She switched off the desk lamp, and Carl waited outside the building while she set the alarm, locked up and brought down the shutters.

Eyam looked gloomy in the greyness of the late November afternoon skies. It was starting to rain, and they hurried through the church gate. Kat pulled her hood up to give some protection to her hair, and

Carl followed in her tracks as she wove in and out of gravestones. She pointed out a couple of them as she passed, explaining who they were and why she brought flowers to them. When she showed him Danny McLoughlin's grave smothered in flowers as always, he smiled. 'He was certainly loved,' Carl said.

'By the whole village. It's his friends as well as his family that bring the flowers, because he was a gardener for the entire village. He worked in many of the gardens, not only mine. He was so lovely, Carl. I miss him.'

They skirted the edge of the grave, and headed down a slight incline to Craig Adams' small headstone. Carl stood to one side, waiting until Kat had knelt and placed the flowers then said a small prayer for Craig. She remained with her head bowed for a short while, and then he offered his hand as she moved to stand up.

She frowned. 'What on earth's happened over there? Look at the piles of mud.'

Carl looked across. 'You maybe need to have a word with whoever opened the grave. They've left a bit of a mess after filling it in. Whoever the relatives are of the new incumbent, they won't be best pleased, I'm sure.'

Kat hesitated. 'I'm pretty sure there's no new incumbent.' She squeezed his hand. 'Come with me. Let's check this out. I do all the funeral visits, take most of the funerals as you know, and I've not done either a burial or an ashes blessing there. Let's check the register to make sure nobody else has taken one.'

The rain was coming down heavily and they ran hand in hand across to the church. They paused in the porch to catch their breath, then headed inside to go to where the records were kept.

Kat ran her finger down the list of five people who had been buried or cremated in the past two months and all of them were on the west side of the churchyard, not the north. She looked at Carl.

'I have to go back. I have to look at this grave.'

'*We* have to go back,' he said. 'You clearly think something is wrong, and I might have to pull rank here. I'm a DS in my other life, Kat Rowe.'

'Oops. Sometimes, when you're walking around my house naked, I forget that.' Her grin lit up her face as her thoughts wandered.

He pulled her hood back onto her head, and took her hand once more. 'You're incorrigible.'

'Spell it.'

'I can't.'

They stepped outside into the deluge pouring from the dark grey clouds and once more ran across the churchyard. With closer inspection, it was clear that the grave had been disturbed with a significant amount of soil left by the side and around the back of the headstone.

'This soil hasn't been left like this since the 1800s,' Carl remarked drily. 'I have a choice to make. Do I ring Tessa? Or do I get my soft hands calloused and get digging down myself.'

Despite the discomfort of rain dripping down her face, Kat smiled. 'Don't touch anything. I'm here, and Tessa will only nag me if I disturb the scene. Are you thinking it could be somebody's pet dog or something?'

'Not really. I mean, that's a possibility of course, but there's still a missing girl... and unless it's an Irish Wolfhound this grave is a bit big for a pet dog.'

'I know. Shall I ring her, or shall you?'

'You. Tell her I've gone back to the car to get some crime scene tape. We can always take it down if it is a pet dog, but I've a feeling, a bad feeling, about this. See if she wants us to do anything else while we're waiting. If she's in Chesterfield, it'll be the best part of half an hour by the time she gets here, and I'll have it cordoned off by then.' He kissed Kat, and trekked his way back to the main church path, before setting off to run down to where he had left his car outside the Connection office.

Kat took out her phone and within seconds was explaining to Tessa the odd appearance of the burial site, the copious amounts of soil surrounding the ancient grave and the fact that it was virtually hidden from view unless you had reason to pay a visit to this small northerly section of the churchyard.

'Is Carl there?'

'He's gone to his car to get some crime scene tape. He's taking no chances. It may be somebody's pet dog they wanted burying in consecrated ground, or it could be a body. The tape will be up by the time you get here.'

'I'll be there in ten minutes. I'm in Castleton. I'm contacting forensics, they need to do the excavation, not me. If Carl has an evidence bag on him, ask him to take a sample of the soil on the surface before it gets disturbed. Remember the RTA victim? The one covered in mud?'

'I'd already connected the two,' Kat said. 'And this mud stands out a mile. I think whoever has done this was in the dark and not able to see the mess they've left behind.'

'Okay, thanks, Kat. Didn't I specifically say don't find me any dead bodies?'

'I knew you'd bring that up.'

Kat heard a chuckle. 'Don't touch anything. Within the next half hour you'll be overrun with people.'

'Okay, Tessa. Oh... you'll need one of Samuel Fox's umbrellas. It's pouring down.'

Again she heard the chuckle. 'I'll commandeer Hannah's brollie. See you in ten minutes or so.'

Kat disconnected and watched as Carl's car appeared at the end of the church drive. He parked it out of the way, and then ran up towards her.

'Before you do anything,' she said, 'have you got an evidence bag to take a sample off the top of the mud? Tessa wants it for comparison purposes with that young man who died in the RTA a couple of nights ago.'

'Of course,' he said, and took one out of his pocket. He used a twig to scrape some soil into the bag, and then affixed the crime scene tape. He was still rolling it out when Marsden's car pulled up, parking behind his. Kat set off down the path to meet Tessa and Hannah, and led them back up to where the blue and white tape was fluttering in the wind.

CHAPTER NINE

Doris stood at Mouse's lounge window, staring out into the grey dampness of the evening. The rain was heavier than earlier and she was feeling pleased that she had decided to stay the night at Mouse's flat rather than venture out into the type of rain that soaked through to the skin within seconds.

She reached up to close the curtains and noticed the police car coming down the hill at speed, no sirens but blue lights flashing. She watched it head up the hill and pull in across the road from the church. Church. Kat. Doris felt a shiver run through her and the curtains remained open. The second car followed within a minute, again with its blue lights brightening the riverlike streets with a Christmas effect. It stopped behind the first one and a steel dread began to fill Doris.

She left the window with the curtains still open and went to get her phone. She had to make sure Kat was safe.

When Kat answered, Doris's legs felt very weak, and she sat down on a kitchen chair.

'Thank God you're safe,' she said. 'I knew you'd taken flowers to the churchyard, and now it seems to be filled with police.'

'I'm still here,' Kat said. 'I'm leaving Carl to do his job, but I'm going to walk down to the office, my car's there. I'll come up to the flat and fill you in on as much as I know. I need to tell Tessa where I am. I'll be about ten minutes.'

'Tessa? Tessa's there?'

'She is. And a couple of the press have already arrived so I'm not saying anything they could misinterpret. If Mouse is awake, tell her to stay that way. See you in a few minutes.'

Kat stood in the hallway of the flat, took off her coat and draped it over the radiator. She shivered as Doris came through.

'Good grief, you're soaked. Go and jump in the shower. I'll get you some spare pyjamas and a dressing gown, we need to get you warm. We can talk when you're drinking some hot chocolate.'

Kat dropped all her clothes except her underwear in a heap on the floor in the hall. Moving slowly into the bathroom, she stood under the shower, letting the hot water wash away the mud, the rain and the pain of finding yet another body. Another link to another death. She knew Tessa believed it to be the missing girl from Castleton, and Kat's heart ached. Her tears mingled with the shower cascading over her, and she eventually switched it off. Time to report to Doris and Mouse.

Mouse was curled up on the sofa, her head resting on a cushion, looking nothing like her normal self. 'Hey, that's my dressing gown.'

'And your PJs,' Kat smiled. 'You're alive then?'

'Barely. Go to bed, you both said, go to bed and stay there till you're better. You didn't say go to bed until we find another dead body.'

'We don't know it is one yet,' Kat said. 'The forensic team hadn't confirmed anything when I left. Tessa said she would ring when they knew more. I know what she thinks, but thinking isn't confirmation.'

'It is now,' Doris said quietly. 'Tessa rang while you were in the shower – it appears to be a young girl, her description matching that of Mandy Williamson. That's as much as Tessa would say over the phone, but she's calling here later before she goes home, to fill us in on it. She was heading off to Castleton to tell the girl's mother first, to warn her that it appeared to be her daughter. I don't envy her having to do that. I'm staying here tonight, so I'll make sure Mouse has a good sleep. Can you stay until Tessa gets here, Kat?'

'I can. I'll let Carl know, and I'll ask Mum to keep Martha overnight.'

Tessa arrived half an hour after Carl, and Doris fed them with cheese and toast, the only food available from the sparse contents of Mouse's fridge. Mouse made no apologies beyond saying *I am what I am,* and even that was said with a croaky voice.

'It's definitely our misper, Mandy Williamson. And I don't think we need to be looking any further than Jacob Thorne for her killer. The boot we found with him was a match for the boot on our corpse, and I'm certain we'll be able to match the mud from the grave with the mud that was all over the interior and exterior of his car, and thick on the soles of his wellingtons. We can also tie Mandy to his car with fingerprints recovered from the passenger side. They've taken her away, and I've been promised a post-mortem tomorrow morning. Zoe Williamson is devastated, obviously. It's such a shitty job at times, this one.' Marsden ran her fingers through her wet hair then sipped at her hot chocolate. 'I'm frozen, weary to the point where it's painful, and sick of never being able to give people good news. And tomorrow I'll be expected to face the press and not show how upset I am at the discovery of the body of a young girl who had her whole life in front of her.'

Mouse, Doris, Kat and Carl stared at her. Tessa didn't normally show her feelings quite so much.

Kat leaned across and put her arm around Tessa's shoulder. 'Stay at ours tonight. Don't go home to that empty house, you'll only feel worse. You can get up early tomorrow morning and then head home to get changed for work. If you want to talk anything through we'll be there for you. Please?'

Tessa looked at her, then brushed away a tear. 'Thank you. I will. It's been such a hard bloody day.'

Kat smiled. 'Good. We'll finish our banquet, drink the nectar that's hot chocolate, and go home. Tibby will think I've left anyway, so be careful he doesn't attempt to kill you when we walk in. He tries to trip up any visitors by twining around their ankles – you have been warned.'

In the labs at Chesterfield, DNA tests were starting to produce results; the first forty showed no matches with the foetal DNA, and that included the one provided by Paul Carr.

CHAPTER TEN

Sleep didn't come easy to anybody except Mouse. She had so much slumber-inducing medication in her she was unconscious by midnight and woke up around ten. As a result she felt much better.

Doris had waited in the flat to make sure her granddaughter wasn't in need of more professional help, and was pleasantly surprised to see the tousled hair appear around the door jamb.

'Could there be a cup of coffee on the go?' Mouse's voice was still husky, but she gave every appearance of being alive.

'You want some toast to go with it?'

'No thanks. Not fussed about food yet, but I'm thirsty. Feel much better though. Any news?'

'Not really. Tessa stayed at Kat's house last night, but Kat said she'd gone by seven, wanted an early start at work.'

'Is Kat in today?'

'She is, and making vague threats about going on the Internet to start searching for Ewan's missing son.'

The two women smiled at each other, knowing that within half an hour of Kat using her computer, she would be saying she had broken the Internet – again.

'I've got my laptop with me,' Mouse said. 'I'm not going downstairs today, because I suspect I'll keep nodding off and I've no intention of fighting that, so I'll start doing searches, see what I can come up with. Tell Kat to stop panicking, I can work but I'll do it from up here. Are you staying tonight, Nan?'

Doris blushed. 'Erm... No. I've something already booked.'

Mouse's head shot up. 'Something already booked? What does that mean?'

'I'm going out.'

'You have a date?' Mouse's face showed shock.

'Not really. Kind of. No, I don't think so.'

'Is it with a man around your own age?'

'It is.'

'Then it's a date and I need to know more. Do I need to vet him?'

'Go to sleep, Mouse. You're looking tired again.'

'I'll ring Kat. She'll tell me what you're doing.'

'She doesn't know.'

'Will you be safe?'

Doris deliberately kept her face deadpan. 'Don't worry, I have enough condoms.'

'What?' The word came out like a cracked shriek, and the shock at her nan's tongue-in-cheek statement was evident in Mouse's voice, her expression and the way she jumped up from the settee she had recently occupied.

'Something wrong, Mouse?' Doris asked, deliberately winding up her granddaughter and enjoying it. 'You think seventy-year-olds don't have sex? I'll tell you about it tomorrow. I'll make us that cup of tea.' She headed towards the kitchen area, struggling to hold in the laughter, keeping her back to Mouse.

The ensuing conversation between Kat and Mouse caused Doris to struggle even harder to rein in the laughter. It seemed the two girls intended talking to her, and both definitely wanted to know the identity of this philanderer with whom she had seemingly made plans that involved sharing a bed.

She handed the cup of tea to Mouse, and Mouse said *I'll talk to her again* before disconnecting.

Mouse placed Doris and her paramour on a temporary back burner, while she began the research that she hoped would eventually lead them to Michael Fairfax, if that was his name.

She inputted Helen Fairfax along with her date of birth, 10 October 1948. She very quickly came up with a hit for her, scribbling down the address in Holmesfield that was on her birth certificate. She ordered a copy of the certificate, then inputted Michael Fairfax, with the birthdate Ewan had given them, passed on to him by Carla Blake. Mouse could find no logical trace; there were two entries with that name, a Michael Ian Fairfax and a Michael Adrian Fairfax. Michael Ian had been born in Scarborough, and Michael Adrian in Inverness.

She didn't rule out either of them, accepting that Helen could have travelled to anywhere in the world to have her baby, but the little boy was born in 1968 and travel at that time was more for business than any other reason. She would start with the nearest, geographically, when she felt up to tackling it. Scarborough it was.

Mouse pushed the laptop away from her with a sigh.

'Beechams?' Doris asked.

'I think so. I feel rubbish. I'll have the hot lemon then have a sleep. Don't think you've got away with things, we need to talk, but I need to sleep again right now.'

Doris made her the drink and handed it over without a word.

Mouse fell asleep very quickly following the medicated drink, and

Doris headed downstairs to check that Kat was managing on her own.

'You're going out with Ewan, aren't you?' Kat said, the second Doris stepped through the door.

'I am.'

'That makes things a bit awkward. He's a client.'

'He's not my client. I'm not an employee, a part owner or anything.'

'Shall I shut up?'

'Think so.'

'Okay. You'll be careful? You don't know him.'

'Kat, I'm going for a drink with him to the Bowling Green. It's two minutes at the most from my house. I am not eloping, I don't want a man in my life, but I simply thought it might be nice to do something normal like going out for a drink.'

'And so it will be. Nice, I mean. Subject closed.'

'Good. Everything okay down here?'

'It is. I've almost finished that forensics course you said would be boring but handy. It certainly wasn't boring, been quite enjoyable really.'

Doris looked around. 'We're going to need bigger offices to hang all these certificates we keep getting.'

'Mouse asleep?'

'She is. She's a bit better than she was last night, so I've sent her back to her

bed. She's made a start on Ewan's son. I imagine she'll carry on when she wakes up. Heard anything from Tessa?'

'Not yet. It seems really strange two girls from the same village, virtually the same age, yet killed by different people on probably the same night.'

'She'll talk to us about it when she needs to organise her thoughts.'

.   .   .

Marsden sat at her desk, her screen on and telling her that the post-mortem for Amanda Williamson was scheduled to start at eleven. She wanted to change the name to Mandy; her brain kept saying she's Mandy, she's Mandy.

It had been hard telling Zoe Williamson they thought they had found her daughter. The meltdown had been instant; the news was what Zoe had expected. It proved to be even more difficult saying where they had found her, thrown into an existing grave and covered with mud.

The time on Tessa's screen was telling her she should be heading to the autopsy suite, and she heaved a huge sigh. She hated attending them, and when it was a young person it made it doubly hard. She left her room feeling tired and unhappy.

Marsden sat in her chair and laid back her head. She closed her eyes for a minute, reflecting on everything she had heard and witnessed.

There had been evidence of rape, scratches, post mortem bruising reaching the surface of her skin, and detritus under her fingernails that, along with the semen evidence, would hopefully lead them straight to her murderer.

Tessa felt in her heart that it was Jacob Thorne; it had cut her to the bone when she had heard that Mandy had been a virgin prior to her death on that cold rainswept evening.

It seemed obvious that Orla French's murder was unconnected and yet Marsden knew it would be unprofessional of her to make that decision. Two girls missing on the same night from the same village... coincidence? She lit up her screen and scrolled through reports. She needed to tie up loose ends on the Mandy Williamson death; Zoe Williamson had been escorted by Siân Dawson to formally identify her daughter; the FLO's report showed that Zoe had been quite calm, almost accepting of her daughter's death until they had got outside into the car park after the identification. She had then fallen apart, and Dawson had opted to remain with Zoe for as long as she needed her. Tessa read through other reports almost mechanically; there was only one report that was missing, the DNA report on the semen traces and the fingernail scrapings.

She clicked onto the Orla French file and was reading through it when an email arrived, from the pathology lab. She opened it, then leaned back and closed her eyes once more. She remained like that for a couple of minutes, then pulled the physical file of Orla's case towards her, temporarily closing down her screen. She wanted no distractions while she read through this particular statement.

DS Hannah Granger was sitting at her own desk repeating Marsden's actions. Reading through all the reports sometimes flagged up inconsistencies, or even consistencies, and she had taken her time, checking every word carefully. Alibis were of the most importance. Every minute had to be checked and double-checked, and she had spent the morning doing that. Again. For the third time.

A movement distracted her and she became aware that Tessa was waving an arm in her direction. Hannah pushed back her chair, and headed for the office tucked into the corner of the large room.

'Grab your stuff, Hannah. Let's go have a chat to somebody who has been less than truthful.' Tessa slid the DNA report across the desk towards Hannah, and waited while she carefully absorbed it.

'Bloody hell.'

'You surprised? I was.'

'Gobsmacked, more like. How's he going to talk himself out of this?'

'Let's go and find out, shall we...'

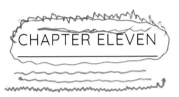

CHAPTER ELEVEN

Hannah drove, and they headed towards the Peak District, each deep in their own thoughts. Two dead girls, and DNA results seemed to be the one thing that connected them – their murderers would be convicted mainly on that evidence.

Perhaps.

Tessa gave a huge sigh. She turned to look at Hannah. 'You enjoy your job, Hannah?'

'I enjoy the part where we get doughnuts brought in, and where we go out for a drink sometimes, after we've finished for the day. And I enjoy seeing someone go down for a serious crime, but in the main I don't "enjoy" it.'

Tessa stared down at her fingers. 'Neither do I. When I became a DI, I decided I wanted to be an out in the field DI, not a deskbound one, and I've stuck to that. I'm not chasing promotion, because that would definitely keep me indoors, but these two cases are testing me, for sure. I'm not overthinking the Mandy Williamson one yet, because in my heart I'm sure it's the Thorne lad. We can place her in his car, he had her boot tucked into his jacket, and the mud is a match for the mud around the gravesite. But this one, Orla, is a bit baffling.'

Hannah gave a slight nod of agreement. 'Andy Harrison's alibi is rock solid. He's always with other people. He works in an open-plan office, so everybody can see everybody else. It's confirmed he didn't leave until six, exactly the same as every day. Ten people have confirmed he was in a meeting with them when his wife rang to say Orla was missing and up to that point he was behaving perfectly normally. The doc says she was killed between four and six the previous afternoon, and he was definitely in Manchester.'

'And now we've seen the DNA result from him and the foetus...'

'Exactly. He can't be the one who killed her, but this could have turned out so well for him. If we hadn't taken his DNA sample, Marnie Harrison need never have known he was screwing her daughter as well as her.'

Tessa frowned. 'So why did she die?'

'What?'

'Why did she die? To me, it looks as though Andy Harrison was the only person who needed to get rid of her. She was carrying his baby; clearly nobody else knew because we haven't even had a suggestion that she was pregnant from anyone interviewed so far. What's the motive?'

There was silence from the DS.

Tessa was relentless. 'And why there? She supposedly was going to Hope, to Emily Carr's house. Peakshole Water where she was found is in the opposite direction. There is no way she would have been there if the intention was to walk to Hope. Could she have arranged to meet someone without mentioning it to anybody? Paul Carr, the potential new boyfriend, was at his mother's house, along with his mother and Emily, waiting for her arrival, and had travelled home with Emily, having collected her from work. Both their alibis are as solid as Andy Harrison's. So why, why, why was she at Peakshole Water, and on such a horrible night? Don't go straight to the Harrison's, Hannah, let's go to the pub.'

.   .   .

Hannah pulled into the pub car park and they got out, Hannah grabbing her umbrella as the rain had intensified over the previous five minutes. They ran, Hannah stopping in the doorway to close the umbrella, and then followed her boss into the pub. They took their orange juices across to a table near to the warmth of the log-burning fire, and studied the menu.

'We've about an hour to kill,' Tessa said, trying to decide between meat and potato pie or a gammon steak, 'because I reckon if Harrison's gone to work that's about the time he'll be home. If he's still staying at home with Marnie he'll be there now and he'll keep. We need food.'

'Okay, forget what I said about not liking my job,' Hannah said, making her tone serious. 'The meat and potato pie has swung it. I love my job.'

'Me too,' Tessa said. 'That's pie for two, then.' She walked to the bar, placed their order and returned to the table.

'You don't want to get Marnie on her own then?' Hannah asked the question, because she knew that given the same set of circumstances she would have driven straight to the Harrison home, and taken whatever the situation was.

'No. We would end up having to tell her, before he arrived. That's not what I want. I want to see her face when she finds out he fathered her grandchild.'

Hannah sighed. Every day a school day; she learned so much from this woman.

The meat and potato pie was truly delicious and filling, so much so that they both declined a dessert.

'I think,' Hannah said without smiling, 'that is the first time I have ever refused treacle pudding.'

'Me too,' Tessa said. 'But think of the calories we've not eaten.'

She glanced at her watch. 'We'll give it another ten minutes, then go. You want another orange juice?'

'No thanks. I want to get this over with. We're probably about to destroy someone's marriage, and that's not a good thought because she clearly loves him, but we're also going to be telling the poor woman that he's been having sex with her daughter and we don't know if it was rape, or if she welcomed it. He, of course, is going to say she welcomed it, he's never going to admit to forcing her, is he? And she's not here to tell us the truth.'

Tessa smiled at Hannah and reached across to touch her hand. 'That could have been me speaking, Hannah. I would have used those same words, and you're right about every aspect. It is going to be difficult, but I'll need you to watch Marnie very carefully, I'll be concentrating on Andy Harrison.'

'No problem, boss.' Hannah picked up her coat, nicely dried and warmed. 'Let's get this over with.'

'Have you let David know you're going to be late?'

There was a brief moment of hesitation as Hannah paused in putting on her coat. 'No.'

'Do you need to let him know?'

'Not really. We're not together anymore.'

'But...'

'But I didn't tell you. I know I didn't. It's still a bit raw. It was our anniversary the day we took out Leon Rowe, and I missed the meal David had organised. To spite me, he rang his PA and took her instead. It was the beginning of the end. They're together, he moved in with her and I kept our flat on.'

'Oh God, Hannah. This bloody job isn't good for any marriage. The only ones who stay together are the ones where they're both in the job. I'm so sorry you've gone through this.'

Hannah smiled. 'Next time I'll go for somebody who's already a copper. Maybe the Chief Constable.'

'Good idea,' Tessa laughed. 'I'll be your bridesmaid. Let's get this out of the way. Drive around to their house, but make sure you park across the bottom of their driveway.'

Hannah held up a thumb, and they left the pub, calling good night to a landlord immersed in his crossword.

Andy Harrison's black BMW was on the drive, parked almost touching the rear bumper of his wife's much smaller cream-coloured Aygo.

Hannah pulled up on the roadside, blocking the escape route should anybody choose to leave the Harrison house in a hurry.

The two women sat for a moment, and surveyed the scene. A bedroom light was on, the lounge room similarly illuminated. The car in front of Hannah's was Nadine Bond's blue Micra, and Tessa felt a slight feeling of relief. Nadine was an excellent officer, fully trained in caring for bereaved families, and to have her there when she confronted Harrison about his fun and games with his step-daughter was a bonus. Tessa suspected Marnie was going to need extra support any time now.

'You ready?' Tessa asked.

'Nope,' was Hannah's response.

'Me neither. Come on, let's go confront the bastard.'

They climbed out of the car and headed up the drive. Tessa noticed the movement of the bedroom curtain, and knew that Andy Harrison had seen them. She also recognised that he must have known that his DNA sample, taken from him almost with the element of surprise behind the action, would show he was the father of his stepdaughter's baby.

'Hannah.' There was urgency in her voice. 'He's clocked us. Back door.'

She watched as Hannah sprinted around the corner of the house, then Tessa waited a minute before knocking on the front door.

Andy Harrison opened it, and Tessa felt relief wash over her. He wasn't running – yet.

'Mr Harrison,' she said. 'I'd like a word with you.'

He hesitated, then opened the door wide to allow her to enter. Nadine was in the hallway.

'Nadine, can you open the back door and let DS Granger in, please?'

Harrison's face showed surprise but he merely led her into the lounge. 'Marnie's having a nap,' he said. Do you need her?'

'Yes, please. I'm sure Nadine can get her.'

Nadine, escorting Hannah through to the lounge, inclined her head and went upstairs.

Marnie Harrison looked dreadful. Her hair hung in greasy tendrils around her face, her eyes dead in their sockets. She didn't acknowledge their presence, merely sat on the settee. Her husband settled by her side, and took hold of her hand.

Nadine remained standing by the door, and Hannah stood by the armchair that Tessa had taken.

Tessa opened her bag and removed a file.

CHAPTER TWELVE

Doris checked her appearance in the long wardrobe mirror, somewhat critically. Still slim as she had been all her life, but with much greyer hair than she would have chosen for herself, she knew she was still of a much younger appearance than her almost seventy years.

'Okay, Doris Lester,' she murmured, 'you'll do.'

She headed downstairs and poured herself a small glass of wine. She recognised it for what it was – a courage booster.

She debated whether to wear a jacket or a longer coat, then decided on the longer one. It might only be a two-minute walk to the Bowling Green but it was bitterly cold. She zipped on her boots and left the warmth of her cottage for the short walk around the corner. Ewan was waiting for her in the car park. He stepped towards her and smiled.

'I'm so pleased you could make it,' he said, and leaned towards her to give her a gentle kiss on her cheek.

'I've been looking forward to it,' she admitted. 'My usual companions are Kat and Beth. Seeing you tonight is such a welcome change.'

'Then let's get in the pub before we freeze to death.' He put his arm around her shoulders and guided her towards the door.

'Mr Harrison,' Tessa began. 'It appears you haven't been totally honest with us.'

Andy glanced at her but said nothing. His wife acted in a similar manner but didn't seem to be taking anything in.

'Andy?' Tessa's voice was insistent.

'I've no idea what you're talking about. You've spoken to my work colleagues, you know what time I left work. I didn't stop off and kill my stepdaughter, I didn't have fucking time.' His voice grew in volume the longer he continued to speak.

Marnie Harrison remained sitting, holding her husband's hand, expressionless. Tessa guessed she was on some sort of antidepressant, prescribed to get her through the horrific few days around her daughter's death.

Tessa opened the buff file and removed the email copy that had given her the DNA results. 'Then if you won't speak voluntarily about the issue, Mr Harrison, I have to ask you if Orla told you about her pregnancy and asked you for help.'

His face hardened. 'Neither of us knew. It came as a complete shock when you told us about it. You know it did.' He let go of Marnie's hand, put his arm around her shoulder and pulled her close.

Okay, Tessa thought, *play it like that, Mr Innocent. Let's see how you react in a second.*

'Mr Harrison, I have the results of your DNA test, plus the results of the foetal DNA, and they are a match. You are the father of your stepdaughter's baby.'

Marnie Harrison's head moved slightly to look at her husband. His face was devoid of colour, and her hand came up with some swiftness, hitting him hard across the cheek.

'Bastard,' she growled. 'Absolute bastard.'

Antidepressants no longer working then, Tessa conceded to herself.

Nadine moved across to separate husband and wife, and still Andy hadn't said anything.

'Didn't you realise when we swabbed you for DNA that this would be the end result?'

His face was still blank and she wondered if this was the last thing he had expected to hear, or if he was a superb actor.

'Andy?' Her gentler tone seemed to bring him out of his trance.

'Once,' he said. 'Only once. I didn't think for one minute...'

Tears were flowing down Marnie's face, and Nadine helped her to stand and took her to the dining table at the far end of the room. Marnie sat, and sank her head onto her arms on the table. Nadine left to get her some water.

Tessa stared at Andy. 'Talk me through it, Mr Harrison.'

He moaned, almost a growl. 'It was months ago, or at least I thought it was. That's why it didn't occur to me I could be the father. Marnie went to the theatre in Sheffield with a friend and they stayed over, rather than driving back here, made a bit of a holiday of it. I was sitting watching television in here and Orla came in with a towel around her. She said she'd had a shower.'

He paused, his mind going back to that time. Tessa waited.

'She handed me a brush and asked me to detangle her wet hair. She sat on the floor in front of me. I thought nothing of it. I've always done it. I finished, handed her the hairbrush and she stood, but she left the towel on the floor. I bent to pick it up, trying not to look at her. As I handed it to her, she leaned forward to kiss me.'

He dropped his head and stared at the floor. It occurred to Tessa that he was probably sitting in exactly the same spot as he was on that night.

'Go on,' she encouraged him.

He shrugged. 'She was beautiful. Stunningly beautiful. And

leaning over me, naked, pushing me down onto the settee. She said she needed to be taught how to make love, and she trusted me.'

There was a moan from Marnie and she rose from her chair. Nadine put a hand on her shoulder and eased her back down.

Tessa continued. 'So you had sex with her?'

He nodded. 'I did, to my utter shame.'

'Where? In her bed? Your bed?' Tessa was relentless. She could see Hannah taking notes out of the corner of her eye and hoped she wasn't missing anything.

'No, here. On the settee.'

The noise that came from Marnie's throat was akin to someone being strangled.

'Why, Andy? Why did she need to be taught?' Tessa felt breathless, as if she was on the verge of something.

'She said there was somebody at church who she was interested in, and she thought they would be going all the way, as she put it, before much longer. She didn't say who it was, and I was in no fit state to ask her. The next day I texted Marnie, who was still in Sheffield, to say I had to go to a three-day conference. I booked myself into the Hilton in Manchester for the time I needed to come to terms with what had happened.'

'What happened when you came home?'

'Nothing. She acted as normal, never mentioned it again, and I tried to put it behind me.'

'And this person at church?'

'I know nothing of who he is. You said she was at the very beginning of a relationship with Paul Carr, but he doesn't go to church so it couldn't have been him.'

'Didn't it occur to you that you should maybe have used protection?'

'No. I had a beautiful eighteen-year-old girl coming onto me, totally naked. You reckon I had time to think about contraception?'

'Okay,' Tessa said. 'I'm taking you back to the station now. We need a statement. You will be kept overnight, but I can see Marnie needs time away from you anyway.' She put away the file, and five minutes later he was in the back of the car, the two policewomen in the front.

Marnie was left with Nadine; unable to stop the tears, unable to forgive him.

Doris waited outside her home with Ewan until his taxi arrived. He gave her a swift kiss on the cheek, and climbed into the rear seat. 'Call you tomorrow,' he said, and the taxi departed.

She stood for a moment watching as its tail lights disappeared, then turned and hurried indoors, suddenly feeling the cold. She locked the door behind her, then put another log in the wood burner, hoping it hadn't burned down too low, before heading for the kitchen.

She cradled a cup of hot chocolate and wandered into the lounge. Thinking back over her night out gave her a great deal of pleasure; he had been wonderful company, knowledgeable, funny, and he didn't once mention his quest for his son. Doris appreciated that. It hadn't been a night out to discuss work, it had been a night out for enjoyment.

Picking up her book, Doris settled down for half an hour of reading time, but even Daphne du Maurier couldn't keep Doris's mind off the man with the beautiful white hair and Mediterranean sea-blue eyes. In the end she gave in, slipped her bookmark back into the book, and simply sat and stared into the flames.

From the depths of her bag her phone pinged, and she ferreted around in the bottom to find it.

Thank you for tonight, I hope you enjoyed it as much as I did. x

Staring at the phone didn't help the rush of pink to her face, and she touched her cheek with her hand. This was silly, she was nearly seventy and grinning inanely because she'd had a text from a man. She answered the text and put down the phone, then picked it up again.

Should she ring Mouse? Check how she was? Doris put the phone beside her once more. Best not ring her granddaughter, there would only be a spate of questions.

The phone rang. She glanced at the screen. Kat. Doris was tempted to ignore it, but knew Kat would keep trying until she got an answer.

'Hi, Kat.'

'Nan, it's me.'

'I know. It said so on my screen.'

'Oh... sorry, I'm functioning with my mummy head on at the moment so my brain's in meltdown. I have a child over my left shoulder.'

Doris sat up. 'Is everything okay?'

'It's fine. She's a bit crabby with this cold. I rang to tell you not to ring Mouse, she went to bed about nine with half a pharmacy inside her, because she says she's coming into work tomorrow. I think it's kill or cure for her tonight,' she laughed.

'Okay, thank you. I was wondering whether to ring or not. I'm glad I didn't. See you tomorrow?'

'Er... one second. You've not said how your evening went.'

'It was good.'

'And that's it?'

'It is as far as you and Mouse are concerned.' Doris's laughter echoed in Kat's ear.

'Oh. It's only because we love you, you know.'

'Kat, I'm seventy...'

'Sixty-nine...'

'Okay, sixty-nine, and I know my way around this life. Stop worrying about me. I'm not going to do a Henry and Clara and elope to Peak Forest. I've been out for one drink with him. Well, maybe three.'

'Who's Henry and Clara?'

'The lovers who were killed on Winnats Pass. In the 1760s, I believe. They were eloping to Peak Forest because her father wouldn't let her marry Henry. Five miners killed them. Remember?'

'Aha! Vaguely. Can you still marry without permission at Peak Forest then?'

'I believe so.'

'So it's no good Mouse and I withholding permission for you to marry him?'

'No good at all. I'm over eighteen.'

'Okay, I'll take that as a good enough reason. But you've enjoyed your night out?'

'It's been lovely. He's a really nice man. Go and get that baby in bed. I'm safe and I'm home, and my hot chocolate is turning into cold chocolate.'

Kat laughed, they said goodnight and Doris disconnected at her end.

CHAPTER THIRTEEN

Andy Harrison felt devastated. How could his whole life have been demolished in four months? That evening when Orla had given herself to him seemed almost a fantasy, not something he'd ever thought about, prior to that night. She was a child, Marnie's child.

Pregnant with his child.

He had been taken from the cell and placed in an interview room. He felt sick. It was obvious they would assume he had murdered Orla, but he hadn't even been in bloody Castleton, for fuck's sake, he'd been in Manchester.

His chin dropped almost to his chest as he thought of what everything would mean. He would lose Marnie, for sure, and he wasn't convinced he could bear that. She was the woman he had waited for, ever since his divorce from Catherine.

And work? What would it mean for his job? At the very least he would be suspended, pending completion of the investigation. And it would forever be a pall hanging over him, no matter who was convicted of Orla's murder.

Because he knew the paternity of the baby would be a factor at the trial.

He looked up as the door opened.

Tessa Marsden did the tape requirements, then opened her file. She didn't believe for one minute this man was directly guilty of the murder of his stepdaughter; his alibi was solid to the point of cast-iron rigidity. It didn't mean he was innocent.

'Tell me about your friends, Andy.'

'What?' The question clearly took him by surprise.

'Your friends. The people you and Marnie go out with, ring up when you've got a problem.'

He looked even more puzzled. 'We don't really have any. We rarely go out, and if we do, it's the two of us. We used to take Orla, but that dropped off when she turned sixteen. She preferred to stay in and read...' His voice shook. 'I'm sorry, it's hard to come to terms with.'

'No friends at all?' Tessa was persistent.

'No. I have friends at work, obviously, but they're colleagues rather than friends. We go out once a year with them to the Christmas meal, but neither of us seem to need anybody else.' And then the shutters fell. 'You think I paid somebody to kill her? My God, DI Marsden, I wouldn't have your job for the world. What a nasty evil mind you must have to live with every minute of your life.'

'There are a lot of nasty evil people in this world that have made it like that,' Tessa answered, keeping her voice flat.

'Well,' Andy's voice was grating, 'it might surprise you to know that I tend not to mix with killers, not in my private life, my work life, or any other life. Check my mobile, my phone at home... check my bloody extension at work, you'll find I'm the most boring person on this planet.'

'We're already in the process of checking them, Mr Harrison.' Hannah stepped in with the remark.

He turned to glare at her. 'Then good luck with that, Hannah. I rarely phone anyone other than my wife. It won't take you long to do that job – not as long as it's taking you to find Orla's killer, anyhow.'

Marsden turned over a sheet of paper. 'Let's move on. The night when you had sex with Orla... let's go through it one more time.'

'Why? Does it turn you on?'

'No, Mr Harrison. It sickens me. But hey ho, it's my job. Begin at the beginning, please.'

Harrison sighed and leaned back in his chair. 'I was sitting on the settee – no, I wasn't, to be truthful I was lying on the settee – reading my book.'

'Last night you said you were watching television, sitting watching television.'

'And I was. I had the television on, but was reading at the same time. And I was lying down, prior to Orla coming in, wrapped in a towel. Then I sat up because she asked if I would brush her hair to get out the knots. She sat on the floor, between my knees, and I worked on her hair for about five or six minutes. I handed her the brush, and she stood. The towel remained on the floor. I remember edging forward to pick up the towel, but she leaned towards me and kissed me.'

He paused and shook his head. 'But none of this makes sense. Did she die because I made her pregnant? That can't be the reason, surely. She said nothing to me, nothing to Marnie. Maybe it didn't occur to her the baby was mine. Maybe this chap at church she told me about thinks he's the father, and she thought the same. What if he's a married man? That would be a motive, a pretty hefty one, wouldn't it?'

'Leave the detection to us, Mr Harrison. Continue with your story. When you've finished, Hannah will type your statement for your signature, so don't miss anything out. You will be given the opportunity to amend it before you sign it, of course.'

Harrison stared at her. She was so cold, so unfeeling... 'As I said, she kissed me. I was still sitting down, and as she kissed me, she pushed me backwards and I was then lying down, my feet still on the floor. In between kisses she told me she needed to learn how to make love, how much she trusted and loved me, and she had chosen me to teach her. I know this sounds stupid coming from a forty-something man, but I was in a right state. I didn't know how to handle the situation, and I knew deep inside that if I tried to stop what she was doing I would have to touch her, to put my hands on her naked body, and I would be lost. So she pulled down the zip on my jeans.'

He lowered his head, then raised a hand to his eyes. 'I'm sorry, that was the undoing of me, and she knew it. She ended up underneath me, and I was the one who took her virginity. I'm not proud of it.'

'And how did she behave around you after that?'

'She went back to being exactly the same as she had been before that night. She knew there was no romantic connection between us, I was somebody she had calculatedly used so that she wasn't a complete novice when she went with this man, and it got her virginity out of the way at the same time.'

I made sure I was never alone with her, but I genuinely don't think it would have made any difference at all. She needed that first time so that she knew what was happening to her body. It affected me so much more. I started working later, so Marnie started to get a bit iffy about that, and I stopped taking Orla anywhere. Marnie used her little car if Orla wanted to go out. Everything changed in my head, yet it didn't seem to in Orla's head.'

'And you're absolutely sure you don't know who the man is at church?'

'No. She never said a word. And of course Marnie knew nothing about him either. She wasn't the one Orla spoke to about him, was she.' There was bitterness in his tone of voice. 'I was singled out for that honour.'

'When we told you Orla had been found, what did you think?'

'Initially?' That she had slipped into the river. The rain was torrential. Even when you said she had died before going into the water, it never dawned on me it had any connection to that night. Even when you said she had been pregnant, I assumed it was the chap at church. I couldn't tell you that, because of how I knew about him, but I guessed eventually you would track him down. It never occurred to me for a minute it would be me you tracked down as being the father.'

Tessa closed her file. 'Mr Harrison, you can go home once you've signed your statement. If you think of anything in the meantime that can lead us to this man who Orla spoke about, please contact us immediately. I'll leave you in this room until Hannah gets back to you, and I'll have coffee sent in. Thank you for your cooperation. Will you be going home?'

His short bark of laughter said it all. 'I have no idea, DI Marsden. If I can't stay there, I'll let you know where I am.'

Mouse walked into the shop, followed closely by Doris.

'Morning, you two,' Kat beamed. 'You feeling better, Mouse?'

'Much better, although I'm still growling like a lion. If I nod off, leave me. I'll wake up eventually.'

'So what's the plan? I need a couple of hours to wind up the paperwork for that forensics course, then if you need me to input data or anything, I'm your man. Woman.' Kat sounded too bubbly, and both Doris and Mouse stared at her.

'What's going on? It's only nine and you're bouncing. You don't even talk until ten. How much coffee have you had?'

'It's the champagne from last night, probably.'

'Champagne? You drink cheap rosé, or, at a push, even cheaper white. Carl got a promotion?'

'Two.'

'Two promotions? Good Lord, is this on the back of the work

he's done for Pam Bird?' Mouse asked. Mentioning Pam's name brought memories back to all of them of the investigation into finding Pam earlier in the year, and the recovery of some of the money that had been stolen from her.

'That's the first part, yes. He's been promoted to DI. The second promotion is to husband-in-waiting.'

There was a silence in the room while Doris and Mouse processed her words.

Mouse spoke first. 'You mean...?'

Kat held out her left hand. The solitaire diamond was a sparkle of fire, casting shards around the beautiful stone. 'I had no idea,' she said. 'I knew the DI was a strong possibility, and he gave me that news first. Then he produced this, and asked me to marry him.'

'Group hug, I think,' Doris said with a smile. They held each other, savouring the moment.

'So where is he, our handsome DI?'

'At work. He says people are still defrauding other people so he has to stay and do his job. Fair enough,' Kat said with a laugh. 'But on Sunday, if you're both free, we'd like to take you two and Mum and Dad out for a meal to celebrate. Thursday today, Mouse, so you've three days to get better.'

'Don't worry about that, if there's a meal on offer, I'll be fighting fit.'

Doris held Kat's hand and inspected the ring. 'It's beautiful, Kat. Many congratulations, my love, may you have much happiness with our Carl. Coffee to celebrate?' And she moved across to begin their Thursday.

CHAPTER FOURTEEN

Mouse looked at the monitor, then turned to her second screen and clicked on Google. She brought up the document stored in OneDrive, and stared at the two names.

Michael George Fairfax born in Inverness, and Michael Ian Fairfax born in Scarborough. The two babies born on the right day and with the right names, but different middle names.

It had taken an hour to find out that Helen Fairfax had married and become Helen North, but that it hadn't lasted – divorced three years later – and she had reverted to Fairfax.

Helen's town of birth was Holmesfield, a suburb on the very borders of Sheffield and the Peak District, according to her birth certificate.

The little boy born in Scarborough suddenly seemed to be a fair possibility, although Helen Fairfax had clearly not kept her promise to use Ewan for the middle name. Ian was as close as it could get though, if you felt you needed to salve your conscience...

Mouse laid her head back and rubbed her forehead. Although she felt much better than she had, she didn't feel up to searching and having to be careful not to be seen searching.

She updated their files with the information she could add to it, then closed her eyes for a second.

Doris opened Mouse's office door. 'Mouse, Tessa's here. Do you... oh!'

Mouse jumped, stared around in panic, then rubbed her eyes. 'I fell asleep! I had a nanny nap. Am I suddenly an old woman?'

Doris smiled at her granddaughter, who was frantically trying to gather her senses. 'Stop panicking, Mouse. You're not old, you're ill. Are we in here, or Kat's office?'

'Has Kat got coffee?'

'Probably. Kat's never without coffee.'

'We'll go in there.' Mouse stood and felt pain in what seemed to be all of her body. 'Don't let me fall asleep in a chair again, will you?' she said ruefully, rubbing her arms and legs in an attempt at getting her circulation moving again.

Tessa and Hannah were in reception, and both looked at Mouse sympathetically. 'You look rough,' Tessa said.

'Thanks. Cheer a girl up, will you... It's no consolation that I feel as bad as I look, but honestly, you should have seen me yesterday. Today, this is perfection.'

'Coffee's poured out,' Kat called from her larger office.

Even in Kat's office, it was overfull with five people sitting around the one desk. 'Everything okay?' Kat asked. 'How's Amanda Williamson's case progressing?'

'It's progressed,' Tessa said. 'I've had confirmation this morning that the semen trace was a DNA match with Jacob Thorne, so we're officially not looking for anyone else in connection with that murder. My DCI went to notify Thorne's family this morning. I can't imagine how they must be feeling. I've been to tell Zoe Williamson, but I think she felt relief that she has some sort of closure. We're releasing Mandy's body this afternoon, so Zoe can lay her to rest properly, and spend the rest of her life coming to terms with it, probably.'

'How would she feel if I went to see her, do you think?' Kat asked.

'I'm sure she would welcome it,' Tessa said. 'You've a very calm and soothing touch, Kat, and I suspect she needs that at the moment. I don't know this for certain, but I think she's a regular churchgoer, as well as Mandy.'

'Then I'll ring her, I'll not turn up on her doorstep.'

'Good,' Tessa said. 'We're progressing in an odd sort of way with the Orla French murder. We know who the father of the baby is, but I'm a hundred per cent sure he's not her killer. He has an alibi that nobody could break.'

'So you're excluding rather than involving?'

'We are. However, before I go any further with that, who's taken away the real DS Carl Heaton and sent us a new one? For a start he's turned up as DI Heaton, but there's something else. He's bouncing all over the place, cracking jokes, singing... singing! It's just not him. So what have you done with our Carl, and why have you sent us a substitute?'

Kat felt the blush begin to deepen, and she placed her left hand in the middle of the table.

Hannah and Tessa stood as one, and leaned over to inspect the ring. Equally as one, they said, 'Wow.'

'Last night,' Kat said. 'After he'd told me of his promotion.'

'Congratulations, Kat, That's wonderful,' Tessa said. 'I'm so pleased for both of you.'

'Right that's enough of the mush,' Doris said. She didn't want any semi-romantic talk heading in her direction, and thought it expedient to fixate on the crime scene in Derbyshire. 'Let's go back to Orla French.'

'There's not a lot to go back to,' Tessa frowned. 'It seems that Orla wanted to take her first sexual lessons with her stepfather because she trusted him, and she was planning on having sex with someone at church. Unfortunately for us, she didn't say who it was. And I honestly think Andy Harrison's penis was governing everything, he wouldn't have even thought to ask her who she was planning on seducing. So, in a way we have a suspect, we simply don't know who he is. Tomorrow we go to church. And if we don't get answers in the morning, we'll go back on Sunday when all the congregation is there. If necessary we'll lock the doors until we've spoken to each and every one of them.'

'Were there any defence marks on her? Did she fight back?' Doris looked troubled, imagining how scared the young girl would have been.

'It seems not. She was knocked unconscious before she was strangled. She was definitely dead before she went into the water, but we've no way of knowing if that was the location where she died, or if she was killed elsewhere and then brought in a vehicle to be dumped in the water. It was running very fast because of the rain, so she could have been dumped higher up. She was wedged between the bank and the bridge.'

'Man or woman? Any feelings on the matter?' Kat asked.

'Not really. She was a very slim girl, nothing about her, so it could easily have been either. Strangulation isn't usually a method chosen by women to kill people, though. It's actually quite hard work subduing somebody enough to strangle them, but she was whacked on the head with something to knock her out, so that tells us it could be either sex. She would be easy to strangle if she wasn't moving.'

'It could be a very angry woman,' Kat responded. 'I wonder if this man at church is married...'

Marsden beamed. 'Now *this* is why I like to come here. One of you always sets me off on a different tangent. One thing's for sure, I have to find out who this man is. I hope somebody in that congregation has seen something, or is uncomfortable about something.'

Mouse closed down for the day, a thoughtful expression on her face. She needed to have a conversation with Ewan, find out exactly what he could remember about Helen's early years, before jumping in with both feet. If they ever needed to contact Helen, they didn't want her pre-warned. The element of surprise was important in most cases. If Ewan could help, it would be to their advantage.

She would ring, make an appointment either at his home, or ask him to drop by for a general chat.

She waved Kat and Doris off, then trudged upstairs to her own flat. It felt cold so she switched on the heating, boiled some water, and made herself a hot lemon. She hated the taste but they did seem to be making her feel better, so she suffered the tang of the lemon mixed with the strange flavour of the medication and sat on the settee with a fleece blanket wrapped snugly around her, watching the news.

While cuddling the fleece, she rang Ewan, explained she needed to chat to him as she hadn't really met him and needed his take on one or two things, and he said he would call into the office the next day. She thanked him, said she hoped she wouldn't infect him, and disconnected the call.

Within five minutes she was asleep and didn't wake up until midnight. Her stomach felt empty and she knew she wouldn't sleep without food inside her.

Two slices of toast made her feel better and she went to bed, her mind awake enough to wander off in several different directions. She sorted out the world in about half an hour, and slept the rest of the night without waking.

And so Thursday ended; slight progress on many fronts for all investigators, and the beginnings of a newly invigorated Mouse for Friday morning.

CHAPTER FIFTEEN

The church was a warm, welcoming place; as soon as they entered they were greeted by a tall lady, possibly in her sixties, who glanced at Tessa's ID and immediately offered to go and get the vicar from the vicarage.

'Is it about Orla's murder?' she asked, her face serious, intense.

'It is. Did you know her?'

'I did. Quite well, actually. I run the choir, and both Orla and Emily, her friend, are members. It's hit all of us quite hard, we will miss her. At first we thought it was an accident, but it seems that she was killed. That, of course, makes it a thousand times worse.' She held out her hand. 'My name is Annabel Knight – Mrs – and if I can do anything to help...'

'Thank you, Mrs Knight. We understand Orla was seeing someone at church, a fairly new relationship. Would you know who it was?'

'Seeing someone? A boyfriend?' Annabel hesitated, and it was obvious. 'Not that I'm aware of, but she was a very pretty girl. I don't think it's anyone here though.'

'No young men showing a special interest in her?' Hannah asked.

The older woman laughed, a little uncomfortably. 'No, it's not that, it's more that there are only old men. I think the youngest male member of our church is the vicar, and he's thirty-five. The oldest male here is Tommy Landers and he was ninety a few months ago. All the other men are somewhere between those two ages. Young lads don't seem interested in church happenings, not these days.'

Tessa gave a brief smile. 'Thank you. Do you think you could get the vicar for us, please? Or would it be easier for us to go to the vicarage?'

'I'll go get him. His wife Ruby is quite ill, and she's really going through it at the moment. I'll send him to you, and I'll sit with Ruby until he comes back.' Annabel nodded as if agreeing with herself.

'She's seriously ill?' Tessa asked.

'She was diagnosed with Multiple Sclerosis shortly after they married, ten years ago. It seems to be quite aggressive, and it's particularly bad at the moment. I'll nip across to the vicarage, and send Steve over here.'

Annabel left by a side door, and Tessa and Hannah strolled around the church, reading plaques on the wall, the floor, even on the pulpit. They were the only people remaining by the time Steve Barksworth joined them. He walked up to them, held out his hand and introduced himself.

'I guessed you would visit at some point,' he said. 'Orla was a very active member of our church, did loads in the community as well. She will be much missed by a lot of people in addition to her immediate family. I called to see Marnie and Andy this morning. Andy wasn't there, but Marnie looks ill. I'll ask Annabel to call tomorrow, Marnie may respond to a woman more.'

Tessa doubted that Marnie would respond to anyone. So Andy Harrison wasn't at home... Tessa hoped he'd left word at the police station of where he was staying.

Tessa felt a little guilty that she could see both sides of the issue – Andy Harrison hadn't chased Orla, Orla had chased him. Marnie had reacted in a way that maybe any woman would react, she had withdrawn from her husband.

Tessa didn't believe it was permanent; she thought they would eventually talk, and she thought Marnie would see the situation as it should be seen. They needed to find this man Orla was intent on seducing, put the whole thing into perspective.

'Reverend Barksworth,' Tessa began.

'Please, call me Steve. You make me feel old giving me my full title.'

'Okay, Steve, thank you. We won't keep you long. I understand your wife is unwell.'

He dipped his head, then looked at her. 'Indeed she is, but she would want me to help you if I can.'

'We believe Orla was seeing someone from the church. Do you know who it was?'

He paused before speaking. 'As far as I know, it wasn't someone from the church. I thought she had met up with Emily Carr's brother... Paul, I think he's called, but he doesn't attend church.'

'No,' Tessa pushed him. 'It wasn't Paul, this was definitely somebody from church. She told her stepfather, but didn't say who he was.'

Steve Barksworth frowned. 'But we have no young men of Orla's age who attend church. Could it have been a different church? Maybe it's somebody who attends Hope, or Bradwell. They're all within two or three miles of each other, so maybe you need to widen the net. I honestly can't come up with anyone from here.'

'We'll check them out, of course. Did she attend either of those churches?'

'Occasionally she went to Hope, and I know she went to Bradwell for instruction when she was confirmed, because they were running the course there for the area. So she did have links with them, but not as big an attachment as here.'

'Okay, thank you, Steve. I'll let you get back to your wife, and free up Mrs Knight to return here. We'll see you Sunday.'

'Sunday?'

'Yes. Maybe you could tell your congregation during the notices that we will need to speak to all of them before they go home.'

He looked shocked, but then his face lit up with a smile. 'Of course I can, but you can deal with Clarice Travers, not me. She scuttles out of this church so fast when the service is over, it's like a high-speed train barrelling through. She has to get home to do her Ernie's Sunday dinner, you see.'

Tessa laughed. 'I'll have a PC stationed on the door to stop her. Roughly how many attend, Steve?'

'On a good day it's around thirty to forty people, including the little ones. On a bad day when the weather's rough it's around ten.'

'Okay, we'll be here for about half past nine, we may get a chance to talk to some people before the service starts.'

'No.'

'No?'

'Definitely not. When people arrive early, it's because they need to, either to have a time of peace with God, or to ask for His help. You will not speak to anyone before the service. Afterwards it's a time of socialising. We have coffee and cakes and biscuits in the church hall and then people will respond to you. I mean it, DI Marsden, leave your arrival until five minutes or so before the start of the ten o'clock service.'

Tessa swallowed. She should have listened to Kat more, she would have known the pre-service time was sacrosanct. Tessa had better check she wouldn't be treading on any other toes on Sunday, before she actually arrived here. Kat would tell her.

Tessa shook hands with Steve, thanked him for his time and they walked back to the car.

'Jumpy, wasn't he?' Hannah said.

'And I walked straight into it, didn't I?' Tessa sighed.

'Oh, don't worry. Vicars don't bear grudges. Behave yourself on Sunday and everything will be fine.'

'Well, you'll need to behave yourself as well.'

'It's my day off!'

'Not now it isn't. I'll teach you to laugh at my mistakes, young woman. And what's more, you'll be driving.'

Hannah put the car into gear, turned to Tessa and gave a mock salute. 'Okay, boss, but don't I always drive?'

Ewan arrived at the office and with Mouse standing by the side of Doris, he greeted them both with a circumspect 'Good morning.' When Mouse moved away, he winked at Doris and blew her a kiss.

She couldn't stop the smile, didn't particularly want to.

He followed Mouse through to her office, and they sat facing each other across the desk. She placed her voice recorder in the middle and asked his permission to use it.

'Whatever,' he said, and waved his arm to say go ahead.

'Thank you, Ewan. I won't keep you long. We've come across some information that may be helpful, and please don't ask what it is. We don't feed out titbits, we wait until we have concrete proof of something before disclosing true facts. What we do need to know is anything you can tell us about Helen's early years. We know she was born in Holmesfield, but did she always live there?'

'No, she didn't. She lived on the coast until she was eleven, then came back to this area so she could go to the school her parents wanted for her.'

'Where on the coast?'

'Scarborough, I believe. Why?'

Mouse ignored his question. 'Did she have relatives there?'

'I'm reasonably sure she did, but you're asking me to remember something from many years ago, you know. I think that's why they moved from Holmesfield to Scarborough, I think Helen's mother had a sister who lived there.'

'Thank you. And can you think of anything else from her early years?'

He frowned, as if deep in thought. 'I don't think so. She said she couldn't remember Holmesfield, she was only about two when they moved to Scarborough, and they were back in the Hope Valley by the time she was eleven. I'm sorry I can't tell you more.'

'Don't worry about it,' Mouse said with a smile. 'You've confirmed what we need to know. As soon as we have news we'll be in touch.'

He picked up his coffee. 'Then if you've done with me, I'll go and chat up that beautiful lady out on reception.'

'Feel free,' Mouse said, and switched off the recorder. 'Hurt her, and I'll kill you.'

He laughed. 'You think I don't know that? And I promise you, I'll never hurt her, not in any way.'

CHAPTER SIXTEEN

I t didn't take Mouse long to come up with an address for Michael Fairfax; he still lived in Scarborough, although it was on the outskirts.

She put the information into her phone, and dropped her head onto her arms, acting as a desk pillow. She knew she wasn't well enough to be working, she wanted to sleep, and yet there was a yearning inside her to be doing what she had grown to love, the investigative side of the work at Connection.

She closed her eyes for five minutes, and then moved to give some relief to her back. Her headache was still present, but nowhere near as bad as it had been three days earlier.

She rummaged around inside her bag and produced a strip of paracetamol, popped two out of their blisters and swallowed them down with the dregs of her coffee.

Pulling up a map of Scarborough onto her screen, she checked out the address for Michael. It appeared to be on a cul-de-sac, the second building on the left. It was a detached residence, although she couldn't tell if it was a single or double-storey home. She logged the postcode into her phone, and then sat back once again. Her aches and pains were easing slightly, and it occurred to her it might be a good idea to go out for a short walk, blow some cobwebs away.

She left her office and found Ewan deep in conversation with Doris. 'Nan, I'm going upstairs to get a coat then out for a little walk. I'll call and pick up some food or something at the Co-op. Do you need anything?'

Ewan took out his wallet and removed a five pound note. 'Can you bring a couple of packets of Garibaldi, please?' he said with a laugh. 'I seem to have eaten most of your supplies.'

'You'll be okay?' Doris couldn't hide her worry. She'd never seen Mouse look so ill.

'I'll be fine. I'll only be ten minutes, I feel as if I need some fresh air. I'll have a coffee when I get back.'

She let herself out of the door, and Kat's office door opened.

'It's like Keystone Cops in here,' Doris remarked. 'Doors opening, doors closing, a different door opening, I feel quite dizzy.'

Kat smiled. 'We have a meeting in five minutes, Nan. DI Marsden is coming.'

Ewan stood. 'Then I'll be on my way. Thank you for your hospitality, ladies. I'll ring you later, Doris.'

Doris watched Ewan's car pull away, and turned to Kat. 'Do we know why Tessa's coming?'

'I think she has some questions about church protocol, because she's going to Castleton church on Sunday to interview the congregation. And she probably wants a coffee, it's blooming freezing out there today. Is Mouse okay?'

'She's gone out. Said she needed some fresh air.'

'Okay. We'll go in my office, shall we? I'll put on a fresh pot of coffee. I hope Tessa hasn't trodden on any toes this morning, I know she was going to see Steve Barksworth. Maybe I should have gone with her.'

'Did you ring Zoe Williamson?'

'I did. I'm going to see her tomorrow morning. I'm taking the service on Sunday, so couldn't do it then, and I didn't want to leave her until Monday. She sounded grateful that I wanted to visit her, said her vicar has a very poorly wife, and she didn't like to trouble him. I could have cried for her. She's lost her only child in horrific circumstances, and she doesn't want to ask her own vicar for help because his wife is ill. I'm going for ten o'clock, so I'll ask Mum to have Martha.'

'Hey, I thought we had an understanding about Martha! Isn't it my turn to have her?'

'But you've only been moved in a couple of days. I thought you'd have things to do.'

'She needs to try out her new cot. Please, Kat, bring her to me. Or do I have to kidnap her?'

Kat held up her hands. 'I'll bring her for about half past nine. That okay?'

Doris beamed. 'It's wonderful. I do miss her. And don't rush back.'

'So it'll be okay if I go and do some shopping after I've been to Castleton?'

'Too right it will. Martha and I will be fine.'

'Thank you,' Kat said, and leaned forward to kiss Doris. 'You're a star. And don't forget we're taking you out Sunday evening. We'll go in Carl's car, we can get all six of us in that, and it now has a child seat as a permanent fixture.'

'Martha's going with us?'

'She is. I can't leave her out of Mummy's engagement celebrations, can I.'

The door opened and Mouse, Tessa and Hannah walked in,

Hannah carrying shopping bags. She dumped them behind the reception desk.

'She's not well enough to be carrying them,' she said, staring at Doris and Kat accusingly.

'Whoa, in our defence,' Doris said, 'we didn't know she was doing a monthly shop. We sent her for two packets of garibaldi biscuits and some cheese to restock her fridge.'

'Well, I'll take them upstairs for you before I go, Mouse.' Hannah helped Mouse off with her coat, and Mouse smiled weakly. More a grimace.

'That's knackered me,' she said. 'I need caffeine.'

They sat around the desk, coffee in front of them, and Tessa finished telling her story of seeing Steve Barksworth.

'He was really nice, but he didn't half jump down my throat when I said I would go in before the service started on Sunday morning to question any early arrivals.'

'Good Lord,' Kat said, 'you can't do that! The church spire would probably fall off. That time before the service starts is used for either setting things up for the service, or for quiet contemplation and private prayer. I bet it's a mainly elderly congregation, and they'll do what they've done all their lives, have half an hour of peace with God before the service starts.'

'I know that now,' Tessa said. 'Barksworth said a very definite "No" when I made my suggestion. And then he explained everything you've said. I felt as though I'd committed an unforgivable sin.'

'You had.' Kat tried not to smile.

'Tell it like it is, Kat, why don't you.' Tessa looked a bit put out. 'So is there anything else I need to know?'

'Yes. I'm assuming Steve will be telling them about you needing to talk to them while he's giving out the notices. Tell him he must stress that nobody can leave until you've spoken with them, because there's always a couple of people who can't get out fast enough.'

'I've already been pre-warned about one of them, Clarice somebody or other, I think he said. I'll grab her first, then she can go. I will have a policeman on the door though, I need to speak with them all. It may be that one little meek and mild old lady who noticed something, or can come up with a name – it's so important I get them all, and ideally get a list of regular attendees who, for one reason or another, aren't there.'

Tessa leaned forward and picked up her coffee. 'Anything exciting happening here?'

'We've a lot of work on, mainly background checking of people wanting top jobs, but I'm off to Scarborough on Monday,' Mouse said.

Doris looked surprised. 'And I'll be going with her to do the driving.'

'I'll be fine, Nan,' Mouse said. 'Surely I'll be better by then.'

'I don't want you going to a strange house on your own. I'm assuming it's to see this Michael Fairfax?'

'It is. I've not really had a chance to discuss it with you two yet, I've only recently confirmed where he lives. I won't be going until the middle of the afternoon, catch him as he comes home from work.'

'You're not letting him know you're going?' Tessa asked.

Mouse shook her head. 'No, I don't want to give him the chance to say he doesn't want to know. We don't know what his mother's been telling him all these years, about his father. I need to speak with him, to put our client's side.'

'You're probably right.' Tessa sighed. 'I forget you can't go blundering in and demand he speaks with you. I could, but it's not advisable you do that.' She finished with a smile. 'Softly softly catchee monkey. But your nan is right. Don't go on your own. You don't know this man, you know nothing of his life…'

The smile on Mouse's face said a lot. 'Okay, maybe you know all about him, but you can't tell from a computer whether he's a psycho or not.'

'I take your point,' Mouse said. 'I was winding you up. Of course I'll take Nan. It's nice to be chauffeured around. And I'll be honest, if I'm still feeling as I am today, I'll put it off until I'm well. This has been flu, and it's been bloody awful. I'm sure our client will understand.'

'I'll man the office,' Kat said. 'Martha can come with me to keep me company. It'll only be for a couple of hours anyway, if you're not going until mid-afternoon. But we'll make all decisions Monday morning when we see how Mouse is feeling.'

'Anything else happening in Castleton, Tessa?' Mouse asked.

'Yes,' Hannah jumped in, 'I'm allegedly working Sunday.'

There was general laughter around the table at Hannah's disgruntled and fast response.

'So am I,' Tessa added. 'Bring your Bible, you might need it for admission.'

'Steve couldn't help you with any names?' Kat was curious. She liked Steve Barksworth, had met him at a couple of conferences, and had even taken two services at his church when he had been forced to miss them because of his wife's illness. She felt sure if he could have come up with something, he would have done so.

'No, he basically said they're all old men in the congregation. He mentioned that Orla had connections with Hope and Bradwell churches, but she was a quiet girl who didn't speak much to anyone except Emily. And Orla clearly didn't speak that much to her best friend because the only name Emily could come up with was her brother, Paul.'

'Which actually makes it sound quite unreal that she could be contemplating seducing somebody at church. She rather sounds a bit of a miss goody two-shoes, doesn't she?' Kat's face was thoughtful.

'You're dead right, Kat,' Tessa acknowledged. 'Which makes it all the more difficult ferreting out who the man is. Nobody knows anything because she kept it all to herself, except for the small bit of information she released to Andy Harrison when she really had to say why she wanted to learn how to make love.'

'What a mess.' Doris stood to get the coffee pot to refresh their mugs. 'And how is Marnie Harrison handling everything?'

'She's not. According to Nadine, her FLO, she's in pieces. Andy isn't there, so she's clearly not able to even look at him, even though she knows he's not the one who killed her daughter. It's the sex thing, I suppose. But I really hope they work through it, it was obvious how much he loved her, and she him.'

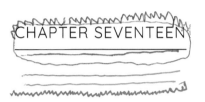

CHAPTER SEVENTEEN

A ndy Harrison wasn't feeling loved. In fact he would go so far as to say he was experiencing deep unlovement, if that indeed was a word. If it wasn't, it should be. It described exactly his current state of mind.

His hotel room wasn't particularly spacious, but it was particularly cheap. He'd notified Chesterfield Police Station of his change of address, saying it was temporary until things became resolved, and then had let Nadine Bond know of his whereabouts, in case Marnie needed to get in touch with him.

He lay down on the bed and closed his eyes. He'd also told his company he needed leave of absence until everything was sorted, and he felt that his boss had been a little bit huffy about it. *She was only a stepdaughter, wasn't she?* had been his first comment. *You been dipping your wick in places you shouldn't have?* had been another question, and he had terminated the call as quickly as he could.

It bothered him that maybe that's what everyone at work was thinking, and he could do nothing to refute any of the allegations. When news of the pregnancy came out at the trial, and he knew Tessa Marsden would make damn sure there would be a trial, he would have to find another job anyway. He wouldn't be able to face his colleagues.

He sighed and rolled over onto his side, hoping to drop off to sleep. He'd been awake, then asleep, then awake, then asleep all night long; he needed an hour to refresh him, but more to give his brain the blankness he craved. He wanted to stop thinking, to stop feeling regretful at what had happened between Orla and himself, to wish he hadn't been ruled by his dick, and more by his head. He should have walked out of that room, locked himself in the bathroom if necessary, but he couldn't have stayed in there all night. At some point he would have had to face Orla. For fuck's sake, he should have said no.

He was almost at the point of sleep when he heard the ping emanating from his phone. He groaned and scrabbled behind him on the bed without opening his eyes. He located it, and then looked at what the text said by opening his right eye. It was from Marnie.

Can we talk? x

Doris slid the casserole into the oven, then headed for the lounge. The new Stephen King was proving irresistible, and she made herself comfortable on the settee. Pulling a lusciously soft pale-blue fleece across her legs, she picked up the book.

Five minutes later, she put the book onto the coffee table. If she read any further she knew she would have to go back and reread it. Something was nagging at her mind, and she had no idea what it was. She let her thoughts meander through everything that had happened during the day, and still nothing became obvious.

Picking up her phone, she dialled Mouse.

'Hello sweetheart. How are you?'

'I'm getting there, Nan, honestly. I'm over the worst. I'll stick to the medication tomorrow, then we'll see how I go Sunday without taking anything. If I don't need so much as a paracetamol, we'll head for the coast on Monday.'

And then Doris knew why she felt uneasy.

'When you tracked Michael Fairfax down, did you also track down Helen Fairfax?'

'No. We're not looking for her. I might have done if Michael had been hard to find, but he wasn't. Ewan specifically said he didn't want to find Helen, it was simply his son he needed to meet.'

'Okay, here's what's going to happen. I'm going to look for her. I'm feeling uneasy. What if Michael still lives with her. We walk in there prepared to talk to him about his father, and possible inheritance issues, and Helen could be listening to every word.'

Mouse was silent.

'You see, Nan,' Mouse said eventually, 'this is why I need you working with me. Why didn't I think of that? If he's still living in Scarborough then it's odds on his mother is as well.'

Doris laughed. 'Under normal circumstances you would have thought of it. Let's not forget how poorly you've been this week, shall we. I'm going to start tracking her. I'll text you instead of ringing, in case you've fallen asleep. Love you.'

Doris pulled her laptop towards herself and searched for the information she needed.

Thirty minutes later, she texted Mouse.

She lives next door.

A conference call between the three members of Connection was speedily set up, and discussions followed regarding the way to tackle the issue without Helen Fairfax being made aware of anything.

Having a car pull up outside her son's house and two ladies emerge would possibly alert her to something out of the ordinary happening, and it would be a strong possibility that she would shoot around to his house, wanting to know what was going on.

They talked about maybe ringing him prior to the visit, but if he told his mother, she would probably insist on being there. Their loyalty was to their client, Ewan Barker, not Helen Fairfax. Having her know they were there could prove counterproductive.

'How about we park up nearby, and walk to his house,' Mouse suggested. 'At least there won't be a car to alert her.'

'That would certainly be better than parking outside, but what if he has a wife. If she's there, it's highly likely she'll ring Helen. We really could do with knowing where he works, and see if that's a possibility for talking to him.' Doris sounded thoughtful.

'Leave it with me,' Mouse said. 'I'll delve deeper. I'll leave it until tomorrow, but we'll know everything about him by then. Helen living next door has made it so much more difficult, but it's not insurmountable. Go to bed, you two. And good luck with your visit to Zoe tomorrow, Kat.'

They closed down their laptops, Kat grinning inanely that she had survived a conference call, her second one, without managing to disconnect the other two participants.

Saturday morning was yet another grim day, cold, dark grey and with the ever-present threat of rain. Kat walked up the path to Zoe's house and used the door knocker to announce her arrival.

Zoe Williamson looked ill. Her hair, with its streaks of grey, was screwed up onto her head in an untidy bun, and she looked as though she hadn't slept for weeks.

'Come in, Reverend Rowe,' she said. 'I'm not very tidy, can't seem to do anything...'

'It's Kat, and please don't worry. I'm here to see you, not your house. Come on, let's go and talk about Mandy.'

Zoe nodded without speaking and led Kat through to the

lounge. 'We'll sit in here, it's tidier than the kitchen.' A small smile flashed briefly across her face. 'Would you like a cup of tea?'

'That would be lovely, thank you.'

Zoe disappeared down the hallway, and Kat moved around the room, picking up one or two of the many photographs dotted around. Most were of Mandy, some of Mandy and Zoe.

Mandy had certainly been a beautiful girl, with a smile that told of shyness. The photographs showed how she had grown and matured, from being a tiny baby in her mother's arms to the Bambi-like grace of around eighteen, ready to take on the world.

Zoe returned with the drinks and they sat together on the settee.

'Mandy was beautiful,' Kat said. 'She had your eyes, your build, everything about her really was you. I'm so sorry, Zoe, I can't begin to imagine how you're feeling.'

'I think you can, Kat. I think you know exactly how I'm feeling. You couldn't do your job if you didn't recognise grief, and when it's murder it's doubly hard. I'm never going to see my girl again, and I'll never see her killer punished. I thank God every day he didn't come from Castleton, that Jacob Thorne. At least I don't have to put up with seeing his family around the place.' Tears rolled down her cheeks, yet she seemed oblivious to them.

'Would you like to take communion?' Kat asked. 'Would it help?'

Zoe shook her head. 'Not yet. I'm still at the point of asking why God would allow this to happen. And don't come out with the old mainstay that God never gives us more than we can handle, because He has this time.'

Kat put her arm around Zoe's shoulders and held her. 'Zoe, I'm going to leave my card with you. Anytime, anyplace, if you need to talk, you ring me. Don't struggle alone. Will you be in church tomorrow?'

Zoe shook her head. 'I'm not convinced I'll ever go in a church again.'

'I wouldn't normally say this, but it's good you won't be there. DI Marsden and her team are going to be questioning the congregation about Orla French's murder, and you're not ready to be faced with that.'

'Thank you for letting me know,' Zoe said with a sigh, then reached forward to pick up her cup. 'Is Marnie okay? Is she getting the help she needs? I know she'll not be getting it from him.'

'Who's him? Her husband? They seemed to be a very loving couple.'

'No, I don't mean Andy, he's a nice chap. Settled in well when they first got together, although, like me, they don't mingle much. I meant...' She hesitated.

Kat held her breath.

'The vicar, Steve Barksworth.'

Again Kat waited.

'There's something about him. I know he's got a poorly wife, and he takes care of her, but I've always felt there was something about him... The way he was with Orla, following her everywhere, singling her out for praise, pushing her to take her faith to another level with the one-to-one courses he devised, I always felt it wasn't good for the girl.'

'Have you said anything of this to DI Marsden?'

'No, I'm not a gossip, Kat. And really, would she bring up Orla's murder in my presence? She's a nice lady, is DI Marsden, and I don't think she'd be that insensitive, do you?'

'No, I'm sure she wouldn't. But I'll be telling her what you've said, so she'll probably be around shortly for a bit more detail.'

'You think it's important?' Zoe looked startled.

'It could be, but if you're asking me if I think Steve Barksworth is a murderer, then the answer is no.' She smiled at Zoe. 'Now, let's talk about Mandy. Was she a good little girl?'

Finally a proper smile appeared. 'She was brilliant. An easy child, gave me no worries. Her teachers basically always said the same comments all the way through her school life. Mandy does well in every subject, she takes part in class activities and she has a beautiful smile. I used to ring her father to give him the report every time I went to a parents' evening, and it always caused a laugh between us.'

'She had a father?'

'Yes.' Zoe's tone was dry. 'The story of the immaculate conception was accurate in only one instance, you know. Mandy had a father. He was married, so when I told him I was pregnant I also told him to forget me and go back to his wife. He did, but I kept in touch because of Mandy. She didn't know about that, she thought he had died before she was born. And then he did. Die, I mean. Two years ago, he had a stroke. Lingered for a while, then had a much bigger one and he was gone.'

Kat squeezed Zoe's hand in response, and they sat and talked quietly of momentous points in Mandy's life, the laughter and joy she had shared with her mother, and Zoe's worries that Mandy's dreams of a fulfilling life had been squashed because she didn't want to leave the family home, and therefore leave her mother to a lonely life.

Kat stopped at the door on her way out and turned to Zoe. 'You may not be ready for healing prayers yet, but you will be firmly in mine, Zoe. God bless, and as I said, be aware that DI Marsden will probably visit you after I've spoken to her.'

Zoe nodded. 'Thank you for today, Kat. I feel much better.'

Kat walked down the path, climbed in her car and drove out of the village before stopping, taking out her phone and calling Tessa.

'I have some news for you.'

I t transpired that Michael Fairfax was CEO of a medium-sized manufacturing company, based half an hour's drive away from his home, and making suitcases, handbags and other leather objects. Mouse figured this might be the better option of speaking with him on his own, rather than going to his house; a simple phone call would confirm his presence at work.

It would be logical to leave early morning for the trip to the coast, rather than later in the afternoon, but before consulting Doris, Mouse added it to the list of the few things she had uncovered. She knew very little about Michael Fairfax; he had no Facebook account, and his company banked with Lloyds. She didn't go into that feature, deciding she couldn't really care less how rich he was, and it was irrelevant anyway.

However, they had no authority to walk into his place of work and expect to see him there and then, they would need an appointment which could potentially lead to him discussing it with Helen. Mouse sighed. It didn't matter who the hell he told after they had spoken with him, but she wanted the initial conversation to be a complete surprise.

Decision made. They would go to his place of work, and blag

their way in. No appointment, simply a power-dressed young woman and her nan. What could possibly go wrong?

The church doors were closed to keep in the warmth, but opened easily when the large iron handle was depressed. Tessa had instructed Ray Charlton and Fiona Ainsworth to remain in their car until she sent them a text towards the end of the service to move into position outside the doors.

Tessa and Hannah, "grumpy Hannah", as her boss had laughingly called her, moved onto the pew and simply sat, taking in as much as they could, people-watching as the parishioners came in, chatted with others then gravitated towards their favourite pews.

It occurred to Tessa that they could possibly be sitting in somebody's lifelong seat. She hoped not and had deliberately chosen the one at the back of the beautiful church, so that she could observe everyone there.

Steve Barksworth acknowledged their presence with a nod and a smile; no words were exchanged.

It occurred to Tessa how different it was being in a church purely for a Sunday service, than it was for an interment, normally the only time she set foot in a church. Both of the girls the village had recently lost to murder would no doubt have their services in this church, and she would once more be sitting on this same pew for those funerals. The thought saddened her and strengthened her resolve at the same time.

Orla French's killer would be found, and soon.

Tessa and Hannah found themselves singing along to the hymns and both of them actually listened to Steve's sermon. It wasn't the unpleasant seventy-five minutes they had expected, and as Steve said the blessing at the end, Tessa clicked on the pre-written text for Ray Charlton.

The congregation sat back down, having been made aware of

the police presence by Steve during his reading of the notices. Only one lady moved, and moved quickly. Tessa guessed she was Clarice, and she smiled at the thought of this tiny woman being blocked by Ray's bulk. She wouldn't take bets on who would win the encounter.

Tessa and Hannah moved out into the congregation carrying pre-prepared question sheets on clipboards, and worked their way through the twenty-two people who had attended the service.

By the end of the questioning, which only took forty-five minutes, they had nothing concrete to look at. And Clarice hadn't returned. Both Hannah and Tessa had given each person their business card with instructions to show it to the officer on the door and he would then let them go home, but if they thought of anything, any minor little thing, they could ring the number on the card.

Steve brought in Ray and Fiona and made everyone a hot drink. 'Did it go well?' Steve asked.

'It did, but it seems nobody knows anything,' Tessa said thoughtfully. 'So what happened to Clarice?'

'She went home. It seems she doesn't rush off to cook her husband's Sunday lunch, he's actually in a wheelchair, very poorly, and she leaves him for an hour and a half every Sunday but has to get back immediately.' Ray handed Tessa a piece of paper.' This is her address, boss. She said you can call anytime, she's always in except for Sunday mornings.'

'Then we'll call round later, give her time to sort him out. I'm going to Zoe Williamson's after leaving here. Ray, Fiona, you can head back when you've had your lunch. Hannah, do you want to go back with them?'

Hannah shook her head. 'Not likely. I want to meet this woman who's managed to ignore everything and go her own way. I think I probably aspire to be her.' She laughed.

· · ·

Hannah and Tessa spent half an hour with Zoe, but gleaned nothing beyond what Kat had passed on – that Steve Barksworth favoured Orla above anyone else, and his eyes followed her constantly.

Zoe also sang Kat's praises, saying how much better she felt for having spoken to her. She had seen nothing of her own vicar, "slimy Steve", as she called him.

The two officers sat in the car after leaving Zoe's house and talked through their morning.

'Did the vicar come across as slimy to you?' Tessa asked.

'A little. He was keen not to disagree with us. I did think it was nice that he mentioned the families of both girls in the prayers, but at the back of my mind was the info we'd received from Zoe Williamson and that kind of coloured how I saw him.'

'Tomorrow we need to go through these forms and really scrutinise them. There may be some tiny snippet that's sneaked in, that can tell us who Orla was seeing. I can't believe it was the vicar, it would be too easy. And he's got a really poorly wife. Orla would have known that.'

Hannah gave a huge sigh. 'Why can't somebody confess and get it over with? Then we could do normal things like eat, instead of having to do strange things like going to church.'

'You hungry?' Tessa sounded surprised.

'I am. I had breakfast before seven.'

'Right. Come on, let's go down to that tea shop in the village, the one where Orla used to work. When I interviewed the staff, I thought how nice it looked. Let's go and grab something there before we go to see Clarice.'

They locked the car and walked down the hill towards the main road that ran through Castleton. The tea shop was almost on the bend, with no parking facilities at all, yet it was busy. They squeezed into a tiny space that held a table for two slim people, and ordered food almost immediately.

Tessa didn't recognise the waitress; she had spoken to all members of staff, so assumed this girl had replaced Orla. 'You new?' Tessa asked conversationally.

The words brought a smile to the face of the waitress. 'Not really; nearly three years.'

Tessa took out her warrant card and showed it to the girl. 'Before I go, can I have a word with you, please.'

The girl nodded. 'Lucie Davison. How can I help?'

'So you knew Orla French.'

'I did. It was quite a shock to come home to that news.'

'You've been away?'

'Got back yesterday, from Cornwall. Mum's been poorly, so I went down for a couple of days and apparently it all happened the day I went.'

'That explains why I've not seen you before,' Tessa said. 'Please don't disappear home. I need to have a chat with you.'

'I'm here until five,' Lucie said, and turned away to continue taking orders.

Clarice could tell them nothing, but her husband was quite scathing about Steve Barksworth.

'Never been to see me once,' he said. 'All these years my Clarice has gone to church, and he's never set foot over this doorstep.'

Clarice smiled in agreement. 'I know they all think I shoot off because Ernie demands he has his Sunday dinner on time, but we don't eat till Countryfile is on TV that day. I dash home because I can't trust this daft bugger not to get out of his wheelchair. When he does he falls, and can't get back up. But nobody knows that, so keep it to yourselves. It's our business, not theirs.'

Hannah wrote down everything that the couple said, and the two officers climbed back in the car.

They parked outside Zoe's house for the second time that day, and once again walked down to the café.

With the arrival of darkness, the café was much quieter. The tourists had departed for home and Lucie immediately came over to join Tessa and Hannah.

'I'm glad you've come back,' she said. 'I can go home as soon as I've spoken to you, it's slowed down now.'

'Thank you for waiting,' Tessa said, and Hannah took out her notebook.

All three sat, and the café owner mimed to ask if they wanted a drink. A shake of the head from Tessa told her no, and they both looked at Lucie.

'You knew Orla well?'

'I did, as much as anybody could know Orla. She was quiet, like a little mouse. I didn't mix with her outside of work, except at Christmas. I like to go to the Christingle service at church, and there's always cheese and wine and stuff after the service. It's a bit of a social event for the villagers. Orla and I, along with Emily Carr, always spend the evening together. We'll certainly miss her this year.'

'Did you talk much at work?'

'Not a lot. She told me she'd met up with Emily's brother Paul a couple of times and that she liked him. In fact, the last time we spoke was on the night she went missing. It was a dreadful rainy day, and really quiet in here, so Orla asked if she could get off early, she had something important she needed to do. And before you ask,' Lucie held up a hand, 'I have no idea what it was. She left here around four, although that may not be accurate. I went home around five and we closed up.'

Hannah continued to make notes. It seemed pretty obvious that Lucie had probably been the last person to see Orla alive, before she met up with the person who had ended her life.

'And you didn't hear from her?'

'Nothing. I set off from here at five the next morning, and have been in Cornwall since. This is my first day back at work. I really know very little. If you've been to Cornwall you'll know what it's like getting a phone signal there, so I mainly kept it switched off. I'm going to miss her, we worked well together, had a bit of a routine going if one was busier than the other. And she was... nice. That sounds like nothing, doesn't it, but nice is the right word. She wouldn't hurt anybody, always polite, and super intelligent. She was wasted in here, but she had a really close relationship with her mum and I don't think she wanted to leave home to go to uni or anything.'

'Thank you very much for waiting for us, Lucie. Hannah is going to write out your statement covering everything you've said today, so if you can hang on and sign it, it will save you having to come into headquarters to do it.'

While Hannah dealt with Lucie, Tessa nipped into the ladies and stared at her reflection. Orla must have looked in this mirror a hundred times, and simply stood and let her thoughts drift. A new love on the horizon? An illicit love? Or a perfectly reasonable love that would make her life enriched by its presence in it...

She sighed, applied some lipstick purely for the hell of it, and went to rejoin her colleague. Lucie was signing her name as she reached them.

Tessa handed over her card. 'Thank you for your cooperation, Lucie. If you think of anything else, please give me a call.'

Lucie slipped the card into the top pocket of her white blouse and stood. 'I hope you find the disgusting person who killed her very quickly. It makes everybody scared, knowing there's somebody out there capable of this sort of stuff. Our village lost two girls on the same night, and the general feeling is that if it can happen to them it can happen to anybody. That makes you feel uncomfortable.'

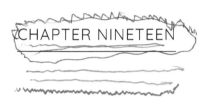

CHAPTER NINETEEN

Mouse and Doris left early on Monday morning. At nine o'clock, Mouse rang to make an appointment with Michael Fairfax, only to be told he was fully booked all day.

'Then can I ask you to check with him, because this is a personal issue for Mr Fairfax, and it's important we see him today. Very personal,' she added.

'I'll try,' the smooth voice at the other end of the phone said, and Mouse sat back to wait. Who would be able to resist a meeting that was about something personal?

'Hello? Mr Fairfax has a small window at ten o'clock. He has another meeting at ten thirty. Will that be long enough for you to conclude your business?'

'I'm sure it will,' Mouse said. 'Thank you for your cooperation.'

She disconnected and turned to Doris. 'We've to be there for ten. He's apparently got another meeting at half past, so we could be paddling on Scarborough beach by eleven.'

Doris looked at the grey skies. 'You'll be paddling on your own, Mouse. And will you remember, while you're getting your toes wet, how poorly you've been? If you so much as sneeze once on the way back, I'll make you walk home.'

Mouse settled back into her seat. 'Okay, old wise woman, maybe I won't paddle. Can I have fish and chips?'

'You can count on it,' Doris said. 'I thought that was why we came.'

The foyer of Fairfax was sleek, modern and warm. There were display cabinets showing one handbag per shelf, and Doris heard Mouse gasp.

They approached the reception desk, and Mouse handed over her ID. 'We're here to see Mr Fairfax,' she explained. 'This is my colleague, Mrs Lester.' Doris handed her ID to the bewildered employee.

She bent her head to check a diary. 'You don't have an appointment today.'

'I rang about an hour ago, and spoke to the secretary. She booked us in. We'll sit over here while you check.' Doris and Mouse wandered over to a settee and sat down.

'Nan,' Mouse whispered. 'These bags are Ciao! I had no idea. When I checked him out it said he was CEO of Fairfax Ltd, makers of fine bags and suitcases. It said nothing about those fine bags being Ciao bags. They are somewhere up in the stratosphere when it comes to price, certainly as expensive as Prada and the likes, and equally as much sought after. I bid for a second-hand one on an auction site, and dropped out at four hundred pounds.'

'Good lord,' Doris said. 'Think he'll give us a free sample?'

The receptionist walked across to them, and pointed to the far side of the reception area. 'If you follow me to the lift, I'll send you to the correct floor and Julia will meet you. I'm sorry about the confusion, the booking was so recent nobody had thought to put it in my diary.'

Mouse smiled at the young girl, who was looking a little put out that her system had been compromised. 'Don't worry about it. These things happen.'

Doris and Mouse followed her across to a small lift at the back of the foyer, and the receptionist sent them to the third floor.

Julia was slim, and anyone would have classed her automatically as a secretary. Her hair was neatly formed into a bun, her make-up was perfect and her fingernails shone, yet without colour.

'Good morning,' she greeted them. 'Mr Fairfax is waiting for you.'

She led them through an outer office that was clearly hers, and knocked on a door leading into the inner sanctum of Michael Fairfax.

Doris felt Mouse tense, and they moved towards the man they had researched. It occurred to Doris that it was a pity they hadn't been more thorough in that research. They had concentrated on tracking him down, and yet it seemed they had the wrong Michael Fairfax. They had both been expecting to see a medium-height man, possibly with fair hair as both his parents had been blessed with blonde hair; they hadn't been expecting a tall man, black hair, brown eyes, and a beautifully coffee-coloured skin. A remarkably handsome man.

This man couldn't possibly be the child of Helen Fairfax and Ewan Barker.

Mouse felt sick.

She held out her hand and shook his. 'Mr Fairfax, my name is Bethan Walters, and this is my colleague, Doris Lester. We are private investigators, and we have been asked by our client to find his son.'

Fairfax nodded, and indicated the two seats in front of his desk. 'Please, sit down. Can I offer you tea? Coffee?'

'No, thank you, we're fine. Do you mind if I take notes?' She waved her iPad around. 'Although, I rather think we might be wasting your time...'

'Oh? Did you believe I was the son?' He smiled. 'I probably am. I've never seen my father, and my mother assures me I did have one.'

'Is your mother Helen Fairfax?'

'She is. So that's a start, isn't it?'

'It is. Does she ever mention your father?' Doris ploughed on gamefully with the questioning.

'Not really, no. I've always understood she became pregnant but didn't want to get married, so left Sheffield, which was where she was living at the time. She moved to Scarborough to have me. We have lots of relatives here, and they helped her get back on her feet after the birth.'

'So you never met him?' Doris persisted.

'I've never seen so much as a photograph of him. Mum always said she didn't have one, and I accepted that. I... erm... I feel a little bit shocked by this. Don't really know how to handle it. Mum is still alive, and I wouldn't want to hurt her by having some sort of relationship with my father. How did you track me down?'

'Our client understood your name was Michael Fairfax. It seems your mother and our client discussed you having his Christian name as your middle name, although that isn't the case. We tracked down two babies born on the same day, a Michael Adrian Fairfax who lives in Aberdeen, and you, living in Scarborough. Our client remembered your mother having relatives here, so we made this our first port of call.'

'It all fits, doesn't it. I feel quite pleased, I think,' Fairfax said. 'Do you have a photograph of him, this man? My father?'

Mouse wriggled uncomfortably in her seat. She felt truly grateful that Doris had come along with her, she had controlled the interview admirably. Now what would she do?

'I do,' Doris said slowly. 'It's a small one on my phone. However, there is something you should know. Can I double-check something with you first... is your mother white British?'

'She is. I get my colouring from my father.'

'Then I'm afraid I can't show you this picture. It would breach data protection laws. Our client is white British, Mr Fairfax, and therefore can't be your father.'

He looked stunned. 'I've actually dreamed of this day for many many years. When I was told by my secretary that you wanted to see me about something personal, I knew. And you're telling me you're wrong.'

'Mr Fairfax,' Doris said gently, 'I believe you are the child we are looking for. I believe that everything your mother says happened to her, really did. Except I also believe she knew the baby didn't belong to our client. She couldn't marry him, as he wanted, because it would have been obvious at the birth that he couldn't have fathered you. I'm so sorry. If you really want to see your father, you are going to have to get the truth out of your mother.'

He shook his head. 'Then the secret will go to the grave with her. She has four to six months to live – cancer. I can't ask her about this, not now.'

Doris stood and Mouse followed her lead. 'Thank you for seeing us, Mr Fairfax. I'm sorry we couldn't unite you with your father. We'll make our report back to our client, and as far as we are concerned, that will be an end to the matter.'

He nodded without speaking, and they left the office, Mouse carefully positioning the iPad as she stood up and taking a photograph of Fairfax. The photograph she took didn't reflect the smile on his face that appeared as they left the office.

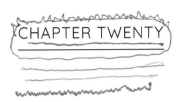

CHAPTER TWENTY

Tessa and Hannah had led the briefing, filling everybody in on the results from the previous day, which were negligible. They sat at their individual desks, going through every form gathered in the church. Nobody had anything good to say about the vicar, but equally nobody had said anything detrimental except Ernie Travers, Clarice's grumpy husband.

In fact, it was becoming clear to Tessa that every person interviewed in the church would probably have to be interviewed away from that environment. Who, in the whole of that congregation, would have had the guts to say we think our vicar is a bit of a perv? Absolutely nobody, not while he was standing within about six feet of them. As he had been. Offering his support to them. Making sure they knew he was there.

Steve Barksworth had given them a short list of seven people who normally were regular attendees, although hadn't been there the day of the interviews. They mainly lived in Castleton, with a couple travelling from the nearby village of Hope. One of the non-attendees living in Hope was Emily Carr.

With hindsight, Tessa reflected that maybe it hadn't been such a bright idea to interview in the church; the list should have been obtained from the vicar and they should have visited them in their homes, where they would have been more relaxed. And maybe more communicative.

'Hannah,' she called across the room, 'let's go talk to some people. Starting with a vicar.'

The three women – and Martha – were holed up in Kat's office, the outside shutters down temporarily, announcing they were closed. Martha's eyes roamed between Kat, Winnie the Pooh, Tigger and Eeyore, then finally settled on Eeyore, the tiny dangling creature attached to the hood on her pram. She began to eat him.

'Martha's eating Eeyore,' Mouse said. 'Does it matter?'

'Depends how good he tastes,' Kat said. 'If you notice she's getting down to the bones, let me know.'

Doris laid out the picture of Michael Fairfax on the desk. Mouse's further research in the fish and chip café had revealed nothing of the CEO of Fairfax. There was lots of other information online about their products that she hadn't discovered before, considering it irrelevant. She had been investigating the man, but now she drank in the exclusivity of their range, the brand name Ciao. All the articles and advertising focussed on the goods and the ethics of the business, not on people. Mouse had breathed a sigh of relief as she swung her iPad around to show Doris the photograph she had taken. At least they had this and they could show it to Ewan.

Kat pulled the picture towards her and stared at the man Ewan believed was his son. 'We have to show him this photo,' she said, tracing a finger across the face staring up at her. 'He's our client, and we have to pass all information on to him. I think the story will end there though. Helen Fairfax left him because she didn't know who the father of her baby was, not because she didn't want to get married. What's the betting that if the baby had been white, she would have returned and claimed she'd had a change of heart and she wanted to be with Ewan?'

'That's cynical of you, Kat,' Doris said. 'Although,' she added with a sigh, 'I suspect you're right. And I'm sure Ewan will see it that way as well. He's believed he had a son for all these years, and we're going to wipe him out.'

'So what do we do?' Mouse spoke with a frown creasing her forehead. 'He's such a nice man, and we're going to give him a final report that demolishes any hope of a descendant. Don't forget he had a plan. He wanted to make sure he contacted his son so that he could leave everything to him when he died. We've taken that away.'

'We haven't taken it away. Helen Fairfax did that by not being honest with him.' Doris touched Mouse's hand. 'He has the freedom to sort out his affairs, to leave his money to any charities he may support, and then to enjoy the rest of his life. Yes, it will be a shock to have his beliefs crushed, but once he accepts he has no offspring, he'll bounce back and get on with life, I'm sure of it.'

'I'll do the report, but I'd like you both to check it. We have to be a bit careful in that we don't give anything away about Michael. What do we do when he asks if we tracked Helen?' Kat waited, knowing they would have to consider their answers.

Mouse spoke first. 'I'm inclined to say we know where she lives, and leave it at that. If he wants to contact her, we can be the inter-mediary, as we had to be with Pamela Bird. We can't simply hand over Helen's address, not without her permission, but then we have the issue of her illness. Do we tell him about that?'

'I think we have to,' Kat said. 'Once we give him the news about Michael, Ewan can simply say use the remaining money to find Helen for me. Maybe he won't pursue that if he knows how near she is to the end of her life.'

There was silence around the table as the three of them thought everything through.

Finally Doris spoke. 'We need to get Ewan in for a discussion.

We can give him the final report, not say anything about Helen's whereabouts and deal with it if he mentions her. But he does need to know our findings from this trip. I'm seeing him tonight, so I'll ask him to come in tomorrow. Ten okay with everybody?'

They nodded, and Kat picked up the paperwork on the table. 'I'll get on with doing it now. Is he a nice man?'

'Michael? He seemed to be really nice. Because we had said our appointment was a personal one, he'd kind of got himself to a place where he thought it might involve his father, and he was obviously disappointed when we said our client couldn't be that person. I do wonder what the conversation will be between him and Helen, or if he'll simply let it go.'

'Who knows. I like him, he seemed like a gentle, considerate man, but this is massive, isn't it,' Doris said. 'Kat, do the report, keep it fairly clinical, and we'll see how it goes tomorrow.'

Steve Barksworth was surprised to see the two women back in his church. He crossed his fingers and hoped whatever they wanted wouldn't take long; he'd left his wife having physio and knew he hadn't got long before he needed to be back at the vicarage.

They walked down the aisle towards him and he forced a smile to his face. 'How can I help, ladies?'

'Is there somewhere we can go to speak privately?'

'Yes, of course, but I only have ten minutes before I have to be home.'

'No, vicar.' DI Marsden was DI Marsden, no longer Tessa who had been in his church on Sunday. 'It will take as long as it takes. If you prefer, we can wait until you've arranged cover for your wife, and make it official in Chesterfield. Today.'

Without another word, he led them to the vestry.

Once inside, he pointed to the sofa and indicated they should sit. He moved behind his small desk.

'Thank you, Reverend Barksworth. Information has been given to us following our investigation into Orla French's death.'

Hannah was watching his face carefully and saw the blood drain from it.

'Can you tell me about the relationship between you and Orla, please?'

'She's a member of our church, our fundraising group and our choir. I therefore meet up with her quite a lot.'

'In here?' Tessa indicated the confines of the vestry with a wave of her hand.

'No, I don't think so.'

Hannah wrote rapidly, making notes of his words, but also of his body language. He was nervous.

Tessa nodded, and temporarily shelved the vestry issue. 'So where did you see her?'

'In the church and in the church hall.'

'Was she alone or with others? Emily perhaps?'

'Occasionally alone, but usually with Emily or any of the choir members.'

'Why?'

'Why what?'

'You don't have anything to do with the choir. Isn't that the remit for Annabel Knight? When I spoke to her she indicated she trained the choir.'

'I've always got something that needs attention in here,' he said. 'And it pleases me to hear them. It's better to do paperwork with a choir singing in the background.'

'Reverend Barksworth, did you go to our mobile headquarters at the school and give a DNA sample?'

He looked startled. 'No, I didn't. Why would I? I've done nothing wrong.'

'It doesn't matter, we'll take one now.'

He tried to protest but Hannah was waiting patiently for him to open his mouth for her to access his inside cheek.

'Thank you, vicar,' Tessa said. 'The tests are used for elimination purposes.'

He looked at his watch and then at Marsden. 'DI Marsden, I really do have to go back to my wife.'

'We've almost finished, vicar. In fact, I think I've only one more question. I expect you to answer it truthfully, but taking your career into consideration, I'm sure you will be honest. Have you ever had sex with Orla French?'

Way to go, boss, Hannah thought, *say it like it is.* She watched as Steve Barksworth's face turned red, then he stood and turned his back on them as he looked out of the vestry window.

There was silence, and Tessa held up a hand to indicate she didn't want Hannah to speak.

They waited.

It seemed like forever as they watched the man of God battle with his conscience; both women knew that was happening. His face had told the story.

Finally he turned to face them. 'Yes.'

Marsden's eyes never left him. She was aware of Hannah taking notes, aware of the utter stillness in the room following the one word Steve had spoken, yet Tessa held back, waiting to see if he would say anything else.

When it seemed he wasn't going to expand on what he had said, Tessa spoke. 'Did you kill her?'

He sank down onto his chair, and covered his face with his hands. 'Of course I didn't kill her.' His words were muffled. 'I loved her.'

.   .   .

He asked Annabel Knight to come in and sit with his wife while he went into Chesterfield to police headquarters. He explained he had to give a statement, but gave no further details.

Annabel watched as the police car pulled away, and gave a small smile before setting off towards the vicarage. Did he really think he could fool her? He was lucky that policewoman hadn't asked her the direct question of was your vicar screwing the pretty blonde chorister, because she might have had to answer honestly.

CHAPTER TWENTY-ONE

Steve Barksworth arrived back at the vicarage to find Annabel watching an old episode of Silent Witness.

'Thank you, Annabel,' he said, his voice raw with emotion. 'Have you said anything?'

'To your wife?' she asked.

'No, but she did ask where you had disappeared to. I told her it was parish business. They've not arrested you then.'

'Clearly not,' he snapped. 'I haven't actually committed any crime.'

'Legally, I suspect you're right,' she said, her own anger bubbling to the surface and reflecting in her voice. She could have spent the night at home with her husband. 'But morally, ethically, that's another thing altogether, isn't it. You have a wife, Steve. I've seen you and Orla together...'

The look of alarm on his face spoke volumes.

'Oh, don't worry, I didn't say anything. But somebody obviously has, so I can't be the only one who knows about it. And when the police do ask me the direct question I will answer honestly. That young girl was a virgin, Steve, and you took advantage of her.'

He sank down onto the settee and stared at the television screen without seeing it. When DI Marsden solved this, it would become a court case. He would be called as a witness and the whole sordid mess would be in the public domain. He doubted he would keep his job; he hoped he would keep Ruby.

In everyone's eyes he would be the one to blame, that was obvious. He was older than Orla, double her age. But had nobody seen her glances, the winks as she said something outrageous, the flirtatious smiles, the low-cut tops she wore all through the summer? He had, and he had responded.

His mind went back to the first time they made love, that night in the vestry when everybody had gone home. She had made the first move, almost as if she had planned it carefully. He had tried to explain to her that it was out of the question, but her smile lit up the room as she said it was going to happen.

And it did.

They talked afterwards, and she had confessed to him that she wasn't a virgin, but she had only done it once, and that was so that she would know what she was doing when it came to making love with him. He loved her open attitude, her frank honesty.

Steve was vaguely aware that Annabel had put on her coat, and as she said goodnight, she paused in the doorway.

'Go to Ruby, Steve. I'm sure she'll still be awake. Tell her, don't tell her, it's your decision, but I'm guessing at some point everybody will know.'

He stood and followed her from the room. 'Thank you for tonight, Annabel. I'm going to have to tell Ruby, I know that.'

She wished him goodnight, and left the vicarage, reflecting on how much easier life had been in the Reverend Brewster days, when all he did was take the Sunday service and bury people.

. . .

Steve poured himself a brandy, and sipped at it, dreading the moment when it would be finished. He held the cut-glass goblet to the light, saw there were dregs still in it and tipped them into his mouth. He took the glass into the kitchen then opened the bedroom door.

'Are you awake?' he whispered.

'Of course,' Ruby answered. 'Did you really think I would be asleep with my husband heaven only knows where?'

His heart sank. 'Well, I'm home, sweetheart. Do you need anything?'

'You.'

He hesitated. 'And I need you, my love, but there's something I have to tell you.'

'Orla French,' she said quietly.

'You knew?'

'It's my body that's giving up, Steve, not my brain. I had to pray you hadn't killed her. It seems my prayers have been answered as you're back here with me. You've been with the police, I take it?'

'Yes. They wanted to know what my relationship with her was, and whether or not I had killed her.'

Ruby turned her eyes towards him. 'Orla went missing, and presumably died, on the night you went to the Cathedral in Sheffield to meet the new bishop. I'd already worked that out. It's why you're still here, Steve. If you hadn't got such a strong alibi – and how much stronger can it be than a bishop vouching for you – I would have told that DI everything. I know you didn't kill Orla, but I also know you had sex with her. Don't deny it, it's not fitting that a man of the cloth should tell lies.'

'There'll be no more lies,' he acknowledged. 'We did have sex, several times, and in a way I loved her. But it wasn't anything like the way I love you, it was more enjoying being with her. I'm so sorry,

Ruby, and if you don't want to be with me any longer, I'll understand. I won't be happy, but what happens next is your call.'

She turned over in bed, clearly in pain, and lay with her back to him. 'That's a big decision, Steve, but plan on sleeping in the spare room from now on.' She reached out and switched off the lamp.

Steve stared at her for a moment, then left the room, closing the door gently behind him.

CHAPTER TWENTY-TWO

E wan pulled up outside the Connection office, watched by three pairs of eyes. He wasn't aware of them; his mind was on the previous evening. The meal with Doris had been special. They had many shared interests and they laughed and talked constantly. It had taken all his willpower not to ask questions about their trip. Now he hoped to get answers.

He locked the car and walked across to the door. Doris opened it for him.

'Thank you,' he said, giving a mock bow. 'That's the sort of service women should offer.'

'Oh, and we do, at all times,' Mouse said. 'It's in our genes.'

Kat burst out laughing. 'Well said, Mouse, well said. It's a pity nobody believes you. Ewan, would you like to go through to my office. We're ready for you.'

Doris had decided not to be in on the discussion, and moved to her own desk in reception. Ewan looked a little surprised, but made no comment.

He followed Kat and Mouse through into the office, and Kat made coffees for all of them. She knew she was putting off the point when they would have to destroy his hopes.

Eventually they settled, and Mouse spoke. 'On Monday Doris and I went to see a man we believed was the best contender out of the two possible ones, for being your son. We did a brief background check on the second one, but there were no links to you. The first one, however, had a mother called Helen, was born on the birthdate you gave us, and lived in Scarborough, a further link.'

Ewan smiled.

Mouse took a deep breath. 'We went to see him at work, after deciding it might be better to keep it away from his home life until he said it was okay. He is CEO of a manufacturing company, and we were lucky to get an appointment, but we did. Here comes the difficult part, Ewan.'

Ewan's face changed. The optimism disappeared at some speed, along with his smile. 'He doesn't want to know?'

'No, it's not that. He can't be your son. Yes, he is the baby Helen was carrying when you were together, but you didn't father him. This is probably why she left; not because she didn't want marriage, but because she didn't know if the baby was yours or this other man's. I believe if the baby had been indisputably yours, she would have come back to you, but the baby was mixed race.'

She pushed the picture of Michael Fairfax across the desk, and waited.

He stared at it, then picked it up. Finally he spoke. 'This doesn't make sense. Remember the friend of Helen's? Carla Blake? When the baby was a couple of months old, she went to see Helen. The next time I rang her she told me about it, said the baby was my double, had lovely blonde hair. There's no way on earth this man ever had blonde hair. No way at all. In fact, she had a photograph, one taken with her holding the baby, that Helen sent on to her. I never saw it, but maybe she still has it. You spoke to this man?' He tapped the picture on the desk.

'We did. And he admitted to being Helen's son, and always hoping his father would come for him. I think he was disappointed to learn our client was white British, and therefore couldn't possibly be the man he had hoped to meet.'

There was silence in the office. Ewan was clearly thinking things through. 'Did he say if his mother was still alive?'

'She is.' Mouse hesitated, but said nothing further.

'Can you trace her? And maybe Carla Blake may still have that photo, we don't tend to destroy photos, do we. I don't want this to be the end, because there's something not right here. Why would Carla tell me the baby was white, if it was mixed race? It would have got me off her back, no more phone calls, if it had indeed been some-body else's baby, but she clearly saw it was mine. Please... don't stop. There's something not right about this.'

'Of course we'll try to track Carla. She lived in Sheffield?'

'She did. I don't know which part of the city though. Her boyfriend was called Luke, and I know they were engaged, but I've no idea if they married. She asked me to stop ringing, so I did. That phone number I gave you was her mother's telephone, she lived at home then. And that's about as much as I know.'

Mouse nodded. 'We'll do our best, Ewan. Carla is roughly your age, and there's no guarantee that she is still alive, but we'll try to find her. It does give rise to the question though, if that man we saw isn't Michael Fairfax, who is he? Until we get proof that the baby was not of mixed race, we can't really pursue that, but believe me, we will if we can get that photo.'

'You're not going to contact Helen?'

'No. It would be morally wrong, wouldn't it. I know she will know things we don't know, but it sounds as though she lived a life of secrets. You have to prepare yourself for the possibility, Ewan, that we may never know the full story. But be assured, if this man is Michael Fairfax, he has no genetic common ground with you.'

Ewan stood. 'I trust you. I'll leave it in your hands. Do you mind if I go? I need time out, I think.'

He disappeared through the door, they heard soft words as he spoke to Doris, and then the shop doorbell pinged as he left.

Doris joined them. 'He didn't take it well?'

'Something's not right, Nan,' Mouse said. 'Ewan says there is a picture of Michael as a baby and he is clearly not of mixed race. So who did we meet on Monday? We need a brainstorming session followed by a laptop session.'

Kat smiled. 'I'm up for the first part of that, count me out for the second part. Do we need doughnuts?'

The box of doughnuts sat in the middle of the table, and Mouse had a piece of paper in front of her.

'Nice to write occasionally, instead of typing.' She headed up the page with the words *Michael Fairfax*, then underlined it. 'Any initial thoughts?'

'Gut feeling says he wasn't Michael, but if he wasn't, who was he and why the impersonation? And why are there no photographs of him anywhere?' Doris frowned. 'Do we go back?'

'I think we do,' Mouse said. 'But I think we do it differently this time. We don't let him know we're coming. I would like to do a surveillance session on his home. We can either get there early and see who comes out to go to work, or we can go mid-afternoon and wait for him to return home. Which do you prefer, Nan?'

'Early morning. We're not hanging around twiddling our thumbs then. If we leave home around half past five, that will give us time to find a decent place to park where we can see what's happening. He'll certainly be in work by half past nine at the latest, I would think. Then we can decide what to do next.'

'Okay,' Mouse said. 'You good for tomorrow?'

'I am. Kat, you clear for being here?'

'I am. I might bring Martha though. I'm missing her.'

'Good idea,' Doris said. 'Mouse, you want me to start searching out Carla Blake?'

'Please, Nan. If she does still have that photograph from fifty years ago, it will be a big help.'

'Mouse, you got a plan?'

Mouse shrugged. 'I do, but it's a bit hit and miss. I'm basically going to tear the Internet apart looking for Michael Fairfax; not his name, his face. If the person we saw isn't him, and I don't think he was, there must be a reason for that. The real Michael Fairfax doesn't want to be found, and we were royally fobbed off on Monday. We accepted everything at face value, but Ewan didn't, and as our client we owe him a full investigation into this. Let's get to it.'

It took Doris two hours to find Carla Blake, now married to Luke Newton and living in Chesterfield.

'Gotcha!'

Mouse lifted her head. 'You've found her?'

'I believe so, if all the stars and moons are aligned and in the right order. I've tracked her life, and I'm as sure as I can be that it's her. I also have a telephone number... Do we ring or go visit her? If we ring she might clam up.'

'I agree. I think we need a visit. No word to Ewan yet though, we don't want him to have foreknowledge of this. It may come to nothing.'

Doris gave a slight dip of her head, and sent documents to the printer.

Mouse was feeling frustrated. How could such a successful company have no pictures or information about its CEO? The only item she had seen was that he was the CEO. She had tried newspapers, magazines, everything in which he could possibly be featured, but it almost seemed like a complete blackout on the man.

She gave up with a sigh. 'Nothing. He's like the bloody Scarlet Pimpernel.'

CHAPTER TWENTY-THREE

K at finished the piece of work on blood groups and everything related to it, and saved it to the relevant folder. It briefly occurred to her that she was getting better at this computer malarkey – not so much at the research side, but the general management of the work they had to do was almost second nature to her now, and she felt both Mouse and Doris trusted her to get it right.

It came as something of a shock when the shop bell pinged, and she looked up. A young woman stood in the doorway and Kat smiled at her. 'Can I help you?'

'I... er... don't know. Do you do advice?'

'We do,' Kat said with a smile. The woman looked unsure of herself, and Kat moved around the counter. 'Come in, and tell me what you need.'

The dark-haired woman, who looked to be in her late teens or possibly early twenties, gave a brief glance out of the door. 'Can my partner come in? He brought me here.'

'Of course. He can't stand out in the cold.'

She waved and a few seconds later was joined by a young man who looked about the same age.

'Okay,' Kat said. 'Let's start with names.' She moved across to Doris's desk and took out a client form.

The young couple moved around the reception desk, and sat on the two chairs facing Kat.

'I'm Alyson, Alyson Read.'

'And I'm Ed Danvers.'

'Thank you.' Kat smiled again, at both of them. They seemed ill at ease, scared even. She passed the forms across to them. 'Fill those in and then we'll see how we can help.'

'We've got money to pay,' Alyson said, the words tumbling out of her, as she handed over her form. Apart from his name, Ed hadn't spoken.

'We generally don't charge for simple advice,' Kat responded. 'We charge if it requires further action.' So tell me what your problem is. Do you mind if I record it? It saves me having to remember everything when I'm explaining to my two colleagues later.' She placed the small recorder on the desk.

Alyson reached into her bag and took out a letter. 'Please – do whatever you need to do. This is the problem. Ed has been researching his family history for a couple of years, and we've managed to get back to the seventeenth century with it, but we're a bit stuck. To give us a bit of a break, we decided to start on mine.'

Ed's eyes never left Alyson as she was speaking. He reached across and took hold of her hand.

'I only have one parent, my mum, and no grandparents, so we started mine knowing very little. I'm sorry if this is sounding a bit long-winded, but there's no other way of you seeing the picture.'

'Don't worry, take your time. I'd rather have all the facts. We deal with quite a lot of cases that require delving back into family history, and the more of the overall view we can start with, the better.'

Ed gave a slight nod, obviously in full agreement with Kat.

'We started with Mum. She gave me a box of photographs, black and white ones as well as coloured, and we photocopied her birth and marriage certificates, and the death certificates for all four of my grandparents. My dad's parents had died before he met Mum, but he brought the certificates with him when they married. He died in a motorcycle accident two years after the wedding, when I'd just been born, so she can't really remember anything about his family. And that's all we have for our starting point.'

Alyson paused for a moment, as if collecting her thoughts. 'We've made a fair start on it, gone back as far as my maternal great-great-grandfather...' She turned to look at Ed and he nodded. 'Yes, my great-great-grandfather, but then ground to a halt. We're in a couple of groups on Facebook for genealogy, so we used their request for information and put in Arthur Bennett of Chesterfield. Within a couple of days we had a response, but it came in the post and not online.'

'You gave out your address?'

'No, that's the scary part. We didn't, and it's certainly not available on Facebook, any more than our telephone numbers are. We... erm... won some money six months ago, and immediately made our privacy settings at the highest level. Only close friends, and obviously our families, know where we live.'

Kat felt as though a torch clicked on in her brain. 'Ed Danvers. You picked up a nice little lottery win.'

'We did,' he said. 'It was a joint win, but we asked them to keep Alyson's name out of the publicity, she wasn't comfortable with everyone knowing. We used Alyson's Facebook account to join the genealogy group so that nobody would connect her name with the lottery win, which is why we're feeling a little uncomfortable with this letter arriving. We've only lived at this address for a month, we're not even on the electoral roll or anything yet.'

'Where did you live before?'

He laughed. 'In a tiny little bedsit in Chesterfield town centre. We've now got a four-bedroomed house at Ashford in the Water, and we no longer catch a bus to get to the Peak District, we live in it. We've told nobody where we live, other than people who need to know. We've bought Alyson's mum a small cottage about five minutes from where we are, but she's not moving yet, it'll be a couple more weeks before that is completed. My mum and dad didn't want to move, so we gave them a dollop of cash, and they're currently on a cruise for the first time in their lives. We've been so careful, so private...' His frustration showed in his voice.

'Okay,' Kat said quietly. 'Let me tell you that tracking people down is one of the easiest things to do, provided you have some degree of IT skill. A high degree of it, I must admit.' Her mind drifted to Mouse and Nan, currently working on laptops in the back office. 'You did nothing wrong, you covered your backs as much as possible, but if somebody wants to find you, believe me, they will. May I see the letter, please?'

Alyson pushed it across the desk to Kat.

Dear Miss Read,

I saw your request for information re Arthur Bennett of Chester-field, and I believe I may be able to help you. Arthur is a relative of mine, the great-uncle of my father, and I have photographs of him in army uniform, alongside information of his predecessors.

Perhaps we can meet for a coffee to discuss the items I have – or maybe I should come to your house?

I look forward to hearing from you.

Best wishes,

Jeremy Peterson

Kat read the letter three times, then laid it on the desk. 'I take it you've never heard of him before? Ed? He's never cropped up in your own search?'

Ed frowned. 'No, and I use this particular website a lot. There's usually some information comes out of throwing a name into the ring. I've used it for about five years. Bit of a geek,' he said with a grin.

'So tell me what's making you uneasy about this?'

'It's not normal. For a start, people don't write letters, not when it's so simple to respond within the website. And it must have been a problem finding our address. For what? There's no chance we'd ever have him in our home, we don't know him. And I'm pretty sure neither of us want to meet him for a coffee.'

'You think he's clicked on to the money?'

'I do, but even if he has, how will that help him? There's no way he'd get any of it. We don't know him!'

'Okay, can you leave this letter with me? I'll give you a photo-copy of it and a receipt, but I'd like someone else to take a look at the original. There's no charge for the advice, and I'll contact you tomor-row. Is that okay?'

For the first time, Alyson's smile was genuine. 'It feels as though a weight has been lifted. And you don't have to give us a copy or a receipt, we know you'll do your best with it.'

Alyson stood, and Ed shook Kat's hand. 'Thank you. We'll look forward to hearing from you.'

She watched as they walked hand in hand across the road to where a smart Range Rover was parked, and pursed her lips. They had clearly been unnerved by the letter, and she wondered how Jeremy Peterson had managed to find their address when they hadn't registered it anywhere.

The door at the back of reception opened and Mouse's face appeared. 'All done?'

'Yep, they've gone. I recorded everything, so you two can have a listen to it. They've filled in client forms, but I'm not sure where we go from here.'

'Sounds intriguing. And it also seems you've had a more productive afternoon than we have. We haven't found one picture of Michael Fairfax, not one. Let's lock the door, and have a listen to your recording. Take my mind off this bloody man.'

After a brief explanation, Kat switched on the machine and they sat and listened to the conversation. At the end, Mouse turned to Doris, and simultaneously they both said, 'Estate agent.'

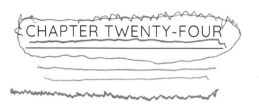

CHAPTER TWENTY-FOUR

Andy Harrison opened the door to Tessa and Hannah, and invited them in. 'You have news?'

Tessa shook her head. 'Not really. I wanted to check in with you, make sure you're holding it together. We will find out who did this to Orla, I promise you. Andy, you're not working?'

'No, I've been suspended until this is all cleared up. I'd rather be here with Marnie anyway. She's going through hell, as you can imagine.'

Marnie, dressed in jogging bottoms and a T-shirt with stains down the front, glanced towards him but didn't speak. It was as if all emotion had been knocked out of her, and she wanted nothing to do with the rest of the world.

'Marnie, has Nadine kept you informed of everything?'

Her face didn't change. 'I have no idea. I don't seem to have any new information, if that's what you mean. I've lost my daughter but it seems I'm the last one to know anything.'

'We do know that Orla was going to see someone to talk to them, on the night she was killed. Do either of you have any idea who that could be?'

Andy spoke first. 'Emily?'

Almost at the same time, Marnie said, 'Paul?'

'No, she had no contact with either of them. Orla left work, and the next time she is seen is when our search team found her. The weather made it impossible to work out a more accurate time of death than between four and six that evening, so we don't know if she did in fact speak to whoever she was going to see, or if she died before that could happen. She definitely said nothing to either of you?'

'No.' Marnie's voice was cold. 'And if you don't mind, I'm going to have a rest. Nobody seems to be taking into account Orla could be a bit of a bitch, are they. Bear that in mind, DI Marsden.' She walked out of the room, and they heard her go upstairs.

Andy sighed. 'I'm so sorry. It's like living on the edge of a volcano at the moment. I keep expecting it to erupt, but so far there's been coldness. I'm back home, but we're in separate bedrooms, speak when we have to, and she isn't eating. She didn't mean what she said. I think she needs counselling... she needs help of some sort. Our lives have changed so much since that evening when Orla died. We had a lovely meal together, even had a glass or two of wine which I nipped out to get while she was finishing the meal, and it was an amazing evening. A rare one, because we're not often on our own.'

Tessa sighed. 'I don't know what to say. We are getting closer, I'm certain of it, but we're doing it by eliminating people. Marnie said Orla could be a bit of a bitch. Was she?'

Andy shook his head. 'No, not in my presence, ever. The only time I've known her argue with us was when we were on honeymoon. I suggested we go on the open top bus, and she said she wanted to stay by the pool. Got really stroppy about it, so we left her at the hotel and went on our own on the bus. She was her normal self when we got back, and she smiled at us and said she thought we needed time on our own, and she was sorry she'd had to get awkward to make us go together. That was what she was really like, not a bitch.'

'Then Marnie was referring to what you two did behind her back.'

'Probably. It's killing me, DI Marsden. Orla had a Harry Potter time-turner… if only it worked.'

Tessa gave a brief smile. 'She liked the books?'

'She loved the books. Didn't care for the films, but she was a reader, didn't watch much television. She could always answer quiz questions on Harry Potter, and if she didn't know an answer she would head back to the books until she found the relevant part.' He sank down onto the settee and held his head in his hands. 'My God, I miss her so much.'

Kat placed a small piece of paper in front of Mouse. 'I rang Alyson and she said this was the agency they asked to find them a home.' Derbyshire Homes Estate Agency.

Mouse keyed in the name and watched as the website appeared on the laptop. Jeremy Peterson, large as life and twice as ugly. She smiled at the memory of the phrase her dad used to use when he didn't like someone. Kat moved to stand behind her, and they stared at the thumbnail-sized photograph of Peterson.

'He looks… insipid,' Kat volunteered.

'The problem is,' Mouse responded, 'he hasn't actually done anything illegal. You can't keep addresses private, not in the way you can a telephone number. Okay, he knows their address because he works for the business that found the property for our lottery winners, but that in itself isn't a crime.'

Kat sat at the desk. This was obviously discussion time. 'Suppose it's a lie,' she said. 'Him knowing Alyson's relative, I mean. Would that make it a crime? What sort of crime? He's not offered to sell the information, or anything like that. Why does he want to meet them? Surely it's not an ego thing... I've met Ed Danvers, the lottery winner.'

'Could be. And while it may not be a criminal activity, I'm pretty sure his employers will be less that happy. Would you trust an estate agent that allowed this sort of activity to happen?'

Kat frowned. 'It might be expedient to ask our resident fraud expert for his take on this. He's seen and heard lots of stuff we couldn't even dream of, so it would make sense to ask him for his thoughts.'

'I agree. Can you talk to him tonight? We'll hang fire until tomorrow, but we need to discuss it then. It's creepy, and if anything happened to those two kids because we didn't act quickly enough, I'd never forgive myself.'

'Those two kids are older than you,' Kat said.

'Really? Dear gods, I feel so old these days. Ask Carl if we should tell Peterson's employers before he tries anything further. Carl might advise us to let it play out, but I don't feel easy doing that without somebody saying do it. Know what I mean?'

Kat laughed. 'I do. We'll ask a policeman. So, tomorrow. You're heading back to Scarborough early?'

'We are. I want to see who walks out of his house, then follow him to work. I'm convinced we were conned, but it won't happen again. What I really want to know is why it happened. Why the secrecy? Hopefully we'll find out tomorrow.'

'I know you changed your mind about visiting Carla Newton, but are you going to ring her before you go?'

'I rang earlier, but there was no answer.' Mouse glanced at the clock. Nearly half past five. She picked up the receiver. 'I'll try again, she may be back from work now.'

Kat nodded. 'I'll leave you to it,' she whispered, and walked through into her own office.

· · ·

Mouse popped her head around Kat's door. 'It's time to go home. Is Martha with Nan and Granddad tonight?'

'She is. You're smiling. Did you get a result?'

'I did. She was really helpful, said the baby was definitely a blonde-haired white little boy and she's going to look for the photo, and message it to me. And that's where the smiling stops.'

'Discussion time? Do we need Nan? We did tell her to go home early, but we could pop up to the cottage.'

'No, we don't need Nan. This, for the moment, has to stay between us. It seems Helen Fairfax left because of Ewan Barker. He was violent towards her, extremely jealous, and before she left Sheffield, he punched her in the stomach. She spent a few days in hospital because she started to bleed. She came out and immediately went to Scarborough and never saw Ewan again. Carla said he pestered her for news of Helen and Carla gave as little as she could get away with, but eventually told him not to contact her again, because she'd lost touch with Helen.'

'But...'

'I know.' Mouse's tone was grim. 'How do we deal with this then?

CHAPTER TWENTY-FIVE

K at barely noticed the drive home, climbing up the hill out of the village and heading to the less inhabited area of Eyam. The outside lights on the driveway had come on automatically at dusk and she could see their glow through the hedge that surrounded the house. It was nevertheless dark and gloomy, perfectly matching her thoughts. What if Ewan hadn't changed over the years? What if he'd used the excuse of tracking down his son to find a way of getting through to Helen? Why? What could he possibly gain from it, especially as Helen was so ill?

Kat slowed down to turn into the drive, and then sat in the car for a few minutes, her mind still churning over so many what-ifs. The biggest one of them all was what if he hadn't changed. How much danger was Doris heading towards, and how the hell did they tell her? But suppose Ewan was no longer the violent man he had been in his teens. There was always the possibility that he was no longer the person Helen had left, in her bid to escape from the anger within him. They could be turning Nan away from a happiness she hadn't sought, but looked as though it could have landed in her lap.

Kat's thoughts drifted back to the only time Leon had hit her, the one punch sending her crashing to the floor, almost unconscious and blood all over the place from a gash in her head. For months she had been afraid, for months she had prayed that Tessa would catch up with him and lock him away for good. His death had allowed Kat to start to live again, but it hadn't taken away that awful memory.

Kat needed Carl to come home. She had the issues surrounding Alyson and Ed to deal with, but more than anything she desperately wanted to talk through the Ewan Barker problem. She glanced at her watch and sighed. At least another hour. Scrabbling through all the junk in her bag, she found her phone.

I love you.

She pressed send and smiled.

The reply was swift.

I love you too. Just leaving work, be home soon.

She breathed a sigh of relief. Climbing out of the car and crossing the driveway to reach the front door, she was aware of tears in her eyes; she angrily brushed them away.

No tears, things required action.

Carl walked out of the station and heard Tessa Marsden call his name. He stopped.

'Slow down,' she grumbled. 'I've been trying to catch up with you all the way through the place.'

'Tessa,' he said with a smile, 'I'm six foot three and you're five foot two, so guess who's going to walk the fastest. Did you want me for something?'

'No, I've not seen the superthree for a few days, wondered if everything was okay, particularly Beth. She looked shocking.'

'She's okay. Don't think she's quite up to dancing the night away yet, but she's back at work. Nan and Kat are good, not managed to catch it from Beth anyway. How's Castleton going?'

Tessa shook her head. 'Slowly. We seem to be ruling people out rather than ruling anybody in. I'll keep tinkering away at it until I know. Will you tell them I'll call in sometime tomorrow afternoon. It's only for a general chat, so if they're not there, it doesn't matter. It's strange, but when I talk to them, particularly Kat, it leads my mind in different directions. It's probably because they're not police. They're not constrained by anything. I can talk to Hannah, or any of my team, but we're trained to think in a certain way. Kat, Beth and Doris are off the grid. And besides, they make good coffee, and feed me biscuits. What's not to like?'

He laughed. 'I'll tell her. I'll even provide some buns. See you tomorrow, Tessa.' He walked across to his car and climbed in, watching Tessa get to hers and start to drive away, before he started his own vehicle. It briefly occurred to him how lonely she had appeared; perhaps it would have been a good idea in retrospect, if he had invited her to go back to Eyam with him for a meal. Kat wouldn't have minded...

He slipped the car into first gear and began the long journey home.

With the clouds covering the moon, the night was velvet black. The streetlights, super-efficient new installations that didn't actually cast a glow, helped to give Jeremy cover, and he sat outside Ed Danver's new house. Jeremy felt this was meant to be. He had followed the purchase of the property by the lottery winner, but then realised it was being bought in joint names, Ed Danvers and Alyson Read.

When Alyson Read's name had showed up on the genealogy site Jeremy gravitated towards every night, he checked out her profile and knew he had struck lucky. It was preordained, written in the stars, and every other cliché out there. They would be friends, names he could drop in conversation; like the two footballers who had bought houses through the Derbyshire Homes Estate Agency.

He had connected with his new friends for over an hour. The

rain was starting to fall heavily, and he was cold, so he decided it was maybe time to go home.

He turned on the ignition, and eased away from the kerb. He thought the following night he could maybe bring some flowers, leave them stuck into the gate. It would let them know he was thinking about them, and meant them no harm.

Kat placed the paperwork on the coffee table, then handed one of the items, the letter from Jeremy Peterson, to Carl. She'd told him the story, stressed that there had been no contact, but spoke of the young couple's worries that their address had already been discovered despite their precautions.

Carl read through the letter and sighed. 'You want me to make this official?'

Kat shook her head. 'No, and I don't think they want it either. However, we do know he works for an estate agency, the same people who found them their house. Thoughts?'

'He's a stalker. Probably collects celebrities. I can make an unofficial visit if you like, but I do think it's important the estate agency is told. Particularly as it's this agency. They find homes for people in the public eye: footballers, TV stars, and all the properties they deal with are expensive. I'll bet anything he stalks more people than your young couple. His mistake this time was in trying to contact them. He perhaps thought he could take his stalking a step further as they're new celebrities, and really befriend them.'

'Can you hang fire for a couple of days? What you're suggesting makes perfect sense, and he really does deserve to lose his job, but Ed and Alyson are our clients, and I need to keep them informed. I'll ring them and ask them to come into the office tomorrow. I'll be on my own; Mouse and Nan are heading off to Scarborough again. And there we come to our second problem. I know you can't help with it, but I do want to talk it over. That okay?'

'Is it a brandy or a hot chocolate discussion?'

'Hot chocolate, I think. My brain's fried enough without adding alcohol into the mix.'

Carl headed towards the kitchen, then paused in the doorway. 'You want to tell me how you know where he works?'

'No.'

'Okay.'

The hot chocolate went cold. It was clear to Carl how upset Kat was, and together they went through everything.

'So why do you think the man Mouse and Nan met impersonated the real Michael Fairfax?'

'I can only guess, but I think it was to close down our investigation. And it would have done. In our heads it was out of the question that Ewan could be Michael's father. It was only when Ewan spoke of Carla's photograph, and the child with blonde hair, that we realised somebody was steering us away. But that leaves us with a real problem, because Ewan is our client. He has tasked us with finding his son and has paid a considerable amount of money to do that. We have this new information from Carla Newton and it was clear from the photo that the child was probably Ewan's. It's a black and white snap with the baby held up towards Carla's face, so there's no doubting that.'

'But all of this is irrelevant, isn't it?' Carl said gently. 'The only thing on your mind right now is Nan. She's started seeing a man who has violent tendencies, and you two have to tell her. Am I right?'

'You are. And she's shooting off to Scarborough in the morning, so it will have to be tomorrow afternoon. We have to fill her in as soon as possible, although maybe we won't be the ones breaking it to her. If they track down the real Michael Fairfax tomorrow, she will find out from him, if what we've been told is true. Helen Fairfax ran away from Ewan, Carl. She must have been terrified. She's never let him anywhere near her baby, not even now that baby is fifty years old. You think she told Michael? I do, and because she is quite close to death, he's following her wishes that he doesn't ever see his father.'

'You're probably right, it does make sense. But what happens when she dies?'

'No idea. I wish we'd never heard of this bloody man. He seems so nice, but leopards and spots and all that...'

Carl pulled her to him. 'Maybe we should have had brandy. Do you want me to go and see this estate agency tomorrow?'

'No, I need to run it by the others first. I won't see them until tomorrow afternoon, so hold off on that until after we've had a meeting.'

'Oops, I almost forgot. Tessa's calling in at Connection tomorrow afternoon. Think she needs input. Every avenue she follows turns out to be a dead end. She's a lot like you, talking it out usually shows the solution.'

'That's good. I'll text Mouse in the morning, let her know. They maybe won't swan off into Scarborough for fish and chips if they know Tessa is coming.'

'You feel any better for the chat?' Carl felt concerned for his fiancée. It seemed to him she looked... haunted.

'I'm fine.' She flickered a smile. 'Hearing about Ewan and his violence towards Helen Fairfax brought the whole situation with Leon back to me. He only hit me once, but it certainly counted. Every so often it overwhelms me, but I get through it. And you help, you know you do.'

Carl pulled her into his arms once more and kissed her. 'Would it help if we moved? It must be a constant reminder, living here.'

'I don't want to move. We'd probably have to leave Eyam, and I don't want to do that. I love this village, its history, the people who live here. But houses coming up for sale are a bit few and far between, so I'll have to get him out of my mind. I can do it.'

'Whatever you say. Bear in mind I've accepted an offer on my house today, so we could buy somewhere bigger, or move just for the hell of it, if we wanted. I need you to be happy, to forget all the bad stuff.'

'The bad stuff goes into the background a little more every day. And life will be a lot better when we sort out this with Nan. I bet Mouse doesn't sleep too well tonight. Maybe I'll give her a ring later, check she's okay.'

D oris chose to drive; Mouse chose to think. Her mind refused to close down to everything they had learned about Ewan, but of one thing she was sure. It was better to wait until today's expedition was over before approaching the subject with all three of them there.

After fifteen minutes of silence, Doris broke it. 'You okay, sweetheart?'

'I'm fine, Nan. It's a bit early. I don't think I've surfaced properly yet. And we've no idea how today is going to pan out, my mind's careering through all sorts of possibilities.'

'Then close your eyes for a bit. It doesn't need two of us to drive this car. And I'm a better driver than you.'

'No, you're not.'

'I am.'

'Nan, if I close my eyes, you'll be doing eighty in about ten seconds.'

'So? You won't need to worry about it, you'll be asleep.'

'I'll stay awake, thanks.' Mouse turned to look out of the window. 'Lovely scenery, isn't it?'

'Mouse, we live in lovely scenery. Grab that cushion out of the back, and lean your head on it. I'll have us there in no time.'

'That's what I'm worried about.' Mouse reached behind her for the cushion. 'No speeding,' she warned her nan, and tucked the pillow comfortably behind her head.

Doris smiled.

They pulled onto the cul-de-sac, and Doris switched off the engine. 'Now we wait,' she said, and glanced at the car clock. 'I reckon he'll be on the move in about half an hour. You still want to tackle him here and not at work?'

'I do. I think he'll be taken by surprise here and that's what we need. Get him to work and he'll have security around him, and I suspect we wouldn't get in a second time. I'll put the bonnet up.'

She reached down and pressed the bonnet release, then got out of the car and stretched her body before walking round to the front and anchoring the raised bonnet in place. She reached down and picked up the cushion that fell out of the door as soon as she opened it, and threw it onto the back seat. 'I'm awake,' she announced.

Doris smiled at her. 'Good. Do we need to go over what we're doing?'

'We could, if we actually knew what we were doing, but I reckon if a different man to the one we've already met walks out of that property there,' she pointed, 'we get out and cross over the road. He needs to hear us call Michael, that will tell us if we've got this right.'

They settled down to wait, and when the tap came on the side window, Doris didn't flinch. They hadn't driven all this way to be side-tracked by a neighbour wanting to know if they were burglars. Mouse dealt with him.

She smiled sweetly and lowered the car window.

'Do you need help?' The small dog to which he was attached gave a low growl.

'No, we're fine, thank you. We pulled onto this cul-de-sac so we didn't affect other cars on the main road. It's jumping about like a kangaroo, so we've called the AA. They've said they'll be here in the next ten minutes.' Once again she smiled.

'Oh, okay... I'll leave you to get on with it then. Can't be too careful these days,' he said, and let the little dog drag him away.

It was two minutes later when the door they were watching opened. A man with light grey hair stood in the open doorway.

Doris and Mouse moved fast. Doris, who was closest to him, immediately headed across the road, and Mouse dropped the bonnet. She caught up with Doris, and they watched as the man walked to his garage.

'Michael!' Mouse called, and he stopped and turned to face them. His head dropped as if in surrender, and he made no further moves towards getting his car out of his garage.

Doris held up her ID, and he shook his head.

'I don't need to see that. I saw you both on CCTV the other day at Fairfax.'

'You are Michael Fairfax?' Mouse asked.

'I am.'

'Then who did we speak to on Monday?'

'My half-brother. My mother married a man called Walter North. Patrice was their child.'

'We really need to speak with you, Mr Fairfax. We can head to your offices if it will be easier for you.'

'No, I'll call and tell them to cancel my appointments for today. I get the feeling I may not want to go to work. Please, come in.' He moved towards his door, defeat written across his features.

. . .

He had a beautiful home, and they moved into the lounge. He headed towards the kitchen to make drinks.

Mouse walked around the room, occasionally picking up photographs. If the one on the windowsill was Helen Fairfax, she was a good-looking woman. As Michael walked in carrying a tray, Mouse turned to him. 'Is this Helen?'

'It is. She's beautiful, isn't she?'

Mouse moved to sit down, and she smiled at him. 'We haven't come here to upset any apple carts, or cause any bother. We're here to give you some facts, and then we'll leave you to decide what you want to do. If you want to do nothing, that's fine.'

'Maybe I should give you some facts, as a starting point. When you called at the office on Monday, Patrice and I panicked. We'd sort of known this would happen one day, and to be honest, if it had happened in six months' time or so, there would have been no need for subterfuge. We thought we could close down your investigation by Patrice saying he was Michael Fairfax. Where did we go wrong?'

'Your mother had a friend, and shortly after you were born, a photograph of you in Carla's arms was taken. Carla still had the photograph.' Mouse took out her phone and found the picture. She handed it to Michael.

He stared at it. 'I've never seen this before. I expect Mum sent her the only copy. But there's no way this baby is anything like Patrice,' he said with a rueful expression clouding his features. 'As I said, it was a spur of the minute thing on Monday, and we actually thought we'd pulled it off. It came as a shock to see you outside my door this morning.'

'I'm sorry, we don't want to cause you any upset or grief, but we have a client, your father.'

'Ewan Barker,' he said quietly.

Mouse felt Doris stiffen and she turned to check she was okay.

'You've been told about your birth?' Mouse asked Michael.

'I have. Do you know, my mother is near to the end of her life, and she's still terrified of him. It's why neither of us have any presence visually on the Internet. His treatment of her when they were together was horrific, and while it's a kind of reaction in me to meet up with him and batter him senseless, it would be pointless. Mum's coming to the end of her life, I don't want to rock the boat in any way. She's still quite mobile, although every day she seems a little more fragile.'

There was the sound of a key being inserted followed by a door opening at the back of the house, and a woman's voice called out. 'Michael? Are you okay? I watched for your car leaving...'

Michael's sigh spoke volumes. 'I'm in the lounge, Mum.'

Helen Fairfax entered the room, and even at such an early hour, she looked beautiful. Michael stood and walked towards her.

'Mum...'

Mouse rose to her feet and held out her hand. 'Mrs Fairfax. I'm so pleased to meet you.'

Helen looked first at Mouse, then at Doris. 'Who are you?' Her body stiffened, and Mouse knew Helen was adding two and two together.

Nobody spoke, and Mouse looked to Michael for assistance.

'Mum, come and sit down. Do you need anything? You've had your pain medication?'

'I have. Is this to do with... him? Ewan is it? Have you looked for him?'

'Mum, slow down and I'll tell you what I know, which isn't very much because we've hardly started talking. These ladies have been hired by... him... to trace me. Not you, me. You don't need to fear anything. He can't hurt you.'

Mouse shot a quick glance towards her nan, but Doris's face was like stone. To continue to be professional was imperative, but Nan wasn't reacting too well to what she was seeing, that much was clear.

'Nan,' she said quietly, 'would you like to go out to the car? I can deal with this.'

Michael turned round at Mouse's words. 'Are you okay?' he asked, but one look at Doris's face could tell him she was far from okay.

Doris took a deep breath. She had to know what had happened all those years ago to cause such fear in this woman, a fear she had presumably lived with all her life, and was taking to her grave.

'I'm fine,' she announced. 'Mrs Fairfax, come and sit down, please, and we can talk, then we can get out of your son's house. I hope you'll feel easier in your mind when we've finished.'

Helen stared at the woman who she presumed to be of a similar age to her, and nodded. 'Tea, please, Michael,' she said, and sat by Doris's side.

Michael carried his mother's cup of tea through, and placed it on the coffee table in front of her.

'Right,' she said, 'let's hear what you all have to say. Michael, tell me how you met these two ladies.'

Michael gave a short bark of laughter. 'They shouted me from across the road this morning, as I was leaving for the office.'

'And is this connected with Ewan Barker?'

'It is, Mrs Fairfax,' Mouse interrupted. 'But he has no idea we're here, and he doesn't know we have located you. I give you my word that we will not be telling him we met you. He has paid us to track down his son. However, it is up to Michael whether he sees him or not. We'll not be disclosing where he lives if he says he doesn't want Mr Barker to know.'

'That man,' Helen Fairfax almost growled, 'very nearly killed me and Michael. He was the most controlling person I have ever known. He wouldn't let me speak to anyone, and if another man so much as glanced my way, I paid for it with a good hiding. I was seven months pregnant, scared of my own shadow, and he insisted I go over to his house where he lived with his mother. He said he wanted to talk about our wedding. I didn't want to marry him, but I couldn't make him see that. I caught the bus, and he was waiting at the stop when I got off.'

She paused, the tears in her eyes evident.

'I said thank you to the conductor who steadied me as the bus pulled up. It was obvious, of course, that I was pregnant. I paid for saying thank you with the hammering of my life. I was almost unconscious when he kicked me in the stomach. Luckily his mother came back from wherever she had been, and rang for an ambulance. They kept me in hospital for over a week, and I prayed every day my baby would be okay. They saved his life, but nobody knew if he would be damaged by the kick.'

Helen took a sip of her drink, her hands shaking.

'Mum,' Michael said, placing an arm round her shoulder. 'You don't have to speak of this.'

'Oh, but I do. I have to make sure that dreadful man isn't fooling these two ladies. He was full of charm when I met him, but within a month he was showing his true colours. Did he marry?'

Mouse nodded. 'He did. I believe his wife died five years ago.'

Doris didn't speak. She couldn't.

'Then I hope they checked for foul play,' Helen said. 'The man is capable of anything. I was released from hospital and the police took me to my aunt's place at Scarborough. They locked him up, but I was too scared to press charges. I thought he would come for me again once he was released, so I backed down. They had to release him but he bothered my friend continuously, trying to find out where I was. In the end we took a photo of her holding the baby, thinking he would stop bothering her if he saw a picture of him. I never heard from Ewan again but I knew one day he would want to meet Michael.'

'And that's why you kept under the radar? No social media, no pictures on your website...' Mouse sounded thoughtful.

Doris finally spoke. 'And that's why he came to us. He didn't know where to start, but he knew of our reputation. He knew we'd find you.'

CHAPTER TWENTY-SEVEN

Marnie stared at her husband. 'I can't stop thinking about it. I don't think we're going to be able to recover from this. I trusted you with the rest of my life, my daughter, my everything, and you had sex with her.'

'And I've explained it all – how it came about, that it was only the once...'

'But what I don't understand is how she could have sex with you in here,' Marnie swept her arm round in contempt, 'then never refer to it again, and carry on as she always had done with you. That's the hardest part, Andy. It seems like I never knew you, and I never knew her.'

He tried to take her into his arms, to offer some comfort, but she pulled away. 'Sorry, Andy, I don't need you near me.'

'Do you want me to move out?'

'Of course not. I don't want the whole village discussing us, and that's what would happen if you moved out. And we'll have a funeral to arrange before much longer, so I'll need you here then.'

'And after that?'

She sighed. 'I don't know. Maybe if we had counselling...'

'So you're quite happy to talk to someone else, but not me? Have I got that bit right?'

The tears that seemed to be a permanent part of her life these days suddenly appeared once more. 'I don't know,' she sobbed. 'I don't know anything. Not anymore.'

'Who do you think killed her?' Ruby's eyes lifted towards her husband's face, and she saw him frown.

'I've no idea, Ruby, but it wasn't me.'

'I'm aware of that.' Despite her pain her voice was clear, and cutting. 'I imagine yours was the best alibi of them all. I can't help but feel sorry for her, to lose her life so young. And I also can't help but feel there's a connection between you having sex with her and her death. Maybe an indirect connection, but it's there somewhere.'

Finally he looked at her. 'And what on earth could that connection possibly be?'

'I don't know yet, but if there comes a day when I do find out there is one, it will be our last day together. It's hard enough for me to know you slept with her, although I half understand that as I'm not much good to you, but if there's anything at all linking you anywhere near the reason why she died, I won't be able to forgive you.'

Steve stood. 'I love you, Ruby. If I could take everything back a couple of months I would do it in a heartbeat, but I can't. It would break me if I lost you. It hasn't broken me losing Orla. Maybe that's something for you to think about.'

Ruby watched him walk out of the room and held up one finger towards his retreating back. She couldn't resist the small smile that said was it right that a vicar's wife should be making that gesture towards her husband, and she decided it wasn't only right, it was spot on.

. . .

Helen Fairfax turned to face Doris. 'And now that you have found us, what will you do? Have you met Ewan? I bet he was so charming. I remember my first sight of him. It was both our eighteenth birthdays, and we'd chosen to spend the evening in the same pub. We didn't know each other, it was pure coincidence. In those days the eighteenth birthday wasn't the important one, as it is today; no, the biggy was the twenty-first. The eighteenth was really only about being able to get a drink legally. We were kind of pushed together once both sets of friends found out it was a joint birthday, and he walked me home. He was absolutely charming. By the end of the first month of seeing him I was head over heels in love. By the end of the third month I was pregnant and he had turned into a monster. The first time he hit me was because I was sick. I didn't know I was pregnant but I did know I felt sick. He took me for a coffee and the smell of the coffee wiped me out. I grabbed as many napkins as I could and vomited until there was nothing left in me. He took me home, very considerate on the bus, helped me into Mum's house, then knocked me to the floor. I had bruises all over, but he was so lovely when he was apologising, promising he would never do it again, it was only because I had shown him up in the café, that sort of thing.

'I put up with a lot. I stopped going out anywhere other than work, stopped talking to any of my male colleagues in case Ewan popped in, and I was within a couple of days of leaving to have my baby, when the final attack came. That bus conductor had no idea what he did when he put an arm out to steady me. When I came to in hospital, the man sitting at my bedside was a policeman, a lovely man who told me to make a statement, then find somewhere to stay out of Sheffield for a while. And so I came to Scarborough. I've been here ever since, still scared to death he'll find me and knowing he could do it through Michael. It's blighted our lives, mine, Michael's and Patrice's. I made them aware from a young age that I had a problem, and they knew never to talk to strangers, particularly men with light hair.'

'And that,' Michael interrupted, 'is why we tried to fool you on Monday. Patrice and I have always protected Mum, and that's what it was about. We figured you would back off when you realised Michael Fairfax couldn't be Barker's son, but we didn't know about the photo you've shown me.'

'Photo?' Helen queried.

Mouse pulled up the picture on her phone and handed it to Helen.

Helen smiled, and touched the screen. 'Carla. This is the photo I mentioned. We went to Chesterfield to take it, got the Crooked Spire in the background, thinking he might decide I was living there. I never saw him again, but he's never been more than a few steps behind me all my life.'

Doris touched Helen's hand. 'I'm so sorry. It must have been such a nightmare. We won't be passing your details on to him, not in any way. However, he has hired us to find Michael, and to negotiate a meeting with him if we do find him.'

'Michael?' Mouse said, and he smiled.

'I want nothing to do with the man. Anyone who can still have this effect on my mother after fifty years is never going to be part of my life. You will convey that to him?'

'I will. Thank you for your time. I'd like to leave my card with you if that's okay. You can contact me at any time if you have any questions. I'll notify Mr Barker of your decision tomorrow morning. We will tell him nothing beyond that.'

'And if he goes to some other agency for help in finding me? You two have been very understanding, and have taken what I have said as what I want to happen, but that won't necessarily be the case with some other business.'

'You should see your solicitor if that happens. You can always take out an injunction to stop him approaching you. I will be writing to you so that you have our contact details, in case you need us for anything, but we won't be troubling you again beyond sending that letter.'

All four stood and headed for the front door. Helen hugged both women; her fragility was evident. Michael shook hands with Mouse and Doris, and they waved as they drove away.

Mouse chose to drive the return journey, and it was almost fifteen minutes before she spoke. 'You have to get rid of him, Nan.'

'He's history,' Doris said. 'I don't want to talk about it, but after we meet with him tomorrow morning, I need you to leave me in the reception area with him. I'll tell him then.'

'We'll be listening from Kat's office with a glass to the wall. Well, maybe not quite that but the CCTV will be on and trained on you.'

'Don't doubt it,' Doris said. 'But don't interrupt us. I can handle him. I seem to remember blowing Leon's hand off, so men don't exactly scare me. And neither will Ewan Barker. So you can stop worrying. Whatever feelings may have been growing for him are wiped out, I promise you. Men who hit women are the lowest, and I might mention that to him.'

'Is that before or after you kick him in the balls?'

Doris thought for a moment. 'After.'

As darkness fell, Jeremy Peterson headed out of his home and down to the parked car. He laid the spray of flowers on the back seat, checked his torch was fully working, and drove away.

He'd had a good day; one of the major players at Manchester United had been in to speak with Mr Kenwright, looking to buy a bigger house. Jeremy had hung around as close to Kenwright's office door as he could get, trying to hear details of areas where they would be showing him available properties.

There had been much laughter; Kenwright was in his element when the celebrities came to call. Jeremy hoped to climb the ladder and be a celebrity estate agent one day, soon.

He had to move quickly when the footballer and his wife left the office, and he felt envious, almost overwhelming, as Leo Kenwright escorted the pair out to their Audi. One day, Jeremy thought, one day.

In the meantime he would nurture the smaller celebrities he encountered along the way, people like Alyson Read and Ed Danvers. Four million, three hundred and eighty-two thousand and sixty-three pounds. He couldn't remember if there were any pennies involved.

He drove through the Derbyshire countryside keeping an eye out for stray sheep that hadn't realised it was bedtime, and who were prone to standing in the middle of the road, waiting to stop as many cars as they could. The moon was a help; it wasn't so ominously dark.

Peterson reached Ashford in the Water and pulled up by the river. In his glovebox he kept a supply of cable ties, and he took three out, ready for tying the flowers to the wrought iron entrance gates. He'd already written a little card to go with the flowers, simply saying with best wishes, JP. He thought they would remember who he was.

He meant them no harm, but he hoped they would forget that he had told them about the fictitious relative. That was a spur of the moment idea that hadn't been right. This one, much more subtle, sending little gifts, would be more appropriate.

Maybe they would even share a coffee, or a pint, one day. He would like that. He climbed out of the car, walked around the corner to the large detached house, and headed for the gates.

It was a bit of a struggle fastening the first tie, because he had to balance the flowers with one hand while wrapping the tie around them with the other, but once that first one was attached, the other two were much easier. He had to stuff the card down inside the flowers; he hadn't thought about stapling it to the paper holding them secure when he was at home.

Finally he stepped back and admired his offering. Red roses. He hoped they would appreciate he hadn't gone for cheap flowers. He wandered back to his car, stood for a moment watching the river flowing to wherever it flowed to, then took his place behind the steering wheel.

An excellent job, he was pleased it had gone so well. He wriggled around until he was comfortable and then turned the ignition key. At first the car wouldn't start, but after some gentle persuasion it fired and he set off for home. The moon had all but disappeared behind clouds, and before he arrived home, the rain had started to fall. By midnight his roses were a sodden mess, water pooling in the bottom of the paper wrapper holding them securely. The writing on the gift card, however, was protected by the Sellotape covering he had placed over it.

The next morning, Ed and Alyson handed it over to Carl Heaton.

CHAPTER TWENTY-EIGHT

Carl was their first visitor of the morning. He joined his fiancée and her two colleagues in Kat's office and laid the sodden bunch of flowers on a towel Kat had hurriedly placed on the desk.

'And which garage did he buy these from?' she mused. 'They certainly look worse for wear.'

'Heavy rain can do that to flowers,' Carl said with a smile, 'but he's rattled our lottery winners, I can tell you. I've told them it will be sorted by the end of the day, but as it's your case and strictly speaking nothing to do with me, I thought I'd bring the evidence here first. My proposal is that I take these flowers and the card to his employers, along with the letter Alyson Read brought in to you. I suspect they'll be horrified he's stalking their clients, but I also suspect Alyson and Ed aren't the first ones he's bothered. I'll then have a word with him, hopefully while I'm still in their offices, and spell it out in words of one syllable that one more action of this kind will result in him being arrested. How does that sound? Or do you want to tackle it on your own?'

'Ordinarily I'd say we'll see to it, but I think it will scare him more if a DI Carl Heaton turns up to talk to him.' Doris and Mouse nodded at Kat's words.

'Okay, I'll head over to see him, and I'll let you know the outcome. I can't see it being a good one for our Jeremy. And can I borrow that towel, please? These flowers are very wet.'

'Help yourself,' Doris said. She sounded weary. She was weary.

A sleepless night hadn't helped at all, and she felt sick at the thought of seeing Ewan Barker again. How could she have been so wrong about him? His charm had fooled her completely, as it had Helen Fairfax all those years earlier. Helen had spent her entire adult life feeling afraid because of him.

Doris recognised she didn't feel afraid of him, but brutally attacking women caused such immense feelings of anger. Seeing Kat lying on the floor with blood pouring from a head wound after her husband had hit her had brought similar feelings to the surface. It had cost Leon his left hand, and at the very least Doris knew it would cost Ewan his dignity. Her words were as lethal as her gun-toting skills.

She watched as Carl rolled up the flowers inside the towel, and gave him a brief smile as he left the office.

Ewan arrived at ten, not in any way disconcerted by the request for a meeting. His assumption that they would have some sort of news for him was written all over his face as Doris showed him into Kat's office.

He looked surprised at Doris not staying, but he sat down and waited for Mouse and Kat to organise some paperwork, and for Kat to take out the recorder from her drawer. She pointed to it.

'Yes of course, I know it helps if you record meetings.'

'Thank you,' Kat said, and switched it on.

'Ewan,' Mouse said. 'We met your son yesterday. You were right about the man we were introduced to as Michael Fairfax couldn't be the child Helen gave birth to all those years ago, he was in fact his half-brother. We spoke at length with Michael, and as a result we have prepared our final statement along with a cheque for the balance of the money left from your deposit.'

Ewan's face was stony. 'He doesn't want to see me?'

'No. We left our card with him in case he changes his mind, but I'll be honest, Ewan, I don't think there's any chance of that,' Mouse confirmed.

'Why?'

Mouse hesitated. 'We also met Helen.'

'And?' There was anger creeping into his voice, and Kat glanced at Mouse.

'And Michael has known for many years about the way you treated Helen, almost causing her to lose the baby you now want to claim as your son. So has his half-brother. She has never hidden it, and I consider you were lucky to escape a prosecution for what you did to her.'

'You do, do you?'

'Yes I do. She spent a week in hospital after that final beating you gave her, and the police took her to a safe place to make sure you couldn't find her. She was too afraid of you to let them charge you.'

Ewan's cheeks grew redder as his anger increased. 'So he's turning down the chance of inheriting my money?'

Mouse thought of the handbag she had stopped bidding on when it reached four hundred pounds. 'He really doesn't need your money, Ewan. He was quite certain that he wouldn't meet with you, so the only thing we could do was leave the door open for the future. We will be writing to him to confirm this, but he was also quite adamant that he would take out an injunction if you seek help from anyone else in finding him. I think you have to accept that you're not going to meet him and make other arrangements for your assets when you die.'

Ewan stood. He snatched up the envelope containing the report and his cheque, and turned to leave the room.

'Thanks for nothing,' he snarled.

Kat quickly switched her screen to the reception area. Doris had given them specific instructions not to interrupt while she was getting him out of her life, but they could monitor the situation in the front office.

They watched as he walked towards where Doris was sitting at her desk.

'Did you know?'

'Of course. I was there with Mouse. I listened to Helen's story, and it killed any hopes of our seeing each other again. Kat has given you your refund?'

'She has. But that's not what I want. I want to see my son. And his cheating, conniving mother.'

'So really that's what it was about. Seeing Helen Fairfax and possibly finishing off what you started?'

Ewan stared at her for several seconds and then moved towards her. She stood.

'I'm not Helen Fairfax,' she warned.

'You're no fucking different. Two bitches. Both running out on me. I thought we had something, but you're no different to her, or my late wife. She was a bitch as well.'

'Why? Wouldn't she obey you in everything either?' Doris knew she was taunting him. She also knew her girls had CCTV recording it all.

'Don't you come the clever know-it-all with me, Doris Lester...' He took another step towards her and she moved away from her desk to face him.

'But I do know it all, Ewan. I saw the fear in Helen's eyes, even as recently as yesterday. Fifty years of terror you gave that woman, being scared of you turning up and beating the hell out of her again. And it must have been permanently on her mind, because she knew exactly why we were there. To bring you into her son's life. And hers. But he's grown up, Ewan, and he doesn't like women-beating men any more than I do, so take your fists and your evil, nasty, malicious brain out of my life. We don't want to see you again.'

He gave a roar, almost of pain, and lunged towards Doris, his hand raised to grab at her. She waited until he grabbed her hair, then punched his throat. His eyes bulged as he tried to breathe, and she brought up her knee.

Even his scream didn't bring Kat and Mouse from Kat's office. They watched as his legs gave way, and he crumpled to the floor.

'God, I love this woman,' Kat breathed.

'Me too,' Mouse said, unable to take her eyes from the screen. 'Think we need an ambulance?'

'We'll think about it if he stops breathing.'

Doris stared at him, his eyes screwed tightly shut. She could see the pain was overwhelming him; a knee in the testicles hadn't been in his plans. His breathing was still ragged, and she knelt down to check his pulse.

'Unfortunately you'll live, Ewan,' she said. 'You have two minutes to recover, then you get out of my life, you keep away from Helen Fairfax and her sons, and you never darken these doors again.'

One eye opened. 'Bitch. I'll sue you.' His voice was hoarse.

'Okay, I'll make sure a copy of the recording...' she pointed to the CCTV camera that was trained on her area, 'is made available to your solicitors. I'm sure they'll be able to see who hit who first. Your mistake was in attacking someone with a black belt in karate. This time it wasn't a seven-month pregnant young girl who wouldn't have been able to fight back.'

He grabbed hold of the back of a chair and tried to stand. Doris moved towards him, and he backed off, doubled over with pain emanating from his crotch.

'Get out, Ewan,' she said quietly. 'Get out and don't ever come back. It's nice to know that the saying "what goes around comes around" is really true. Close the door behind you,' and she turned her back on him.

She half-expected him to move towards her, and she held herself in readiness, but he didn't; the shop doorbell pealed out and he slammed the door with some violence before shambling his way across to his car.

Kat and Mouse remained silent, waiting to see what would happen next. They watched Doris sit down at her desk, then look out of the large office window. Still they waited.

Finally Doris looked up into the camera and blew them a kiss.

She walked across to the shop door, locked it, retraced her steps and went into Kat's office.

'That was fun,' Doris said.

'Black belt?' Mouse queried with a grin. 'It's nice that you promoted yourself, but you have to actually do the grade to claim it.'

'Bethan Walters,' Doris said, 'I do not tell lies. I did the grade six months ago while you and Kat were fussing over Martha. I had no intentions of telling you, because as you know I've held back from taking it because I'm so proud of you having reached it. I was quite happy at brown belt, but one day I knew I had to do it. So I did. Okay?'

Kat was the first to hug Doris. 'Congratulations, Nan. Did it hurt Ewan more to be pole-axed by a black belt than it would have done to be kicked in the balls by a brown belt?'

'Nope, it's just as painful, no matter the colour of the belt.'

Mouse walked round the desk and hugged her nan. 'Congratulations, old woman. I'm so proud of you. We need to celebrate.'

Doris laughed. 'No problem. Let's go out for a meal or something at the weekend. Decide amongst yourselves who's going to be the designated driver, because I certainly will be enjoying a tipple or two. And bring Ferrero Rocher.'

There was a lightness in Doris's step as she returned to her own desk, and it felt good to look out of the window and not see Ewan's car. What did she want with a boyfriend at her age anyway? Mind you, if Tom Hardy were footloose and fancy free...

Carl leaned back in his chair and waited for Leo Kenwright to speak. Instead he sighed.

'I knew something was going on. We've had a couple of minor complaints that weren't really complaints officially, about Jeremy Peterson. He name drops. I know that's nothing in itself, but it's constant. And he does silly things like sending new home cards to celebrities. We have lots on our books, but he particularly likes footballers. Now it seems he likes money as well.'

'I will be having a word with him myself, Mr Kenwright, but he hasn't actually committed a crime so I won't be taking it further. However, I think you may need to take action.'

The two men stood and shook hands.

'I'll speak to him,' Carl said, 'and then you can have your five minutes with him.'

Carl escorted Peterson outside to his car, and held the door open while the quaking man climbed inside.

The DI then talked for some considerable time, telling Peterson what they knew, the proof they had, and warned him in no uncertain terms that he was receiving a caution, but if any further stalking came to light, he would be arrested.

Peterson's words came out in a rush; his promises were wide but not varied. He would never approach the lottery winners again, he would forget he had ever heard of Manchester United and their players, and he would never do anything like this again no matter what he heard or saw in the office.

Carl let him go, and Peterson walked back into work.

Five minutes later, he was out of a job and heading to his car, prior to driving home.

Later that day a huge bouquet of flowers arrived at the Connection office, bearing a card with the immortal words "Thank you! Sorted!". They had to raid Mouse's flat to find a vase big enough to accommodate the stunning display.

CHAPTER TWENTY-NINE

Zoe Williamson stared out of the window at the pouring rain, although not seeing it. The day she had been dreading had arrived, and finally saying goodbye to Mandy was going to be so painful. Too painful.

She had lost everything that had ever meant anything to her. The man who had fathered Mandy was gone... and she had loved him breathtakingly. It had been hard not being able to talk about it when he died; to find out by accident, as she had, had been the worst thing ever. They had spoken every month on the first day ever since they had decided to part, and ringing on that first of October and hearing his wife's voice had been traumatic.

His wife had explained through tears that he had died two days earlier; a stroke had taken him. Even now, two years later, she felt sick thinking about that phone call. Everything was unbearable; Mandy had left her too, and that was the hardest of all.

Zoe felt a mug being pressed into her hand, and she turned with a grateful smile. It was Kat Rowe.

'I didn't know if you would be able to come,' Zoe said.

'Of course I can come. I told you, I'm here whenever you want to talk, or cry, or anything. You'll get through today, Zoe, and it will get easier.'

They stood side by side, each cradling a mug of tea, staring at the rain.

'A damn miserable day all round,' Zoe murmured, her eyes misting with tears and not for the first time that morning.

'It is but look at how many are here supporting you. Your little house is full to overflowing. Stay strong, Zoe. Will somebody be with you tonight?'

'My sister. She says she will stay as long as I need her, but she has a husband and family of her own, she can't be with me, no matter what she says.'

'Good. Let her stay a few days, until you start to recover some form of normality. You will eventually want to be on your own anyway, it's a natural progression.'

'You're a wise lady, Reverend Rowe.' Her sigh was heavy. 'I'd better get my coat on. Mandy will be arriving any time.'

The hearse left for the short two-minute drive to the church, with a snake of friends and family following on behind. A sea of umbrellas covered heads, but Zoe walked without one. She knew her tears were heavier than any rain.

Tessa Marsden and Hannah Granger were standing by the church door when the procession arrived, and both slipped into the back of the church, alongside Kat.

The church was full, with mourners having to stand along the back. Steve Barksworth spoke. The service was warm, all-encompassing, and the choir paid their own special tribute to Mandy by singing her favourite hymn, *Be Still, for the Presence of the Lord*. It was almost too much for Zoe as the last notes of the hymn died away, and her sister held tightly to her, and whispered in her ear.

The coffin was carried around to the newly dug grave, and ten minutes later it was all over. A distraught Zoe was helped back home, and Kat, after having a few words with Tessa and Hannah, returned to Eyam.

'That was a shitty morning,' Kat said as she walked through reception, and slammed her way into her own office.

Doris half-stood, then sat back down again. She'd give her a few minutes to calm down, then take her a coffee through. Maybe she would be ready to talk by then.

Andy Harrison spotted DI Marsden and DS Hannah Granger as he walked home after going to collect the morning paper. They drove through Castleton, so he hoped it meant they were going to the church for Mandy's funeral, and not going to be visiting him and Marnie. His wife was fragile, too wiped out to take much more.

He almost felt jealous that Zoe Williamson had her answers. They seemed to be always in limbo, every phone call a jolt to the system, a scream inside his head, because that call could be the one saying we've found the person responsible.

Marnie was sleeping deeply every night thanks to the ministrations of her doctor, but Andy had nothing to help close his mind down. And his mind drifted continuously to the night that had ultimately resulted in killing Orla – he had no doubt that her pregnancy had been the reason behind her death. Had somebody suspected they were the father of the baby? Or was it that somebody would have liked to have been the father and felt let down by Orla?

It wasn't only during the night-time hours that Andy's mind couldn't switch off, it was all the time. He had no idea whether Orla knew who the father was. If she had slept with the man she intended sleeping with, how quickly after their night of passion had it happened? If it was only a couple of days, then maybe she would have thought her lover was the father...

His heart ached for her. She wouldn't have known where to turn, and when she did turn to the person she expected to have been supportive, he had strangled her. He. It had to have been a he, there was no reason for it to have been one of her girlfriends, no reason at all.

Andy walked into the hallway, took off his coat and fished the soggy newspaper from his inside pocket. If things had been different, they, the three of them, would have been attending Mandy Williamson's funeral. He towelled his hair, and went into the lounge expecting to see Marnie staring vacantly at daytime television. She wasn't there.

He ran upstairs to their bedroom, the one she was refusing to share with him, but the room was empty. He glanced through the window and saw her. She was down in the garden, in her nightie, standing by the swing that Orla had refused to have removed, gently pushing the seat. Marnie was drenched.

Andy grabbed her dressing gown, ran downstairs and out of the back door. She didn't flinch, didn't even look at him as he draped the dressing gown around her shoulders.

She let him lead her up the path and into the kitchen. He sat her at the table, sickened that her face should be so devoid of expression. She shivered and he clicked on the kettle. He needed to warm her, to get her dry.

In his panic to go upstairs to get some dry clothes for her he fell up the top step and took a tumble onto the landing. It hurt. It would bruise. The same as his heart felt bruised.

Picking himself up and rubbing his shin, he went into the bedroom and got her a clean nightie and two towels from the warm airing cupboard.

She let him dry her and change her nightie, then she sat at the table once more, all without speaking. He placed a cup of tea in front of her.

'Drink this as soon as you can, sweetheart,' he said. 'You need to warm up.'

She gave a slight nod and picked up the mug. Cupping her hands around it, she took small sips.

It was when she was halfway down the drink that her brain unfroze. She cried, said her daughter's name over and over again. Andy moved round to sit by her side, and pulled her towards him.

She sank into his strength and he held her. They cried together, and he knew things had changed. Finally they could face this tragedy as one, not two halves.

Kat gave a weak and watery smile as Doris handed over a mug of coffee. 'And I got the big mug. Did I look as though I needed it?'

'You looked as though you needed a bucketful,' Doris said. 'Want to talk?'

'Yes, but not about anything too deep. I think my brain will implode. Tell me something good.'

'Okay. Mouse has gone to Manchester. She took a phone call last night from a friend of a friend of a friend – I think I've got that right – who runs one of the big player companies. His base is Manchester. They're looking to recruit a lot of new people, and the main place will be in IT. Connection was recommended to them as being excellent at background checks and recommendations, specialising in IT, so she arranged to go over and see him today. If this goes through, it may be that we have to put Mouse exclusively on that, and we stick to the investigative side. I know Ewan was a pretty big case, but we pick up lots of minor ones like our lottery winners. I would hate to lose that kind of work, and I really think we can manage that side of the business between us. It may even free you up a little more, so that you get some time with Martha during the week, and not only at weekends.'

'You think we can do it?' Kat looked a bit livelier. 'You know my lack of skills in the Internet department.'

'Stop running yourself down, Kat Rowe. You have improved a hundred per cent since I started to sort you out. But you don't need to worry your head about that, you're our sensible one, the one that sees things that we don't see, the level head we need. I'm the IT expert, remember? I'm certain we can manage and leave Mouse to bring in the big money. We might need to employ a receptionist if I have to start going out more, but the business is doing remarkably well, so it could carry an extra member. We'll make sure we have weekly meetings so that we're all aware of what is happening in general, and of course Mouse needs to come back with a contract for any of what we've discussed to be viable anyway.'

'You're right, but I have every faith in our Mouse,' Kat said, her smile a bit brighter than earlier. 'We've no idea what time she'll be back, I assume.'

'No, she said she'd see us when she saw us.'

Kat sipped thoughtfully at her coffee. 'Tessa said she might call in for a kick-about this afternoon.'

'I'll set up the goal posts then,' Doris said with a laugh. 'I guess she's not after a game of football.'

'No, I can't imagine Tessa would understand the offside rule. She might not even understand the principle behind a net, a ball and eleven fit men. She does seem to get something from talking to us though, it's like she throws everything into the ring, we look at it with civilian eyes and make what we probably consider half-hearted remarks, but she digests them, thinks about them and something gets triggered in her brain. She's a smart cookie, is Tessa, and Hannah looks at her with utter admiration.'

'I know, bless her. It doesn't matter what Tessa asks her to do, she does it. She might grumble a bit, but she'll always do it.'

'Have we got chocolate biscuits? They'll be disappointed if we can only offer them Rich Tea Fingers.'

The smile on Doris's face faltered. 'We're quite low on biscuits altogether. Please don't bring Garibaldi, we won't be stocking them anymore.'

Kat stood, walked round to where Doris was sitting, and placed a kiss on the top of her head.

'No Garibaldi,' she whispered. 'And we'll wipe that man out of our lives. He hasn't contacted you?'

Doris shook her head. 'No, he may not be able to walk or speak yet. I... hit him quite hard.'

Kat hugged Doris. 'I know. We watched it happen. And we've viewed it about six times since then, you were amazing. The control... I would have gone for a killer blow, I know I would, but you, no you hit his throat perfectly, and the knee to his balls was perfection. You think he'll contact you?'

'I think he got the message, but will his ego let it go? He was hammered by a woman, a woman he didn't know was a black belt in karate. I told him I went to a dojo, but I think he thought the little woman likes to exercise. It never occurred to him for a minute that this little woman could kill him with one well-placed blow. That's not going to sit well with him, I can assure you. I think I'll have to be on my guard for quite a long time, but it was worth it. He ruined the last fifty years of Helen Fairfax's life, it impacted on his son's life and business – he's a bad 'un, and I want nothing more to do with him.'

By lunchtime, supplies had been restored to their former glory in the cupboards of Connection, with not a Garibaldi biscuit in sight.

Kat typed up the full report into Alyson Read and Ed Danvers, but didn't file it away in the completed drawer; she wanted Carl to check through it first, ensuring she had all the facts for the part he had played.

She was aware of how quiet Doris had been, and knew the reason had to be Ewan Barker. Kat hoped she wasn't scared, more angry that she had been taken in by him. She had started to leave her office door open when they had no clients in. She didn't expect Ewan to have the balls to come back to their offices, but it didn't mean he wouldn't. She figured he would be more protective of the said balls in the future.

She was mulling over the difficulty, and wondering how they could find the real Doris again, when she heard the ping of the shop doorbell, followed by Tessa Marsden's voice.

'We need to talk.'

'Good Lord, are you here to arrest us?' Doris didn't sound too concerned.

'Why. You done something wrong?'

'Sort of. A little bit wrong. Maybe a tad.'

'Doris Lester! Tell me more.'

Tessa had long suspected that Doris was the muscle behind the three Connection ladies, and wasn't convinced by their denial that Leon Rowe's absent hand was anything to do with them. 'What have you done?'

'Self-defence,' she said. 'Totally self-defence, and it's all on film, so if you ever get a strange man in that police station of yours saying I beat him up, I can prove two things. The first one is I did, the second one is he went for me first. I stopped him. Effectively. But he can't have been in to see you because I don't think he'll be walking yet,' she finished with a smile.

'Can we see the film?' Hannah asked.

'Not if you're going to arrest me.'

'If we promise not to arrest you, can we see it?'

'Maybe. Later. It's coffee time. Do you want to go through to Kat's office?'

Kat tried to stifle her laughter at the conversation she had heard, and went to her office door to usher them in.

'You done anything we can arrest you for?' Tessa said, with an exaggerated wink at Kat.

'As if,' Kat responded. 'I'm a church deacon.'

'And Mouse? She done anything?'

Simultaneously it occurred to both Kat and Doris that even Tessa had taken to using the name Mouse for Beth.

'She's in Manchester, she could be doing anything in that den of iniquity.'

'Then we can safely leave her to the Manchester lads. What

happens in Lancashire, stays in Lancashire. We got chocolate biscuits?'

Doris handed around four coffees and placed a plate of biscuits on the table. 'You're here for a specific reason? Or is it a friends dropping by sort of visit?'

'Friends dropping by for a biscuit,' Tessa said. 'And to talk.'

'Orla French?'

'Orla French. We've interviewed everybody at least once, some twice, some even three times, but I'm leaning towards the random stranger theory. Maybe it was simply a case of Orla being in the wrong place at the wrong time. Do I think she would be so naïve as to accept a lift from a stranger in the pouring rain? Yes, I think I could see that situation with her. However, we've covered every house along that stretch of road between Castleton and Hope – and there aren't many – checking CCTV cameras and not one has showed an image of a young girl walking in the rain. Either she never started to make that journey, or she was actually offered the lift in Castleton, but from her leaving work it seems she disappeared. Nobody saw her once she walked out of that café door.'

Engrossed in Tessa's explanation, they all acted as if they were Hungry Hippos, reaching across the table with one hand towards the biscuit plate and taking one. Nobody spoke, waiting for Tessa to continue.

'It has to be somebody she didn't know, or at least somebody she knew but nobody in her circle knew she knew them. And I realise that's far too many "knews", but you get my drift. I'm thinking off the top of my head here, but if I'm right with that, where the hell do we start looking for a stranger? I don't want to be dragging Orla's name out in ten years' time and working it as a cold case. So, let's throw this around. Who wants to go first?'

The silence was solid until it was broken by the peal of the doorbell. Doris stood and moved towards the door, but Kat blocked her. 'I'll go,' she said.

'I'm on reception, Kat,' and Doris went through.

Mouse was removing her coat.

'Hello, sweetheart. Good day?'

Mouse looked at her nan. 'You thought I was Ewan, didn't you?'

'If I did it wouldn't have worried me,' Doris said with a slight smile. 'In there I have Kat, Tessa and Hannah. He'd have run a mile. You joining us, or have you had enough?'

'I'll dump my stuff in my office, and join you. I'll lock the main door though.'

Mouse watched, a thoughtful expression on her face as Doris re-entered Kat's office. Her nan wasn't right and it was showing.

Tessa quickly filled Mouse in on what she had already covered, and Mouse countered with, 'You don't think it's a stranger murder at all, do you?'

'Not really, no.' Tessa sighed.

'What stops you thinking that?' Kat joined in.

'First and foremost, I think the pregnancy is behind it all. We know she slept with Andy Harrison once, but we've only his word it was once, don't forget. She slept with Steve Barksworth several times... could she have dabbled with someone else? Either willingly or unwillingly? Paul Carr says they definitely hadn't got to that stage, they were simply at the cup of coffee point, no further, so that leads us to other church people, because she didn't do much else in her life. She has connections with Hope and Bradwell churches, but her main worship place was Castleton.'

'Okay,' Kat said. 'You've interviewed everybody in the usual congregation of Castleton church, and I know they're like every other church congregation, getting on a bit. But do they have kids or grandkids who would be about Orla's age? Could she have met one of them at some church function? We have lots of village-based activities here in Eyam, as you know, and I'm sure the others will as well. That could be worth looking at. Talk about it specifically to Steve, he might be able to point you in the right direction. But I'm sure you're right, that baby is behind all of this.'

'We do have another avenue to follow about the baby, funnily enough,' Tessa said. 'I don't know much about it yet, because when I rang to make an appointment, the voicemail message said they are closed today. I'll be going to see them tomorrow.'

'Who?' Mouse asked.

'Oh sorry, my thoughts are all over the place. We called to pick up a sandwich from the tea shop where Orla worked, and the owner produced this from the side of the till.' Tessa took out a letter from her bag and laid it on the table. She turned it over so they could see the name of the sender on the back.

'M B clinic. Don't they do baby scans?'

'They do,' Tessa confirmed. 'What's strange is that Orla didn't use her home address, she gave the café address. This letter arrived two days ago. I don't suppose for one minute I would ever have got it if we hadn't chosen to call in.'

'And what is it about?'

'According to the letter, she gave them the wrong mobile phone number, and emails to her email address are bouncing back to them, so they've had to resort to a letter. It's an appointment for a gender scan. It's rather looking as though the first part of her pregnancy was being taken care of outside of the NHS, with Orla paying for her scans.'

'Do you get the impression this young girl was running scared?' Doris said quietly. 'Nothing about this is normal. Nobody, not even her best friend, knew what was happening. I find it strange. I also think we're going around in circles with it, and I feel we're being less than helpful for you. I think you possibly will have to go back to the beginning. Recheck all the alibis, because if it isn't a stranger who has killed her, it's somebody within her circle of friends or family. And that means somebody is lying, or manipulating somebody else to lie for them. Did you ever find where she went into the water?'

'No.' Tessa shook her head in frustration. 'The weather that night was awful, torrential rain that washed anything vaguely resembling a clue into oblivion. We had no tyre tracks in places where there should have been tyre tracks, nothing that would show us where she went in, no candidates for the person who threw her in... nothing. I might need another biscuit to calm my frazzled nerves.'

Doris pushed the plate towards her. 'Help yourself. I think it's been that kind of week for all of us. Although has it? Mouse, how did you get on?'

'We got the contract. He was impressed. Took me for lunch, and I'm going over next week to go through my suggestions for what I think they need with the questionnaires. I said I'd spend this week putting together a comprehensive package. I talked the talk, and I think he was impressed. He's called Joel Masters, and I'll probably stay over in Manchester because he's taking me for dinner.'

'You'll be careful?'

Mouse was surprised it was Tessa who asked the question, and not her nan. 'I will. Last time I wasn't careful I took a bullet. This time I'll carry the gun.' She grinned.

Tessa shook her head. 'I wouldn't be a bit surprised. Anyway, ladies, thank you for your input this afternoon. I'll be at this scan place tomorrow morning, then at my desk for the rest of the day. I think you're right when you say somebody is lying. I need to find out who it is. That's the plan for the morning.'

Tessa and Hannah left, and Mouse sank back in her chair. 'That was nice. I do like it when they call in, and I always feel as though they sharpen my mind. It's bothering her that she seems to be going round in circles. When she's solved this one, and I'm sure she will, we'll all go out for a meal, yes?'

'I'm always up for that,' Kat said.

Doris remained silent.

'Nan?'

'I'll let you young ones go, I think,' she said, and walked out to the reception.

Doris knew her girls were worrying about her, concerned that she was too quiet, but she also recognised that she needed time out, to recover. Ewan hadn't been good for her and she could never have accepted that it was right to hit a woman, but she had liked the Ewan she hadn't really known.

She sat at her desk, and opened her laptop. Work. That's what would do it. She could immerse herself in it, and never have to think about Ewan bloody Barker again.

Perhaps.

CHAPTER THIRTY-ONE

The plane landed at Manchester airport at half past seven, and by the time she had cleared customs and dragged her suitcase through the milling crowds of departures and arrivals she could have kissed the man she noticed holding a card sporting her name.

'We're not far away,' he said, and led her across a small road to a waiting Peugeot.

Rush hour traffic delayed them so it was almost ten o'clock by the time they reached her hotel, a small one in Bakewell she had stayed in before. She checked in, then dealt with the woman from the car hire company, who was waiting to hand car keys over to her.

By eleven o'clock, she was unpacked and finishing off a welcome cup of coffee.

The greyness of the day didn't bother her, she wasn't here for a holiday in the sun. For the next week or so, she intended disposing of some of the stuff on her bucket list.

It was peaceful in the office. Doris had taken the day off to supervise having some work done at Little Mouse Cottage, and Kat had brought Martha with her, knowing it would be a quiet day and she could spend some time with her daughter while keeping a watching brief on reception.

Kat was reaching to unfasten the harness holding Martha in the pushchair when she heard the peal of the shop doorbell.

'One moment, sweetheart,' she said to the baby, and turned to see who the visitor was.

'Is that my beautiful granddaughter?' Sue Rowe said.

'DI Marsden, and this is my colleague DS Granger.' Tessa held out her ID towards the receptionist. 'We'd like to speak with whoever is in charge, please.'

The place was impressive, white with deep purple armchairs in the seating area.

The receptionist smiled. 'If you'd like to take a seat, I'll get Mr Ingham to you as soon as possible. He's scanning at the moment, but he shouldn't be long. Would you like a coffee while you wait?'

'No thank you, we're fine,' Tessa said, to Hannah's dismay.

They sat side by side on the purple seats and waited.

And waited.

Half an hour passed, and then the door to the side of the reception opened, a man walked through and headed for them. He reached to shake their hands. 'I'm so sorry to have kept you waiting. The scan I was doing proved to be twins, which obviously takes longer. However, all was good and the parents are slightly shell-shocked. Please follow me, and we'll go to my office.'

Once seated, and yet again refusing the offer of a drink, Tessa produced the letter that had been sent to Orla French.

'You scanned this girl recently, then wrote to her at her place of work.'

He glanced through the contents of the letter, then nodded. 'Yes, but this was the address she gave us. I assumed she lived at this place. And for the record, we don't scan girls, or women, we scan pregnancies. Everything was fine, we were able to give her what she wanted, and I said I would contact her with a date for her gender scan. Is there a problem? I can't go into any details of course; her pregnancy is her own business.'

'The day after you scanned her, Orla French died. So we'd like to see her file, please. It is a murder investigation, and we can get a warrant...'

'That won't be necessary.' He spoke into his intercom and a couple of minutes later the file was on his desk. He opened it and glanced inside. 'Now I remember. She was quite specific in what she wanted from this scan. She wanted the date of conception of the baby, almost to the minute it seemed to me. I assumed there was some query over the paternity, but she didn't say that, it was purely my speculation.'

He passed the file to Tessa and it was clear from the date they had given Orla that she must have known immediately that Andy Harrison was the father. Tessa could only begin to understand how Orla must have felt. She had been naïve enough to get the question of her virginity out of the way, but had she been so naïve that she didn't know that the first time of having sex could result in a baby?

'Can you remember how she reacted when you gave her this date?'

'She didn't react. She seemed a quiet person, she thanked me, asked about gender scanning, and I said I would contact her with a date for that. However, when we tried text and email, then finally the phone, it was clear we had been given incorrect information. That letter was a last resort really.'

'And you didn't connect the girl murdered at Castleton with this client?'

He shook his head. 'No, I didn't. We get a lot of people giving us false names anyway, so they don't actually stick in my mind. I know who you're talking about now, but half an hour ago I didn't. I'm sorry.'

Tessa gave a slight nod. 'We're going to take the file with us, but DS Granger will give you a receipt for it. It will be returned to you after the trial.'

He looked startled. 'I'll be needed?'

'Oh yes, every day we get a little closer to knowing who strangled Orla then threw her into the Peakshole Water. It's probable you will be called to give evidence.'

Hannah wrote out the receipt, and took hold of the file.

Keith Ingham said nothing further.

Tessa and Hannah sat in the car without moving.

'Bless her,' Hannah said.

'I know exactly what you mean. I wonder what Orla would have done, had this awful thing not happened to her. And what Andy and Marnie would have done. Andy would have been the baby's father and grandfather at the same time. They came very close to splitting up recently, and Andy was devastated by that. I don't reckon that marriage would have survived if the baby had been born.'

'Do you think Orla had actually gone off the rampant vicar by the time she died?' Hannah spoke slowly, thinking her thoughts out loud.

'He didn't say she had.'

'I'm thinking she was starting to get interested in Paul Carr, a lad more her age. She did take her faith pretty seriously, and it makes me wonder if she was starting to see how wrong it was, sleeping with Andy, then with Steve Barksworth. Maybe she was starting to mature, and realising Paul would be good for her.'

'We'll never know, will we. It's a frustrating case, and I feel as if we're going round in circles. We have a really clear picture of her, her life, her activities, her sex life, her home life – all her bloody life, and yet nobody is an obvious suspect. She was as close as anything to her mum and stepdad, even went on honeymoon with them, so there's no conflict in the home. She had a nice little job that she enjoyed – no problem there either. Her church life was complicated but only because of the vicar and he was with a bloody bishop on the night Orla died.

'And it seems there was nothing else about Orla. A village girl, didn't go out clubbing, one close friend but other friends on the periphery... this should be easy, shouldn't it? When we get back,' Tessa was the one now speaking slowly, working through her thoughts, 'we will both sit down independently and make lists of everybody who has a connection to Orla French. This won't be a quick job, because then we're going to reinterview every damn one of them who confirmed alibis, double-check everything, nit-pick until we get down to the lowest levels. You can take the bishop.'

'Gee, thanks. Do I have to genuflect?'

'You can do what you want, as long as you get the truth.'

'Right, let's do it. Did our talk at Connection spark this little lot off then?'

'It did. Because somewhere in that list is one lie. It may only be a small one, but it's going to convict somebody when we find it.'

Hannah reached forward and turned the ignition. 'Let's do it,' she said, and pulled out into the traffic.

Martha looked at the slim woman with the very black face and smiled. The slim woman with the very black face looked back at her granddaughter and smiled. They became friends.

Kat felt in shock. First of all she had had no idea that Sue was planning a visit, and secondly she wouldn't have recognised her. The last time she had seen her she had been well-rounded with a beautiful smiling face. The smiling face was still there, but she had lost a considerable amount of weight.

'You look amazing,' Kat said, and opened her arms.

Sue hugged her and they stood for a moment, deep in memories. 'Can I hold her?'

'Of course.' Kat laughed. 'I was about to take her out of the pushchair, she woke about a minute ago. Good timing.'

Mouse's door opened, and she popped her head through to the reception area. 'Everything okay?'

'It's fine, Mouse. Can I introduce you to Sue Rowe, Martha's Canadian nanny.' She refrained from saying Leon's mother. She couldn't, not yet. There would be time enough to talk about him before Sue returned to Canada.

'Wow! So good to meet you, Sue. I'm Beth Walters, Kat's business partner. I take it this is a surprise visit.'

'It is. I didn't want to tell Kat because she would have felt obliged to have me stay with her, and that's not what I want. I'm staying in a nice little hotel in Bakewell, and I've hired a car, so I'm sorted. I was hoping we could maybe go out for lunch, but you're working, so would it be possible to have dinner together tonight?'

Kat laughed. 'If you want Martha to be with us, it will have to be lunch. She's in bed by seven and I hate her to be out of routine. Mum and I stick to the same timetable; she has Martha most of the week. I only had her today because we're not overwhelmed with work at the moment. We'll be happy to go for lunch. Mouse can lock the door, if anyone desperately wants us they'll ring and leave a voicemail. We have a system.' Kat smiled.

Sue turned to Mouse. 'Your name is Mouse? Would you like to come with us?'

'I'm good, thanks. I've a big job on at the moment, so I'll take advantage of the peace and quiet to crack on with it. And yes, Mouse is my nickname. My real name is Beth, please – use either. It's really good to meet you at last. You go and enjoy your time with Kat and Martha.'

Kat quickly changed Martha and put on her coat, then they left, taking Kat's car as it had the baby seat in it.

Not once was there a mention of Leon, or indeed his father, Alan, but Kat knew the time would come when they would talk of both. She carefully avoided driving near the place where Leon had met his death, but was unable to avoid talking about Carl. The engagement ring on the third finger of her left hand gave it away.

Sue took the news with grace; she said how pleased she was, that she hoped he would be a good father to Martha, and she would like to meet him.

'Of course you'll meet him. He's amazing with Martha, has been from day one. I was silly not to tell you when we've had our telephone chats, but I didn't want to upset you. I wasn't looking for anyone, we met accidentally through one of our cases – he's a detective inspector and we ended up connecting because of that. He makes me laugh, he makes me feel safe. And yes, I love him.'

Sue reached across the table and took Kat's hand. 'Then I'm pleased for you, Kat, I really am. I wasn't even sure you would want to see me, but you're exactly the same as when I first met you. Now, are we going to have a dessert?'

And the subject of Leon was effectively avoided.

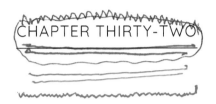

CHAPTER THIRTY-TWO

'So you're telling me that I have a day off and Leon's mother turns up? And out of the blue?' Doris's worry showed in her voice.

'She did, but everything seemed amicable.' Mouse tried to soothe her nan's fears. 'I think she's here to finally meet Martha, and maybe lay some ghosts to rest. She seemed really nice.'

'Huh. Ruth Ellis seemed really nice. They hung her.'

'Oh, Nan.'

'Don't "oh Nan" me. You know I'm right. And why has she come without telling anyone?'

'She says she didn't want to put anybody out, she booked a hotel and a car, and she's free to do whatever she wants without having to check with anybody.'

'Exactly. And I bet she wants to see where her bloody son died; she'll have Kat taking her there.'

'Don't swear, Nan.' Mouse tried to hold in the laughter.

There was a growl down the phone. 'You can bet your sweet life I'll be in tomorrow. I want to see this woman for myself. What's she like?'

'Elegant. And quite beautiful, certainly doesn't look as though she's in her sixties, but she must be. I liked her.'

'But you liked Anthony Jackson, so that doesn't fill me with confidence that you like Sue Rowe. This is bad, Mouse, I can feel it.'

'Nan, stop worrying. Kat can handle herself, she's a big girl. And she's got Carl. I'm going to have my cheese sandwich. That's the substitute for the posh lunch Sue invited me to, then do another hour here before going upstairs. I'll transfer the phone line to me, in case anybody desperately wants us.'

'You're saying she invited you as well? Why didn't you go? You could have protected our Kat and Martha!'

'Nan, they don't need protecting. Sue is Martha's nan, she's not going to hurt her. Or Kat.'

There was silence for a moment, then Doris said, 'Okay, see you tomorrow.'

Mouse disconnected, feeling the icicles coming down the line. She'd not known her nan to be like this before, even at the height of her own troubles with the Anthony Jackson murder. She shrugged it off, hoping she was right to do so.

Connection was closed by the time Kat drove everybody back to the office, so Sue headed towards her car after promising to ring Kat the next morning.

The invitation Kat extended for Sue to eat with them that evening was declined; the long flight had wiped her out so she was intent on having an early night.

Kat gave her a kiss. 'It's lovely to see you, Sue, honestly. I'll keep myself available as much as I can for the week that you're here so that Martha really gets to know you, and maybe you can have her all to yourself towards the end of the week, take her out for the day or something. Once she's comfortable around you, she'll be fine.'

'That would be lovely.' Sue smiled. She stroked Martha's cheek.

'She's so beautiful, a baby to be proud of.'

Sue put the car into drive, and waved as she pulled away.

Kat turned and walked back to her own car, then drove home. It had been an unsettling day; she had got on really well with her ex mother-in-law, but an unease had been present all the time. Maybe they would have to talk about Leon sooner rather than later, get the subject out of the way.

They hadn't even mentioned Alan's death on the day they had buried Leon in Canada. She cursed herself – that should have been a priority, letting Sue know how much she had cared for Alan.

She reached home and took the flowers out of the boot that she had planned on putting on Craig Adams' grave, but how could she have explained to Sue that Craig was possibly the first of Leon's murder victims; she couldn't.

Carl wasn't home, and she sat on the floor with Martha, playing with toys. Martha was crawling, but in a weird fashion where most of her weight was on one knee. It made Kat laugh out loud, but Martha continued to practice, taking no notice of her insensitive mummy.

Kat bathed Martha, gave her a last bottle and put her to bed. Then she rang her mum.

It was obvious from the stilted conversation that Enid didn't know what to say, until in the end, Kat said goodnight, and told Enid she would ring the following day.

Tessa and Hannah went home around five, but took work with them. They had made lists of people who had any sort of link, no matter how minor, with Orla, and took the compilations to work out their strategy for the reinterviews.

They worked until late in the night, each fuelled by a bottle of wine. But both had a comprehensive plan that they hoped would show up something, no matter how tiny, that they hadn't picked up on first time around.

Sue arrived at Connection before eleven and was disappointed to see that Martha wasn't there.

Kat smiled at the downcast look on Sue's face. 'She rarely comes into work with me. Mum and Dad have her most days at the moment, but when she starts walking she will be going to creche during the day. I can't expect them to devote their retirement to bringing up a child, it wouldn't be fair. Anyway, can I introduce you to Nan, also known as Doris Lester. She's Mouse's nan, but I've adopted her as mine. We couldn't manage without her.'

Sue stepped forward, hand outstretched. 'Pleased to meet you, Doris. Kat has mentioned you when we've chatted on the phone.'

Doris smiled and hoped that it didn't show on her face that it was forced. The girls always told her that some of the things she said and did weren't reflected in her eyes and on her face. Doris shook the hand offered, but then felt guilty. She knew she was judging this woman unfairly; Leon had turned out to be evil, but not because of her.

'I was sorry to hear of the death of your husband, Sue,' she said. 'I'm a widow myself, and that feeling of emptiness can last for a long time.'

'It's one of the reasons I decided to come here.' Sue sat down on the seat across from Doris. 'His death wasn't unexpected. He was suffering heart failure, needed a triple bypass, but his health meant he couldn't have the operation. We knew he didn't have long, so I got him a wheelchair and we enjoyed our last few months going out for long walks, seeing friends and suchlike. I think burying Leon was too much for him, but he went peacefully, having an afternoon nap. It felt strange travelling alone to get here, because I've never gone through an airport on my own before, but I did it.'

'I can't remember the last time I went to an airport,' Kat said. 'I think it's time I had a holiday, somewhere very warm.'

'It's cold in Canada at the moment, but you'll be welcome in the summer, you'll get a tan then.'

Doris felt a little easier the more they chatted, and recognised she had judged Sue unfairly. This woman must have gone through hell, knowing Leon was a killer, a drug dealer and everything else the law would have thrown at him if they had taken him alive; but they didn't. Dying by a police bullet had been his end, and Sue had had to cope with that as well, followed by the death of her husband.

Kat decided to finish for the day and take Sue up to see her mum and dad, along with Martha. She hoped that Sue would still be with her when she went home, and would meet Carl.

It was important that Sue met Carl; Kat felt that her ex mother-in-law had to know that Martha would be loved and cared for by her new father.

Hannah and Tessa closeted themselves in Tessa's office and compared lists. Hannah added Lucie Davison's name, the only one that was extra on Tessa's record to her own.

They planned the route they would take so that they could interview everybody, alongside the people who had actually provided alibis for them. It was going to be a long few days, no doubt about that.

They decided Andy Harrison had to be the starting point. It meant a trip to Manchester to speak with his boss and work colleagues; his alibi had been confirmed over the phone the first time around, but they knew that everything had to be face to face, and nothing could be missed. But first they had to see Andy himself.

He wasn't happy to see the two women at the door, but he let them into the lounge and sat down. There was no offer of a drink; Tessa and Hannah realised he was in a bad mood, which became worse when he realised they were once more checking his whereabouts on the night of Orla's murder.

'How many more times do I have to tell you I was in my office? I left around six, came home to my wife, nipped out for five minutes to pick up a bottle of wine to have with our meal, then went to bed. Had sex, if you must know. We thought Orla was safely with Emily in Hope, because the silly girl wouldn't wait for me to come home to take her. As far as we know, she went straight from work, to walk along the main road. I wasn't here, it takes a good hour to get here from Manchester at that time of night, as you well know, and all of my colleagues will vouch for me.'

'Where's your wife, Andy?'

'Asleep. She hasn't woken yet. It seems she can't face the world at the moment.'

'We'd like to see her.'

'I'll do what I can,' he said, and stormed upstairs. He really was in a bad mood.

Marnie's hair was all over the place, and her eyes barely open.

Andy helped her to sit and asked if she wanted a coffee. She nodded without speaking.

'Marnie,' Tessa said gently, 'when Andy arrived home the night that Orla was killed, what was he wearing?'

'His pale grey suit,' she said, after some thought.

'Was it wet? Muddy?'

'No, it had specks of rain on the shoulders from him running in here from the car, but that was all. Why?'

'We're trying to rule him out once and for all,' Tessa said. 'He had no mud on him?'

'No.' Marnie was sounding more awake. 'No, he didn't. I would have noticed, because Andy is always smart. It's why I noticed the spattering of rain on his shoulders, he's usually impeccably dressed. He definitely wasn't covered in mud from murdering my daughter and throwing her in a river in full spate. For fuck's sake...' And she burst into tears.

Andy came back in with a coffee for his wife and glared at them. 'Happy now? Please leave. If you want me again, I'll come to you. You only have to ring. I don't want you here upsetting Marnie any more. Spare our feelings a little bit, for God's sake. We've just lost our daughter.'

They stood and Tessa said a quiet, 'Thank you for your time,' before leaving.

She and Hannah reached the car without speaking, climbed in and sat back, sighing.

'That went well, didn't it?' Hannah said, and turned the ignition key.

'Drive, Hannah, drive,' Tessa said, knowing that Andy Harrison was no more guilty than she was. She felt she had always known that, she was simply creating a stereotypical perpetrator – the stepdad always did it.

'Let's get Manchester over with,' she said, 'and cross Andy Harrison off our list. We both know he didn't do it, don't we.'

'Never thought he did, but we have to follow everything. He was really pissed off with us, wasn't he?'

'A little.'

'From my angle,' Hannah said, 'it was a helluva lot.'

CHAPTER THIRTY-THREE

'When Andy told us he was getting married we all made a joke of it, said it was because his bride had such a beautiful bridesmaid, and we made all the old jokes about stepfathers and stepdaughters, but everybody could see how he felt about Marnie.' Dan Egerton, Andy's boss, shook his head. 'He was a man who enjoyed his own company, didn't mix with the others unless he didn't have a choice – I'm thinking things like the Christmas do, and the team building stuff we occasionally have – so when he met Marnie and they became inseparable, it was a bit of a shock to us all. But, DI Marsden, he's no killer. I don't know many men who are too decent for their own good, but Andy is. He'd recently joined our company when his divorce came through, but he'd kept it to himself. He only told me because he'd made his sister his next of kin, instead of his wife. He said his wife had found somebody new, somebody who didn't work all the hours under the sun.'

'And he still works long hours?' Tessa asked.

'He does, but he leaves here by six every night. Never earlier, but he likes to be home between seven and half past. He doesn't intend losing this wife to too many hours at work. Of course, he hasn't been in work since his stepdaughter died.'

'So, on the night his stepdaughter was killed, he left at his usual time?'

'He did. It was the day after that he did the unthinkable – he walked out of a crucial meeting around four o'clock, and shot off home. That was when Marnie rang him to tell him Orla was missing.'

Hannah was taking notes, but she was aware they were repeated words of their first telephone contact with his work colleagues. She waited until Tessa stood, and then she followed. They thanked Dan Egerton, and asked for directions to Andy's desk. It seemed he had a corner in the open-plan area, only Egerton had an office and secretary of his own.

It was a large room, and they spent time talking with all the men and women, but each told them the same story – Andy was a devoted family man, left at the same time every night, and appeared to live only for his wife and stepdaughter.

Once back in the car, Tessa and Hannah paused for a few minutes to discuss what they had heard. The consensus of opinion was that Andy Harrison should be scrubbed from the suspect list, his alibi would never be broken in a million years. He simply didn't have time to kill Orla French, not even when he nipped out for the bottle of wine.

Hannah started the car. 'Where to now, boss?'

'We'll call it a day but I think our next stop has to be Reverend Barksworth, don't you? Then we'll see if Emily is at home, and hopefully Paul. That will take care of tomorrow. At least we've got the Manchester bit out of the way. The rest of the interviews are fairly local to Castleton.'

'Except for the bishop,' Hannah reminded her with a grin.

'I think we can give him a miss. There must have been other clergy there who can vouch for Steve's attendance, and confirm his arrival and departure. He's another one I know didn't kill her, but that can't influence us. We have to get this exactly right, Hannah, and to be honest, if it means interviewing a bishop, then so be it.' Tessa paused. 'I'd rather not, that's all. We had it confirmed by one vicar, but we need more than that.'

'You scared of the bishop?'

'Of course not. I'm scared of doing the wrong thing, not knowing the workings of the church and stuff like that, but I'm not afraid of the office. After we've completed our checks on this one, the rest will be a piece of cake.'

'Yeah, you hope.' Hannah laughed. 'Somebody's lying, don't forget. And we've no idea who the hell it is.'

Sue was cuddling Martha before the baby was whisked away to her bedroom when Carl walked in the front door. He hung up his coat, and entered the lounge.

'Hello,' he said, 'I take it you're Sue.' He bent down to kiss her cheek in greeting and then kissed the top of Martha's head while he was in the vicinity, and because he liked to kiss Martha's head. 'You obviously have the magic touch, she's almost asleep.'

Sue smiled at Carl. 'Kat's in the kitchen putting something in the oven. I got to cuddle this little charmer. It's lovely to meet you, Carl. Kat's told me lots about you.'

Carl looked at her, and thought what a beautiful woman she was. No wonder Leon had had such dark good looks. 'I'll always take care of them both, you know,' he said. 'You'll never need to worry about that.'

She dipped her head in acknowledgement. 'I know. Carl, there must be no awkwardness about this. Kat and Leon are no more, and I fully appreciate she's moving on with her life. Leon was a complex man, evil in many ways, but he loved Kat and she loved him. He destroyed that, not Kat. I wish much happiness for both of you, and I'll look forward to my invitation to your wedding.'

'I'll post it personally.' He smiled. 'Are you okay with Martha, or should I take her up to bed?'

Sue looked down at her granddaughter. 'Oh, let's leave her ten minutes more, shall we? Go and help Kat, I'll be fine with the little one.'

Doris was pretty much like Martha. Eyes almost closed, her drink of choice almost empty. The main difference was her beverage was a nice little Châteauneuf du Pape. Doris hadn't the energy to top up the glass so remained relaxed, her book sliding off her knee. The fire was sending out many degrees of heat, and despite the hiccup of Ewan Barker, she felt at peace.

The letterbox rattled and she ignored it. She didn't want yet another leaflet from a Chinese takeaway in Matlock; she rather thought it might be a cold meal by the time it arrived at her home. The book dropped on the floor and she left it. Her eyes closed, and didn't open again for an hour.

When they did, they settled on the clock, and she knew she'd have difficulty falling asleep when she went to bed. Maybe another glass of wine would help... She picked up the almost empty one and stood, heading for the kitchen.

To get to the bottle of wine meant traversing the hall and she saw a white envelope on the mat. Not quite the end of November yet Christmas cards seemed to be arriving. She bent to pick it up and continued towards the bottle of wine.

She poured a generous glass, then opened the fridge door, contemplating its contents. Nothing exotic. She sighed. It was starting to resemble Mouse's fridge. A big shop was clearly called for, but in the meantime Doris would settle for cheese and biscuits for her supper snack.

She popped everything, including the envelope, on a tray and carried it through to the lounge, placing it on the side table. A quick top up of wood on the fire, a sorting out of which page she was on in her book, and she settled back onto the sofa.

She read her book while munching her way through the tasty late-night snack, and as she went to pick up the glass of wine to wash down the crumbly biscuits she was reminded of the envelope. It simply said *Doris* on the front, in a hand she didn't recognise.

She picked it up with a smile. She tried to guess which of her Christmas loving friends would have been out hand-delivering her cards at this time of night, eager for the festive season to get under way. Maybe Frances? She hadn't known her long, only since moving into Little Mouse Cottage, but they chatted most days as she lived three doors away and their paths were always crossing. In addition Doris didn't know what her handwriting was like... *Yes, Doris Lester,* she thought, *those qualifications and courses are paying off.*

Except they weren't.

It wasn't a Christmas card. The words on the front said *I miss you* and inside it said *so much.* It was signed *Ewan,* and underneath his name he had written *Please don't freeze me out. I would love to see you again.*

She felt a chill run through her as she read the words, and leaned forward to throw it on the fire. At that point the fear dropped away and she stopped. She put the card back into the envelope, and slipped it into her bag. Her two colleagues needed to see it; this was a result of a Connection case, and as such they had to be made aware of it.

She was more concerned that Ewan had been outside her door, a mere ten or twelve feet away from her, and she hadn't sensed it, known it. She moved at speed into the hall and slid home the bolt.

She echoed that with the back door, and went around the down-stairs, closing all the curtains, lowering all the roller blinds. She finally felt secure.

Doris sank back down onto the sofa, drank half the glass of wine, and picked up her phone.

'Hi, Kat. You busy?'

'Not really. Sue's here, and I'm making us some food. She's in the lounge with Carl, and they're nattering away as if they've known each other forever. Something wrong?'

'Not sure. Will you be in the office tomorrow? I know you wanted to keep work to a minimum with Sue being here, but I thought I'd check...'

Kat had known Doris for long enough to sense problems. 'I'll be in. I'll ask Sue if she can babysit Martha. I gave Mum and Dad a few days off because Sue was here so they're not available. They've swanned off to the Lake District for a break. If Sue has something planned I'll bring Martha with me. Are you okay?'

'I'm fine. It's something I need to discuss with both of you – and Martha if she's going to be there.'

'I'll see you tomorrow then. Nan... if there's an issue...'

'I'm fine, Kat. Honestly. Night, God bless. Oh, I'm not ringing Mouse tonight. I know she'll be there in the morning, she'll have to put this Manchester plan aside for half an hour.'

They disconnected and Kat took drinks into the lounge, a troubled expression all over her face.

'Problem?' Carl asked.

'Not sure,' she admitted. She placed the tray on the coffee table and handed out the glasses of wine. 'That was Nan. She wanted to know if I'd be in the office tomorrow. Something's wrong, I know it is. I'm sorry, Sue, I'll have to deal with this before we can go anywhere.'

'What about Martha?' Sue asked. 'I'd love to take her out, but that's up to you. If there's a problem at Connection, you can stay as long as you need without worrying about anything.'

'You're sure you'll be okay with her?' Kat looked troubled.

'Of course I will. I've even mastered the pushchair. I'll probably take her down into Bakewell, we'll have a walk through the park. As long as I have food for her, and nappies, we'll be fine. This will be my thank you, Kat, for all you've done for me.'

Kat smiled. 'I haven't done anything that wasn't done willingly. You're welcome here anytime, you know that. And next time you must stay with us, not in some hotel. I'll pack a bag for her, and thank you so much. I need to be in work for around nine...'

'Kat, stop worrying,' Sue said. 'I'll be here for around half past eight, you can give me full instructions then. I'm really looking forward to this, it's so much more than I could have wished for.'

'But you're her nan. Of course I'd have encouraged you getting to know her better. And I'm sure you'll get along like a house on fire tomorrow. Can you have her back for around five, so I can bath her and settle her for bedtime at seven.'

'Not a minute later,' Sue promised.

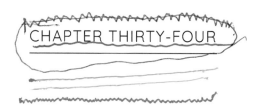

CHAPTER THIRTY-FOUR

There was tentative sunshine next morning. Sue loaded the pushchair into the boot, and watched as Carl transferred the baby seat from his own car to hers. She tucked the overflowing baby bag in beside the pram, then took Martha from an anxious Kat, who was desperately trying not to show how she felt.

With both the baby and her strapped in, Sue gave a wave and pulled out of the driveway and onto the road leading down through Eyam.

Carl put his arm around Kat and pulled her to him. 'Stop worrying. They'll both be absolutely fine, you know they will. You don't get uptight every time your mum and dad take her, so there's no need for it with Sue.'

'But Martha knows Mum and Dad really well, probably better than she knows me. She's only seen Sue a couple of times. Oh well.' She shrugged. 'There's nothing I can do about it.'

She lifted her head and Carl kissed her. 'Let's go to work,' she said, 'and look forward to five o'clock tonight.'

· · ·

Doris was already in the office when Kat arrived, with a full coffee pot waiting. She could see that Kat was out of sorts. 'No Martha?'

'No Martha. She's out for the day with Sue.'

'That explains the hangdog look. You're not happy about it?'

'I'm perfectly happy about Sue, it's Martha. She doesn't really know Sue, and I don't want her to play up. I'm being stupid, aren't I?'

'You're being a mum. Stop worrying. Sue got Leon through his early years without managing to kill him, and I imagine he was a good kid until he found out what money could do for you. But that part wasn't down to Sue, that was all Leon. So trust her, they'll have a brilliant day.'

Kat flapped her hand as if irritated with herself. 'Oh, I know you're right, my wise friend. I'll put it to the back of my mind. Mouse here?'

'Not yet. We'll wait though, or I'll be going through everything twice.'

They sat down at the reception desk, and Doris made some drinks. 'Biscuit?'

'No thanks, Nan. I'm trying to lose a bit of weight before Christmas so that I can binge a bit.'

'Is that sensible?'

'Eminently.'

'Okay. You'll not want the coffee and walnut cake I've made for you to take home then.'

'Nan! That's not fair. I'll be fat as a pig by Christmas instead of sylphlike and gorgeous.'

Doris smiled. 'I'll take it back home with me...'

'No! It's fine. I'll manage. And Carl will. We'll cope.'

'Good.' Doris's tone was dry. 'I thought you might.'

The bell pinged as Mouse walked in, carrying a travel mug of coffee. 'You've started without me?'

'Only in the discussion of coffee and walnut cake,' her nan said. 'Are you going to say no to one as well?'

'As if. I'll have Kat's also if she's said no.'

'Hey, I said yes!'

'Okay. There's one each for you, no more squabbling, children.'

Mouse paused at the door to her office. 'Are we here at this ungodly hour for a reason?'

'We are. I need to show you both something. Can we go in Kat's room, and lock the outer door for a bit?'

Doris placed the white envelope in the middle of Kat's desk. They all stared at it, Doris included.

'It says *Doris*,' Mouse said.

'That's because it was posted through my door last night. About half past eight I think, but I can't be sure. Might have been a bit earlier. I fell asleep before going to pick it up. When I heard it come, I assumed it was a takeaway menu being delivered. When I did get to it, I thought it was an early Christmas card, although I didn't recognise the handwriting.'

Kat reached forward and picked up the envelope. She slid out the card and read it. Without saying anything, she passed it to Mouse.

'First of all I have to tell you that he doesn't scare me,' Doris said. 'I was unnerved by his being outside my cottage and me being unaware of it, and yes, it's kept me awake most of the night, but I'm more concerned that he might approach you two as well, and Kat isn't a black belt.'

'I don't need a black belt to knee him in the balls.'

Doris laughed. 'I know you don't, sweetheart, but why should you have to? His connection is to me, not you two, but you do need to be on your guard. I was going to handle this myself, but realise that would be silly. You two need to know he's been in touch, so that you can be on your toes all the time.'

'What's your next move, Nan?' Mouse spoke quietly, the anger showing in her face.

'I thought I would email him, spell it out in words of one syllable that I don't have any contact knowingly with men who hit women, and ask that he doesn't get in touch with me again. That's the first salvo. If he does get in touch again, if an email comes back where he's still wanting to see me, instead of him throwing in the towel and backing off, then I'll go down the legal route of injunctions and anything else I can find. Maybe even ask Tessa what they can do, if anything. He's not actually committed a crime, I suppose.'

Mouse turned to face Kat. 'That man at church who changed the locks on your house after Leon went in... can we get him in here? We need better security on that front door, the sort where whoever is coming in has to press a buzzer, and we release the door from the reception desk. If it can be super-efficient and have a card scanner on it, the three of us can get in easily, but nobody else can. What do you think? We have to give Nan more protection. And it's not only about Ewan Barker, it could be anybody entering that door.'

'On it,' Kat said. 'I'll tell George exactly what we want. Let's hope he can do it quickly. I'll walk over and see him when we've finished.'

'What did you do, Nan, after you'd opened it?' Mouse was clearly worried.

'I checked everything was locked and bolted, dropped the blinds, closed the curtains. Basically I battened down the hatches, finished my wine and took my book to bed.'

'Did you put a chair under your door handle in the bedroom?'

Doris grinned. 'I did. I know it was silly, but I thought if I felt totally safe I would sleep. I didn't, but that was partly because I'd slept for an hour or so during the evening. My mind wouldn't close down. I was trying to work out how to stop him, but came up with nothing. I finally dropped off about six, and my alarm woke me at half past seven, so if I nod off today, leave me,' she added with a laugh.

'Nan.' Mouse sounded serious. 'Stay with me tonight, please. No arguments, no saying you'll be fine, no quoting black belt at me. I insist you stay in the flat where it's secure.'

Doris smiled. 'Already decided. The holdall is by the side of my desk.'

Kat called in at the small grocery shop and bought some flowers, then headed towards the churchyard. She went unerringly to Craig Adams' grave, took out the babywipes and wiped down the headstone. She offered up a prayer, and arranged the flowers in the small vase she had taken down. The flowers didn't last long when laid as a bunch across the headstone, so now she stood them in water.

She always felt she should apologise to the young man; Leon had killed him for a two hundred pound debt, and Kat knew she would take care of Craig's final resting place for the rest of her life. His mother, without a car of her own, could only visit sporadically, and Kat had promised he would always have flowers.

She stood for a moment then walked away, heading towards the church. She slipped inside and knelt in prayer. Doris was at the forefront of her conversation with God.

Fifteen minutes later, Kat was knocking on the bright red door of George Mears' cottage, almost the last house in the village.

'Kat! What a lovely surprise. You coming in?'

'If you're not busy, George, I will please.'

'I'm cleaning out the hamster cage. You okay with hamsters?'

She laughed. 'I have absolutely no idea. I've never been that close to one. What sort is it? Will it eat me?'

'Shouldn't think so, it's about six inches long, head to tail. Eats seeds, not Kats,' he joked.

He led her into the lounge and she saw the hamster in an empty cage that was at the side of what presumably was its usual home.

'Wow. It's quite strange. I hope Martha never wants one, it's a bit too much like a little rat. I'll stick with Tibby. You got five minutes for a chat?'

'I've got as long as you need. What's wrong?'

She explained what they wanted, but didn't mention anything of Ewan Barker, saying that they preferred to have clients ask for permission to enter, rather than them walking in.

'I can do that for you. And you'll want three cards for you to gain admittance? Is that right?'

'It is. How soon can you do it?'

'Tomorrow morning? Will somebody be there?'

'Yes. It'll probably be Doris and Beth, not me.'

'No problem. If I'm not able to locate one today, I'll keep you informed.'

She stood. 'Thank you so much, George. Can you make your invoice out to Connection, and not to me. I'll leave you to finish off your hamster cleaning. Does it have a name?'

'He does. He's called Hector.'

'Bye, Hector,' Kat called as she left the house.

It was a fair walk as she headed back down through the village, and although it was cold, she enjoyed the exercise. Her mind was on Martha and Sue, and she hoped they were having a lovely day. She didn't notice Ewan Barker's small red Fiesta that was parked on a side road, with a clear view of Connection ahead.

Mouse was in her own office, continuing with the paperwork that was an essential part of the business she hoped to dazzle with the following week. Doris was in reception, unable to concentrate on work. She was sitting reading her book when Kat walked through the door.

'Perfect morning,' she said. 'I took some flowers to Craig's grave, then went for a quarter of an hour in church. I needed some peace. Finally walked up to George's cottage where I met a hamster called Hector, but more importantly he's coming tomorrow morning to fit the new system for us. If he can't track one down that quickly, he'll let me know.'

'He's got a hamster who's coming to fit the new lock system. Wow, I'm impressed.'

'Okay, maybe that didn't come out quite right.'

'I like hamsters,' Doris said. 'We should have one in the office, like a mascot.'

'Can we make do with a goldfish? I'm sure they're a lot less trouble, and they don't look like little rats. George seemed to be going to an awful lot of trouble cleaning the cage out. Nah, a fish is so much easier.'

CHAPTER THIRTY-FIVE

Tessa and Hannah spent their morning repeating every question they had asked Steve Barksworth first time around. He could tell them nothing new, other than giving three names of clergy who would vouch for him having been at Sheffield Cathedral from two o'clock until late at night.

It was a relief that they had the names; no trips to see a bishop were needed. They had spoken to one vicar, Reverend Ashton, as they attempted to find out if Barksworth's alibi was solid. Ashton had ratified what Steve had told them, but they needed more confirmation than one other person. Now they had Reverend Kieran Michaels, and Reverend Isaac Reece.

They had also spoken to Ruby Barksworth, who had corroborated her husband's words, but added the rider that they could believe her above everybody else, because she would dearly like to see him squirm as he was charged with Orla's murder. However, she had added, he simply didn't do it. He hadn't been there at the time they were saying were the crucial hours.

They got back in the car and Hannah turned to Tessa. 'One unhappy woman, yes?'

'Oh yes, I think Steve Barksworth should be grateful she's bedbound and relies on him to get her through each day, because if she was fighting fit, he would be out of a marriage, and a job. She was positively vitriolic, wasn't she. Did you feel like that about David?'

'No, but that was different. I'd stopped loving David. She hasn't stopped loving Steve Barksworth. She's hurting and can't hold that hurt in.'

Tessa sighed. 'You're probably right. We're a funny lot, aren't we, human beings.'

Hannah grinned and started the car. 'Hope? For the Carr siblings?'

'No, we have to interview them at work, I think. They'll not be home for about four hours. Let's go and get some lunch, then head for Emily Carr first.'

Emily stared at the two police officers, a blank expression on her face. 'But I've told you all I know. What more can you possibly want?'

'We're rechecking everything. Can you get somebody to cover for you, please?'

'Actually, it's inconvenient. My relief is on her lunch break.'

'Okay. Close everything down as you would when you go home at night. Get your coat, we'll take you to headquarters.' Tessa's tone brooked no arguments, and Emily stared at her.

'I'll see if Lindsey is on the premises.'

Within a minute, Lindsey had joined them, and Tessa, Hannah and Emily moved to the small room where they had conducted the first interview, before the investigation had really got going.

'Thank you for your cooperation, Emily,' Tessa began.

'Would you really have taken me to the police station?' Emily stared at the two women, disbelief etched on her face.

'Yes.' The answer couldn't have been clearer. 'I'm here to go through your statement, make sure there is nothing you've forgotten. Something you may have thought of later. DS Granger, can you read Emily's statement back to her, please.'

Hannah did so, while Tessa watched Emily for any response. It was only when Hannah reached the part where Emily said she didn't know of any man that Orla was seeing, that was there a reaction. Very slight, but there. She waited until Hannah finished.

'Did you lie, or omit to tell us anything, Emily?'

'No.'

'Are you sure?'

'No.'

Hannah looked up, startled.

'No, you're not sure?' Tessa pushed the girl.

A slight shrug of Emily's shoulders spoke volumes.

'Talk to me,' she urged the young woman. 'There can be no secrets in a murder enquiry. What do you know that you haven't told us?'

'It's not what I know, it's more what I saw.' There was still hesitation. 'It was seeing them together, at church. I saw Orla change, she used to dress quite... primly. I know that's a strange word, but I mean she wore jeans and jumpers, jeans and T-shirts, she wasn't showy, more... ordinary. Know what I mean?'

Tessa nodded, but didn't speak. She didn't want to stop the flow of words in case some nugget came from Emily Carr.

'Orla began to wear low cut tops, hipster jeans, bare midriff, that sort of thing, all through the summer. And he couldn't keep his eyes off her, Mr Godalmighty Barksworth. He followed her everywhere, but she encouraged him. He's married, and with a really poorly wife. How could she do it?' It came out almost as a wail. 'She never told me she was seeing him, but it was obvious. They would disappear into the vestry, and come out looking... different. I don't know how to explain it. One day I asked her if she was sleeping with him.'

'And?' Tessa said.

'She admitted it. I made some comment about her throwing her virginity away for a married man, and she laughed and said I'd got that all wrong. She'd already lost her virginity before sleeping with the randy vicar.'

'You don't like him?' Tessa asked. 'Is that because of his affair with Orla, or for some other reason?'

There was a long pause. 'He took my virginity. That was before Orla started chasing him. He seduced me over about six months, and I eventually gave in. I fell for the smooth talk, imagined I loved him really. It happened twice, and I said stop. I saw Ruby look at me, and knew that she knew. I couldn't bear that. Orla didn't know, I didn't tell her, and I'm pretty sure Steve wouldn't have. Steve immediately moved onto Orla, and I was history. And before you ask, yes it hurt, but it didn't hurt enough to make me kill my best friend. And I know I'm being hypocritical slagging her off for sleeping with a married man when I'd done it with the same married man myself, but I recognised it for what it was, wrong and sleazy. She didn't. It would still have been going on now, if...' Emily wiped a tear from her eye.

Hannah was scribbling furiously, keeping up with the words pouring out.

'Why didn't you tell us this before, Emily,' Tessa asked, her voice gentle.

'I was ashamed. I haven't killed Orla, I was sitting in my mum's house waiting for her to arrive that awful night, not out there killing her. Telling you I'd slept with Steve Barksworth wouldn't have helped anybody.'

The door opened and a tall dark-haired woman stood in the doorway. 'Are you going to be much longer, Emily?'

Tessa held up her warrant card. 'Emily will be as long as it takes, Ms...?'

'Cartwright, Yolande Cartwright. I need Emily back on reception, to free Lindsey up to do some filing.'

'Okay, Ms Cartwright,' Tessa said. 'Keep yourself available because when I've finished speaking with Emily, who is helping us to piece together what happened before a young girl was brutally murdered, I'll also need to speak with you.'

'I'm going out in ten minutes so you'll have to come back tomorrow.'

Tessa sighed. 'DS Granger, please place Ms Cartwright in the back of the car and transport her to Chesterfield headquarters. I'll be there later to take her statement. You'll have to come back and get me once you've placed her in the interview room.'

Cartwright went white, and began to bluster. The outcome was that she went back to her office, Lindsey remained on reception, and they completed their interview with Emily, finally knowing they had the full story.

Yolande Cartwright, feeling full of trepidation for what this commanding woman would say next, confirmed that Emily never left before five, and after checking her rotas said she had been in work on the day that Orla French had been killed. She added that Emily was collected every day by her brother, so actually never left work at five, it was usually ten minutes later as he finished at five and had to have a wash before picking up his sister. Tessa thanked her, and stood. 'Your cooperation has been helpful; we're corroborating alibis and you've been very informative regarding Emily. I trust this will have no comeback on her, she has done nothing wrong, and had no choice in whether to talk to us or not. Is that understood?'

'Of course.' Yolande Cartwright's tone was stilted, but Tessa guessed she'd got the message.

Tessa and Hannah walked out and said goodnight to Emily,

telling her they were going to pop round and speak to Paul. 'Please don't ring him, Emily,' Hannah said. 'We don't want him to wind himself up with thoughts of a second interview.'

Emily smiled. 'I won't. And I'm glad I've told you. As per your request... instructions... Paul and I will be in Chesterfield tomorrow morning to amend our statements. Although his won't need amending because he knows nothing of Steve and me. I'll catch a bus, make a day of it. Then only one of us will lose a day's pay.'

Tessa laughed. 'Oh, I don't think you'll lose pay over this, but let me know if you do.'

Paul Carr had nothing to add to his first statement, and they didn't ask that he report to headquarters. He did decide, however, that he would book a day's holiday and take Emily to make her statement. Until they had caught whoever had killed Orla French, he didn't want his sister out unaccompanied.

Tessa and Hannah discussed events while sitting in the car, both feeling they had done enough. They had spoken to the main people in Orla's life, confirmed times and dates, and both of them felt it was time to move on to the bit part players.

'You certainly get them to cooperate by threatening them with' being taken into Chesterfield,' Hannah said with a laugh. 'Everybody's terrified of you. Good job they don't see you like I do, doughnut smeared all over your face, or half a bottle of vinegar on a tray of chips.'

'Don't be cheeky, young Hannah. You get us back to the station while I organise sending for a car to pick up Steve Barksworth. For a vicar, he's a pretty good liar, isn't he? If it weren't for his wife, I'd make sure we kept him overnight.'

. . .

And so the day passed into late afternoon, heading towards a general exodus of office and factory workers at the magic hour of five o'clock.

Connection had closed their doors at half past four, and Kat arrived home ten minutes later, ready to welcome Martha and Sue back from their adventure.

By six o'clock, she was in complete meltdown.

CHAPTER THIRTY-SIX

'But what if she's had an accident?' Kat said, struggling to hold it together. Carl had arrived home, and was enfolding her in his arms. He had fully expected Martha and Sue to be back by the time he pulled onto the drive, but there was no sign of Sue's hire car. Kat had sounded frantic at half past five, and initially he had given a gentle laugh, but soon realised how serious she was.

'Is her phone still switched off?'

'Yes, it's going straight to voicemail. What do we do, Carl?'

He moved to the phone, and dialled Chesterfield HQ. They had had a report of one road traffic accident, but an elderly black woman and a baby hadn't been involved. Carl then moved on to ringing around all the hospitals, including the Children's Hospital in Sheffield, but there had been no admittances of either a Susan or a Martha Rowe.

'Okay,' he said. 'You stay here. I'll go down to Bakewell, to the Parkside, and see if she's there. If she isn't then we'll bring in the troops. Alert Doris and Mouse, in case they see her car anywhere.'

The Parkside was a small hotel, probably around twenty rooms, and

Carl walked up the front steps and into reception. He'd checked the car park situated to the side and back of the building, but had seen no sign of the hire car.

The receptionist smiled as he walked to the desk. 'Can I help you, sir?'

He held up his ID, and the smile all but disappeared as she realised he wasn't there to book a room.

'You have a Mrs Susan Rowe staying here?'

'Yes we did, she checked out this morning. I understood she was returning to Canada early. She said she would see to the return of the hire car to Jameson's.'

He felt the blood drain from his face.

'Thank you,' he said, turned, and ran back to his car.

He spoke to Tessa on the way back to Eyam, and she arrived within two minutes of him getting home. She had already put in place the airport checks, and Dave Irwin, Ray Charlton and Fiona Ainsworth were all heading back to work to monitor information.

Mouse and Doris were there, both with their laptops. Mouse was at the kitchen table, her fingers flying across the keyboard. Doris was in the lounge, trying to support a distraught Kat.

Carl walked in, and Kat stood, moving rapidly towards him. He held her, stroked her hair, but could say nothing. He wanted to kill Sue Rowe.

Tessa arrived with the news that Sue wasn't booked on any flights to anywhere in the world, let alone Canada. 'She's somewhere in this country, and we've contacted the car hire company to see if she's returned it. She hasn't, so we can at least get that registration out all over the place. Kat, you can take some comfort from the fact that she can't take Martha out of the country, as Martha hasn't got a passport yet. All ports are alerted, and train stations as far as we can. Certainly she'll not get to the continent by train, because we've blocked that avenue.'

'And what if she went as soon as she set off with Martha this morning?' Kat's tearful face turned towards Tessa. 'She could already be on the continent.'

'Kat, in these glorious days of Brexit, she's going nowhere without a passport for that baby. We'll find her for you. Does she have enough formula for Martha?'

'It doesn't matter, does it? She knows what she has, and she can buy more.'

'Think about this, Kat. Is she making you pay for exposing Leon?'

The room went quiet.

Kat's bottom lip trembled. She couldn't focus her thoughts. 'I... I suppose so. She's never said anything, not ever, about blaming me, but that doesn't mean she's not thinking it. But Leon's dead! She's not planning the same thing for Martha, surely.' Her eyes were wide as the implications of Tessa's question sank in.

'No, of course she isn't.' Tessa tried to soothe her friend. 'She's Martha's nan. She won't hurt her. It's probably you she wants to hurt.'

Sue sat on the park bench, watching the baby as she slept in her pushchair. She gave a brief passing thought to Kat, who she knew must be going frantic by now, and smiled. Thanks to Kat, she had spent months wondering where Leon was, not knowing if she would ever see him again. Kat had only had two hours of feeling scared, nowhere near long enough.

Sue took out her phone and looked at it. Smashed, the screen a myriad of tiny cracks. She was pleased she had brought her old one with her, she had known it would have to be shattered at some point, and her shiny new one couldn't be part of the sacrifice. She had rung the car hire people to say the car wouldn't start, then in the middle of saying where she was she had deliberately dropped the phone, then disconnected the call. The small rock had destroyed the screen. It would take time for them to find her, even with the car's tracker activated.

She had set aside a day to pay Kat back, to make her fear for her daughter's life, but Sue had no intentions of charges being laid against her. She had a story of delay, being unable to contact Kat to tell her because Kat's number was in the wrecked phone and she could no longer access it. Oh, silly me, she would say, I never thought of using Directory Enquiries for the landline number.

Sue stood, carefully lifted Martha out of the pushchair and placed her gently in the car seat. She stirred and waved her arms around, then settled back into her sleep. She was fed and changed, and Sue knew the little girl would be fine. She would wrap her pushchair blanket around her to keep her warm, and Martha would sleep until she was eventually returned to her tearful mummy.

Sue reckoned if the car hire people turned up in the next fifteen minutes, she could have Martha home before ten. Kat would be at screaming point by then, as Sue had been when somebody thought to ring and tell her Leon was dead, two days after the event.

Opening her bag, Sue took out two of the tablets her doctor had insisted she needed. *Edge of a breakdown* had been his words as he wrote out the prescription. She swallowed them by using the last of her water, and then watched as the car pulled up in front of her.

It only took the car hire employees a minute to reconnect the loose battery cable that had only taken her a minute to loosen, and they asked her why the police had contacted them about the car. She said she should have been back for five, and her daughter was concerned about her, but she had been in touch so all worries had been dealt with.

She was quite surprised they believed her, but they wished her a cheery good night, said they were going home and not back to the office, and she gave them ten pounds each for their trouble.

It was ten past ten when she pulled onto Kat's forecourt, and was immediately surrounded by police officers.

The tears came easily. She showed them her phone, the broken screen telling its own story of the item being useless.

Eventually Tessa dismissed all the officers, feeling relieved that it was a misunderstanding and that baby Martha was back where she should be, in her mummy's arms. She felt she should have strong words with Sue Rowe, but could see how upset she was, and recognised what a shitty day she must have had from the onset of darkness, with an immobile car and a shattered phone, no access to phone numbers, and reliant on a car hire company finding her.

Eventually they all left, leaving Sue with Kat and Carl. Martha should have been in bed, but Kat was carrying her around, not letting her go. Her fear that she would never see her daughter again had been too strong.

Sue couldn't stop apologising. 'I could do nothing.'

'So why didn't you ask the car hire people to ring us? I know they said they were going home, but I'm sure either they would have lent you a phone, or they would have rung us if you'd asked,' Carl snapped.

'I was cold, I was concerned with keeping Martha warm because at that point I couldn't start the engine to keep us warm, and I wasn't thinking straight. I wanted to get back here.'

'Okay, another question, Sue.' Carl felt he couldn't let it go. Kat was in a dreadful state and he wanted answers. 'Why did you check out of the hotel in Bakewell?'

'Because I didn't like it. I booked a room at the airport hotel, the one I'm staying in the night before I fly back home. I rang them and explained I needed two extra nights, and they sorted me out. I only did it last night, and thought I would fill you in on what was happening when I brought Martha home tonight. I did expect that to be at five o'clock, not ten. You must have known I would never let any harm come to that baby, she's my Leon's child. My grand-daughter.'

'Okay, here's what's going to happen, Sue. You go from here tonight, and you don't come back. Martha is out of bounds to you. I'm going to take her up and put her to bed, so you can give her one last kiss before I do. Then you can say your goodbyes to Kat while I'm doing that. It's up to her what she says to you.'

Carl took the sleeping baby from Kat, who rubbed her red eyes. 'Thank you,' she whispered to him.

Kat went outside with Sue and waited while she fastened her seat-belt. 'Safe journey, Sue,' Kat said. 'I can't forgive you, not yet. I know there's something not right. You might have fooled the police, but you didn't fool me any more than you fooled Doris and Mouse. And you didn't fool Carl, not for one minute. Today you've done some-thing evil. Go back to Canada. Goodnight, Sue,' and she turned and walked back to the house.

'Katerina!' Sue called, 'now you know exactly what it's like to be waiting for news of your child, to hope that the child is still alive, and to cope with the constant pain of having no news. You caused me to feel that pain, I've returned it in spades. I needed you to feel it as well. We won't meet again, Kat, I'm going back to be with my husband and son. I brought Martha home to you alive – you sent me my son in a coffin,' she spat and pulled out of the driveway at speed.

Kat, numbed by the anger and the horror of Sue's words spewing out, felt her head spin, and she staggered back inside.

'Carl!' she called before blackness overwhelmed her.

CHAPTER THIRTY-SEVEN

Doris and Mouse listened with growing horror as Kat told them what had happened the previous night.

'What a bloody evil bitch,' Mouse said, 'and she came across as so sweet and nice. Has she always had this side to her, this nasty side?'

'I used to feel she was a little strange,' Kat said. 'Within a week of Leon and I getting married, they'd moved to Canada. We joked that she couldn't bear losing Leon to anyone, but I'm thinking maybe it wasn't a joke. Rather than see how we were building a relationship that supposedly would last for life, she took her and Alan out of the way. He told me at the wedding he wished they weren't going quite so soon, that he would have liked to get to know me better first before making such a massive move, but Sue wanted to go, and that was that. Then Alan had the stroke not long after they arrived in Canada, and she was on her own, looking after him.'

'She deserves everything she gets,' Doris said. 'Are you taking it any further now that you know this was all planned?'

Kat shook her head. 'No, I'm not. I want her back in Canada, a long way away from us. You know, I'd never understood how Leon could have turned out the way he did, his cavalier attitude towards the law, the murders he committed... but I guess this week has shown exactly where it came from. I thought his parents were lovely, how wrong could I have been.'

Martha, sitting up in her pushchair and nibbling on a biscuit with her four teeth, beamed at the three women, oblivious to the drama in which she had played a starring role. She held up her arms towards her mummy, and Kat unbuckled her.

'I can't leave her at the moment. I'm going to take the rest of the day off, spend it with Martha. I'll only be at home because it's horrible weather, but I'll make sure all doors are locked, so don't worry.'

'Can I get your signature on this Manchester thing before you go,' Mouse asked. 'It's complete, so I can take a couple of days off if you need me.'

'Me too,' Doris said. 'Shout up if there's any problems, anything at all.'

Kat smiled. She loved these two women so much; they had her back totally covered.

'We'll be fine, honestly. I've a feeling Carl will be home early, he really didn't want to go this morning. Sue'll not come back, we don't need to worry.'

'She flies home Monday?'

'She does. And if she wants any sort of access to Martha before then, the answer will be no.'

The other two nodded. Calm, quiet Kat had turned into a bit of a martinet, and they felt like clapping.

'Think you can get rid of Ewan for me?' Doris said.

'Point me in the right direction, and call me St George, slayer of dragons,' Kat said, picking up a biro to practice with. 'Has Ewan bothered you again?'

'No, no... I don't think so. Maybe.'

'Nan?' Mouse and Kat said the word at the same time.

'You know when you get a feeling that things aren't quite right, they're a bit out of kilter? That's how I'm feeling. Maybe it's because of that damn card, it's possible the unease has carried over from that, but...'

'But you don't think so?' Mouse asked. 'You think he's following you, or something?'

'He'd be crazy,' Doris said. 'He only came near me last time, and he ended up unable to walk properly. And next time it would be both feet I used. Surely he didn't believe I simply got lucky?'

'Nan, I'm not happy about this. Next time he may have a knife, or heaven forbid, a gun. So what is it you're feeling?' Mouse asked.

Doris sighed. 'I don't know. Maybe I'm not feeling anything, maybe it's only a reaction. I feel... invaded, as though he's out there watching me. I'm probably being a silly old woman.' Her laugh was shaky. 'You know, this stalking proves Helen was telling the truth when she said his actions aren't normal, and weren't normal all those years ago. I'm well out of it, aren't I?'

'Okay,' Kat said, 'his car is a grey metallic Freelander, isn't it? We need to be on the lookout for it. Nan, you're not to approach him if you see it, we'll talk to Tessa and see what we can do. Are you listening to me?'

'I am, I am. But to follow on from that, I don't want either of you going up to him. Is that understood? We know how violent he can be, and we know about leopards and spots, so this is an instruction that you don't go near him. The sad fact is that even if he is following me – and it feels like that – he's not committing a crime. I don't want to have to ask Carl to warn him off, but maybe we should make it official this time.'

Kat fastened Martha in the baby seat and drove out of Eyam, hoping Mouse and Doris didn't notice she was going the opposite way to her home. She fancied having a little run to Bradwell, maybe a stop close by a small dwelling called Little Mouse Cottage. She wasn't sure that she could do anything if she did spot the Freelander, but at least they would know Doris's spooky feelings were actually spot on and they could take appropriate action.

Within a couple of minutes of setting off, Martha fell asleep, so when Kat reached Bradwell, she turned right at the village green and drove up the road towards the cottage. She pulled into the Ye Old Bowling Green Inn car park, swung her car around and sat facing the road that ran by Little Mouse Cottage. She felt safe there; if Ewan's car did drive past the cottage she would see it, but he wouldn't be looking up the hill towards the car park, he would be too busy negotiating the tight bend in the road.

She pressed play and settled down to listen to her audiobook, keeping a watch on the road. Martha continued to sleep, and Kat almost wished she could join her. It hadn't been a good night, and she was feeling tired. The temperature began to drop and she covered Martha with a pram blanket. Fishing around in the glove compartment gave her a bobble hat, and she put it on, pulling it well down over her ears. The audiobook seemed rather muffled but it didn't matter. She would stay for another half hour, and then head home. She didn't think she would freeze to death in thirty minutes.

The book was good, and she decided it was actually quite a pleasurable thing to do, surveillance. Only one car drove past the cottage, a small red Fiesta, and she smiled. Definitely not even related to a Freelander.

Twenty minutes later, Kat leaned forward to start the car, and saw another car, a small red Fiesta, turn into the car park.

'Good grief,' she said quietly, not wanting to disturb the still sleeping baby in the back, 'two red Fiestas passing Nan's cottage within an hour. And they're the only two cars that I've seen. Come on, Kat, get your act together, there's something odd about this.'

The car headed to the top of the car park, swung around and

dropped back down. It stopped about ten metres away from Kat's car, and the driver cut the engine and the lights.

At the same instant, in the increasing gloom of early evening, the car park lights flickered into life. Ewan climbed out of the car and Kat gasped. He walked up the incline and into the pub, only just opening its doors. He disappeared inside.

Kat pulled up her hood and covered the bobble hat, her hair and a significant portion of her face. Then she took out her phone.

'Mouse, where's Nan?'

'Putting her coat on. We're closing.'

'Bugger. Can you keep her there for a bit? Take her up to the flat or something?'

'Kat... where are you? What are you doing?'

'Detecting. It's in my job description.'

'You've not answered the first part. Where are you?'

'Bowling Green.'

'And?'

'And I'm in the car park. There's only two cars in it, mine and a little red Fiesta. The other driver is Ewan Barker. He's seen my car, but he's not recognised me, and he doesn't actually know my car. I hope he doesn't anyway. It might be all perfectly innocent, he might like to eat here because don't forget he used to live in Bradwell, but it seems odd that he's not in his own car. I'm doing surveillance.'

'We'll be there in ten minutes.'

Kat stared at the phone still clutched in her hand. 'How rude,' she said to herself. 'She's gone.'

She almost felt relieved that they were heading over to join her, because she hadn't actually expected to get a result, and she simply didn't want to go home. Her own home almost felt violated by Sue's actions, and Kat had quite enjoyed listening to the book while Martha slept.

She kept her hood up and waited for the cavalry to arrive.

Doris parked her car at the bottom of the hill, locked it and walked across the road to climb in beside Mouse.

Mouse drove up the hill and parked a hundred metres away from Little Mouse Cottage. They walked back towards the pub, passing the cottage and then moved as fast as they could towards Kat's car. Mouse got into the passenger seat, and Doris the back seat. Both women copied Kat, pulling their hoods up to hide who they were.

Mouse looked around. 'Kat, when he comes out the pub and heads back to his own car we need to act. Start the engine, but leave all the lights off. When he moves I want you to put your foot down and get to the entrance before he does, and block it. He'll not get round this big car, no matter what he's got. Then we'll get out, Nan and I, and you stay in this car with our precious one. Okay?'

'But this is my collar,' Kat argued.

'Your collar is a small white one that fits around your neck, along with your cross and chain. Stop being stroppy, and leave the fighting to the grown-ups.'

They watched as he left the pub and walked back to his car, skirting around half a dozen other cars that had arrived while they'd waited. Martha had woken and they were all trying to keep her amused when Kat spotted Ewan in the brightly lit doorway of the old pub. She nudged Mouse. 'He's walking across to his car.'

They watched as his headlights lit up the scene, and then Kat drove slowly down the inclined car park. He too set off and she put her foot down, swinging the car to the left as she hit the bottom of the slope, effectively blocking the entrance. Either side of the gap was a dry stone wall. He had no way out.

. . .

Doris leaned in the driver door, and looked at him. 'You waiting for me, Ewan?'

'Of course not,' he growled.

'But you've been driving around here today, certainly all afternoon. Hoping for some revenge, are you?' She punched her hand inside the car, stopping the volition two inches away from his nose. He jumped back as Mouse opened the passenger door.

'You upsetting my nan, Mr Barker?'

'No, no, of course not, Beth.'

'Miss Walters.'

He looked terrified. His eyes flashed between the two women and it was clear that he knew he was defeated. 'Move the car, please.'

'Is this a hire car?' Doris asked, her words conversational, pleasant.

'What if it is?'

'Why do you need to hire one? Or did you lie about the Freelander being yours? What's the matter, Ewan? Did you think it would be easier to track me if you had a different car?'

He shifted in his seat, and she knew she had hit on the right answer.

'Okay, Ewan. Here's the information you need. You've seen me in action. When I want to hurt people, I find it to be quite therapeutic. I have a talent for it, along with my black belt. My sensei taught me well. However, that is as nothing, it pales into insignificance at the side of Bethan, who not only achieved her black belt some considerable time ago, she is now a fifth dan.'

His eyes flicked from side to side as if he didn't know which black belt to look at first. And he was deeply scared.

'Are you understanding me, Ewan? If I ever see you within twenty yards of me, you will pay for it. Painfully. Get out of my sight, before I ask Bethan to give us a demonstration. DI Marsden is aware of all of this, as is DI Heaton, Kat's fiancé. You really don't want to tangle with us again.' She slammed Ewan's door shut at the same time as Mouse slammed the passenger door, and the sound echoed around the car park.

Kat backed her own car out of the way, and they could see him fumbling to get his seatbelt fastened. He roared off, and they held it together until they climbed back into Kat's car.

Even Martha joined in the laughter.

'You think that's it?' Kat asked.

'Oh, that's it for sure. He was scared shitless.' Mouse grinned into the darkness. 'But to be on the safe side, I'm going to stay with Nan for a week or so. Fifth dan, indeed, Nan. What were you thinking?'

'How many is it?' Doris frowned.

'Fourth.'

'Oh, that's okay then. I'll remember next time.'

Martha was a little late in bed for the second time in succession, and Mouse and Doris drank a bottle and a half of wine before retiring for the night. Kat snuggled in Carl's arms, feeling much happier than she had twenty-four hours earlier, and silence was present in all bedrooms by midnight.

Ewan Barker was surfing the Internet looking for a two week holiday in the Canaries. He'd see if he could find a nice widow there, who wasn't a bloody black belt in anything. He rather thought he'd had some good fortune in being kicked in the balls by Doris, and not by her know-it-all granddaughter with fifth dan attached to her name.

CHAPTER THIRTY-EIGHT

Tessa led the briefing and it was a good one. There was chatter about the alibi suppliers, the alibi confirmers and the case in general. It was starting to feel as though all loose ends would be tied up shortly; everyone had supplied in-depth statements to attach to their original one – and yet nothing had moved any further on.

Tessa had moved into her own office, and she could see that the main office was thronged with personnel. She was trying to decide whether or not to finish the final round of statement checking with Hannah, or whether to farm it out and she would concentrate on preparing the report. She could send Hannah and Fiona...

But that meant giving up coffee and cakes at the tea rooms. The only interviewees left to be seen were the owner and employees of the said tea rooms, and their lemon drizzle cake was to die for.

Tessa was mulling over the issue when Hannah popped her head round the door.

'You okay?'

Tessa nodded. 'I am. Shall we go for coffee and cake?'

'Sounds good. And once we've done the second statement from them, that will be it for our list. Still no liar that we've come across.

If we don't get a result from anyone in the tea rooms, we can always put all these names in a hat and draw one out.'

'Now there's a good idea, Hannah. You'll make DCI in no time with thoughts like that.' Tessa glanced at her watch. 'Get your coat, let's go and finish this off, then this afternoon I want Irwin, Charlton and the two of us to move into one of the rooms where we won't be disturbed and we're going through this lot all over again.'

'What room do you want for that? A cell?'

Tessa threw a paperclip at her. 'If necessary. But let's try the conference room first. We need a big table, so can you check if it's already booked for something? If it isn't, we'll have it. What did you think to the carry on at Kat's over Martha's abduction?'

'She was lying. Sue Rowe, I mean, not Kat. The more I thought about it after we'd left, the more I saw the holes in her story. She could have rung Kat at any time by using a landline. No, she definitely did it to hurt Kat. And it worked. We doing anything about it?'

'It would be hard to prove kidnap, when it's her granddaughter and she brought her home. The Crown Prosecution Service would laugh at us. No, I don't think there's anything we could pursue, but I'd love half an hour in a room with her where she couldn't get out, and I could detail every transgression her bloody son made, every murder, every beating, all the drugs he sold. I'd like her to see the statements from his cohorts when they all started talking – maybe then she'd see that it was nothing to do with Kat, she'd only known him for five years tops, and he'd certainly kept his business away from her.'

'So we forget it?'

'We do. She flies off into the sunset early tomorrow morning, so let's wish her bon voyage and hope she'll soon be back visiting her son's grave. Sometimes, Hannah, you have to know when to let something go, when it's the right time to ignore something because it's not worth the hassle it would cause. Something like Leon Rowe's missing left hand.'

'You think...'

Tessa held up her own left hand. 'I choose not to think. But Danny McLoughlin would be alive today if whoever shot that hand off had done it to his head instead. Come on, let's go.'

They easily found a table, and Tessa explained to the owner what they were doing. They dealt with her first so that she could release her staff one at a time, until they were finished.

Lucie Davison was the last one to be interviewed. She sat down and smiled. 'Good to see you again. Are you allowed to tell me how Marnie is? She used to be in here fairly regularly, but since that horrible day she hasn't been anywhere near. Too painful I suppose.'

'I don't think she goes out at all,' Tessa said. 'It's hit her very hard.'

'Then I'll make time to go and see her. We can talk about Orla, that's maybe what she needs. It must be an awful feeling to know that the last words she heard from her daughter were "See you after four, Mum", and it didn't actually happen.'

Hannah made a note on the pad.

'Can we go back to that? Orla actually said that? In your original statement you didn't mention it. You said she left here after four, and that her plans were to walk to Hope.'

Lucie closed her eyes as if thinking back to that dark, wet and windy afternoon. Neither of the two police officers spoke. They waited.

'Orla definitely said I'll see you after four to her mum,' Lucie eventually confirmed. 'Then Marnie said she was going home to do some baking. She wanted to make an apple pie for dessert because she was doing a special meal for her and Andy. That was all I heard from them, and I only heard that because I was serving someone near the door when Marnie was leaving. She nodded at Orla, and left.'

'Lucie,' Tessa said, 'I'm going to leave you with Hannah while you sign this addition to your earlier statement. Thank you for your help. I'm going to chat with your boss to see if she heard Orla say it, and then we'll leave you to get on with your job. Is there anything else at all that you've not remembered before? And don't worry about not mentioning this in your earlier statement, this is why we do second visits. The human mind is a fickle creature.'

'I really can't think of anything to do with her mum,' Lucie said, 'but I'm sure it was that afternoon when she rang her dad. Not her dad, Andy, I mean.'

'Did she say why she rang him?'

'No, but she spoke to him, she didn't leave a voicemail. It was obvious it was a conversation, not a quick "Hi, it's me. I'll ring you later" type of thing. Only lasted a minute or so, and she made the call outside, we're not allowed to use our phones in here.'

'Thank you, Lucie.' Tessa stood and walked across to where the owner was serving a customer. They had a brief conversation in which she confirmed she hadn't heard Orla say anything to her mum, but she had seen Orla make the call outside the café.

Back in the car, the two women turned to each other. Tessa spoke first. 'Now all we have to find out is whether Orla did go home before her plan to walk to Hope kicked in, was the reason for going home her pregnancy, and what the fuck did she ring Andy about? Let's go back and get in that conference room. We certainly saved the best till last.'

'And these were the ones really on the extreme periphery of Orla's life, yet they've been the ones to deliver something new.' Hannah shook her head. 'Let's go and grab some doughnuts – it could be a long afternoon.'

'We've left a tea rooms who sell doughnuts. Why do we always complicate things?' Tessa, driving for once, switched on the ignition, and drove carefully through Castleton. The doughnuts were picked up in Hathersage Café, and transported safely to the conference room.

It was indeed a long afternoon. The hot water urn had been set up and was good to go, tea and coffee supplies were by its side, along with bottles of water and the precious doughnuts.

Everyone was present at the specified time, and Hannah handed out bundles of paperwork that she had spent her lunch break photo-copying.

'Thank you for being on time,' Tessa said. 'We'll crack on with it till half past two, then have a half hour break. This is going to be a lot of work and I don't want anybody to have a frazzled brain because of it. Besides, we have doughnuts. So, in your packs you have copies of every reinterview. We must have had some really enthusiastic uniforms on this job, because some of the notes are extensive, but they need reading through carefully. This has been a massive undertaking that is now complete, and so we mustn't miss anything. Hopefully Hannah has put them into the same order, so we'll read the statement, and discuss it. Hannah will take notes of anything that we consider worth a mention, and then we'll move on to the next one. That okay with the three of you?'

Hannah, Dave and Ray said 'yes, boss' at the same time, and opened their file folders. Hannah pointed out that there was order in the way she had collated them – there were only three that hadn't had any changes, and they had been placed at the top.

There was silence as they read Clarice Travers's statement.

'Okay,' Tessa said, 'thoughts? Comments?'

'No changes,' Dave said. 'I think Clarice has too much on her plate with Ernie to take notice of anything, to be honest. Lovely lady, but saw nothing and knows nothing, in my opinion.'

They agreed with his words, and moved on. Tessa was pleased to see the three of them taking notes, and after talking through six of the statements, she called a halt. 'Okay, let's get a drink and talk about something else for a bit. We need to take a step back for a few minutes.'

'Okay, boss, I'll get them,' Ray said. 'Everybody want coffee?'

All three nodded. He made the drinks, handed them around and placed the pile of doughnuts in the middle of the table. 'We need the sugar,' he said with a grin.

'Thanks, Ray. How's your lad doing?' Tessa asked. Ray's son, Ben, had been the one to find Leon Rowe's hideout, which had ultimately led to the murderer's death.

'He's doing fine. Once he'd got over the shock, I think he felt quite proud really. And he's never told any of his pals about his part in it. The good thing that's come out of it is that he wants to join the police force as soon as he's old enough. I can't make up my mind how I feel about that, deep down, but it's his decision without any suggestions from me, so I think he'll do it. It's not an easy job, being a copper, not with the increase in knife crime and gangs of youngsters roaming the streets, but he seems set on doing it.'

They carried on talking about anything but the job in hand for ten more minutes, then returned to the files.

'Okay, to check we're on the same one, this is...' she glanced to the top of the page. 'Rory McIver. There's a good Scottish name. Interviewed by you, Dave.'

'Yes, boss. And it might sound like a Scottish name, but he's definitely a Derbyshire lad, born in the house he still lives in, and he's eighty-two. Sharp as anything. You'll not know him because he wasn't in church on the day we did the initial interviews after the service, but he was on the regular churchgoers list. I spoke to him first in the week following, but he was a bit distracted. His wife had

had a fall, and he was having to do everything – cooking, cleaning, looking after her. It's why he wasn't in church that day, she'd fallen while she was getting ready to go.'

Tessa glanced down at the new section of the old man's statement. 'He saw a car?'

'He did. It started by my saying how fantastic a position his house is in. It overlooks the hills, and it's virtually the last in Castleton, the last before the end of terrace next door. Then there's nothing but hillside. I asked where the road goes after the houses finish, and he said nowhere; it stops about a hundred yards further on, at the spot where the Peakshole Water becomes more than a stream. It widens at that point and it's always fast flowing and what he termed as "busy", before settling down as it reaches the middle of Castleton and becomes more placid.'

'He had no description of this car?'

'I left him thinking about it. He said he would ring if he could remember the make. He knows it was the same night as Orla disappeared, because of the atrocious weather. They've got a dog, a yapping little thing that never stopped all the time I was there, and he normally takes her out about five every evening for a little walk around the village, but that evening he took her as far as the front garden, in the pouring rain, and let her do her business there. While he was trying to shelter under a tree, he heard the car. It carried on past his house, and he said at the time he thought they must be strangers who didn't know they would have a hell of a job turning around, because they would have to come back down. It was a small car, light coloured, and with two people in it. That's all the information he could give me because he returned inside before the car reappeared.'

She looked at him. 'Why didn't you tell me last night?'

'I didn't get back here to pick up my own car till nine. I picked up the memo about attending this meeting this afternoon, and I hoped Rory would come good with the make of the car before we started, so we'd have something more concrete to look at. And I was bloody tired, ma'am.'

She sighed. 'I'm sorry, Dave. You did everything right. It's me jumping on every little point. He hasn't come back to you then?'

'No, but I went from his house up to the end of this road, and that's why I was so late back, ma'am.'

The second time he'd called her ma'am and not boss. Inwardly Tessa cringed. She'd feel better when he reverted to boss. All her team knew she didn't like ma'am, and she knew she was only called that in front of senior officers or when they were pissed off with her. There were no senior officers present...

'I believe we should get forensics up there,' Dave continued, 'but we have to bear in mind it's been virtually non-stop rain since this poor lass died, so tyre tracks are simply not there. However, one thought did occur to me. And this is only a thought.'

The others leaned forward.

'I don't think a stranger would know of this weird little road. Rory says there's only me been up there and I certainly didn't know it. I hadn't clocked it was an unfinished road. That's how Rory described it, anyway, and that's a good description. When you get there it sort of stops and becomes a hillside. To the right is the water, and it was in full spate last night. The side of the road dips down into the water so it would be very easy to roll a body into it, but there's no guarantee where the body will go after that, there's a lot of water at that point. I think the search team found her before they climbed that high, so didn't know of this possible spot for dumping her.'

'Give me a minute to think,' Tessa said.

The others remained silent. Hannah scribbled a note on her pad, but said nothing.

Tessa eventually placed her hands on the table and pushed back her chair. 'Let's go now. Dave, get us a car, will you. Hannah, rebook this room for tomorrow if we can, and I'll hide the doughnuts in my office. Ray, can you quickly print off half a dozen small cars, all light-coloured – say a C1, an Aygo, a Fiat 500, a Fiesta, and a couple of others. Make sure they're small, and we'll see if anything jogs Mr McIver's memory.'

Hannah pushed her notepad over to Tessa. 'I predicted your next words, boss,' she said with a laugh. Written in capitals on the pad was LET'S GO NOW.

'Smart arse,' Tessa said.

CHAPTER THIRTY-NINE

Ninety minutes later, and with Dave driving because he knew where the small road was, they reached Rory McIver's house. Dave pulled up to show them which one it was, but then suggested they head on up to the end of the road as it was already starting to go dark.

They parked where it was possible to turn the car around fairly easily, and then walked the rest of the way. There was no pavement; twelve inches from the road edge, on both sides, was a dry stone wall. Where these walls stopped, the road stopped. The ground rolled away, and there was an incline down to the swollen waters of Peakshole Water.

'Perfect spot,' Tessa said. 'How easy would it be to drag a body out of a car, and simply roll it until it hit the water. Job done, into the car, turn it around and go home. Seeing this, imagining that night, it seems to me it makes a mockery of Andy Harrison's alibi.'

'We know he spoke to Orla that afternoon, and he could have arranged to meet her. It would only take five minutes to kill her, she was tiny, and dump her here before heading off home to wifey.'

'We know that, do we? The phone call?' Dave asked.

'We do.'

'Have we been told, Ray?'

'Oh, shut up, you two. Dave, I apologise for being a dickhead. Now can we get back onto the real stuff. I want forensics out here first thing tomorrow morning. I don't think for a minute they'll find stuff; the rain will have taken anything that would have been helpful, but we have to go through the motions. Hannah, can you ring and organise that? Dave, can you liaise with them, please? Show them where to park vehicles for safety, we don't want any vans rolling into this bloody river.'

Dave grinned. 'No problem, boss,' and winked at her.

'And stop winking at me. Let's go see our Mr McIver. He's expecting us.'

'Bet we get scones,' Dave said.

'So that's what took you so long last night? Scones at the McIvers?'

He held up his hands. 'Guilty.'

Dave turned the car around in five moves, and the others clapped. It wasn't necessary for him to take a quick course in dry stone walling.

'Wait until all the forensic and scene of crime vans turn up tomorrow. Glad I won't be here,' he said. 'It's fairly easy outside the McIver place, but here it isn't.'

McIver was waiting at the door. 'I was watching you from the bedroom window.'

'You can see that far up?'

'Oh, aye. There's nothing wrong with my eyesight, it's my legs that don't do so well these days. Come in, let me introduce you to the wife, Eileen.'

Introductions out of the way, the four officers sat down at the kitchen table and placed the six photographs of small cars on it. Eileen was busy making drinks for them, and buttering scones.

Rory pulled the pictures towards him one at a time, then sat back thoughtfully. 'Give me a minute. I want to bring that night to mind. I saw the back and side of the car, and I'm trying to remember anything else.'

Eileen carried the two teas Dave and Ray had requested, then she paused and tapped the Aygo. 'I've been in one of them.' She smiled. 'Not a lot of room and we struggled to get the boxes of stuff into its tiny boot, but she didn't hang about driving back. Nice little car. It's that colour as well.'

Rory looked at her. 'It's Marnie Harrison's car, isn't it.'

'Yes,' Eileen said, and turned round to get the two coffees Tessa and Hannah had ordered. 'She's been up here a couple of times, always grumbled about the tightness of turning the car around, even the size of hers.'

'Mr McIver?' Tessa said.

'Look, it was a dreadful night, one of the worst we've had in a long time, and I was sheltering under the tree so didn't see it properly. I saw two people in the front seat, I saw the side and back end of the car only, but out of all of these, I would say that one,' and he pointed at the Aygo,' is as close as dammit to what I saw. It has a distinctive set of back lights, shaped like a boomerang. Yes, it was an Aygo.'

The Aygo was collected from the Harrisons' home that night, for a detailed forensic inspection. Marsden ordered a SOCO team into the house, with instructions to pay particular attention to the kitchen and to remove anything that could have been used as a blunt force instrument.

Marnie and Andy Harrison were taken in, and kept overnight in separate cells until they could be questioned the following day.

· · ·

Tessa felt wide-awake, her energy levels at a high peak. At eleven o'clock, as she was thinking about trying to get some sleep, Phil Anderton, the man in charge of the SOCO team tearing apart the Harrison house, rang her. They had found a Nike backpack concealed in an empty plastic carrier bag and covered with other carrier bags, hanging in the pantry. It contained a mobile phone, a scan picture of a foetus, and various cards inside a purse confirming the bag belonged to Orla French. Her name was also written inside the front flap.

He added that the wooden rolling pin found in the cupboard appeared to have dark stains on it, and that if it was blood it would be confirmed as early as possible the next morning.

She thanked him, and walked through to her own kitchen. She considered ringing Hannah, but decided against it – why should both of them have a sleepless night.

Tessa felt sick that they had missed everything for so long.

Marnie Harrison had acted her socks off from the word go. The distraught mother, fooling everybody. Nadine Bond would be livid. She had given every care and consideration to the family, looking after Marnie when she appeared to be at her lowest ebb... Why would this woman, this mother, kill her only daughter?

And then Tessa knew. It was all about Andy. Marnie's love and need for the man had showed from the beginning, and even when she had told him to leave, he had only been away a couple of days before she told him to go back home. She couldn't live without him, and Orla had threatened that. If Orla lived, and had the baby, Marnie would have had to make Andy go. For good.

The fact that the bag was in the house proved that Orla had gone home first, before intending to set off on the walk into Hope. To fill in the picture properly, Tessa knew she had to get Marnie talking, confessing. That meant having as many facts at her finger-tips as possible, before going into that interview room. She needed confirmation that it was blood on that rolling pin, and even more imperative that it was Orla's.

Tessa sat down at the kitchen table, and pulled a notepad towards her. Time to put her brain into the right gear, and plan out the next day's interviews. She would start with Andy Harrison.

She paused for a moment and wondered what he must be thinking. He was probably expecting to be arrested for his stepdaughter's murder, and heading for a major meltdown knowing he hadn't done it. Had he ever considered Marnie might be a prime candidate for a charge of filicide? Was he thinking it now?

Tessa knew that they would probably be releasing Andy Harrison after his interview; they had known from the beginning that his alibi was unbreakable, but he wouldn't be allowed to go home. The house was a crime scene, and would remain so for a few days.

She focussed on the list again, and wrote down questions that required answers. And Castleton could get ready for an invasion of journalists and television crews once this bit of news broke.

Tessa managed two hours of sleep, then showered, grabbed a couple of slices of toast and a travel mug of coffee, and headed into Chesterfield. It was going to be a long day.

CHAPTER FORTY

By ten o'clock, Tessa had the information she needed. Inside the Aygo, they had lifted Orla's fingerprints, very much to be expected as it was her mother's car. They had also found minute traces of her blood on the passenger seat's back, presumably where her head had rested during transport to the dump site. The wound caused by the rolling pin had smeared the seat's back.

The rolling pin bore traces of the same blood; it had been scrubbed, but the stain remained. Tessa gathered up everything she needed and headed to the interview room, where Andy Harrison was sitting quietly.

His stomach was churning; he felt sick. What on earth could Marsden have that could possibly point to him killing Orla? Absolutely nothing – he hadn't done it. And yet he'd been in a cell overnight, and he was seriously worrying that it was the first night of many to come.

And Marnie – they had brought her in at the same time. He hoped she was back home, her fragility was evident, and he didn't want to see a complete breakdown. He shuffled on the chair, not the most comfortable of seating he had ever used. The door opened.

Tessa walked across to the table, placed a couple of files on it, and switched on the recorder.

'Andrew Harrison, DI Tessa Marsden, DS Hannah Granger and duty solicitor Ursula Pentland. Interview room three, 10.05.' Tessa checked her phone and added the date.

Tessa looked through her file, then lifted her eyes to meet Harrison's white face. 'Andy, I want to go back to the night of Orla's murder. I want you to talk to me about Marnie. Tell me what she was like.'

'Marnie?' He frowned. 'She was busy with our evening meal. Just putting in the apple pie, and flapping because she hadn't had time to go out and get the rosé wine we both enjoy. She said she had a headache, and she closed her eyes for half an hour, which extended into an hour, making her late. I left her to her pie-making and went straight back out to get the wine.'

'Where did the wine come from?'

'The pub. I went in Marnie's car, because I intended nipping to the wine shop in Hope, but the weather was so bad I only went as far as the pub, then straight back home. I had a brief chat with the barmaid, so I must have been gone ten minutes at the most.'

'You used the Aygo?'

'I did.'

'Why?'

'My car is too big for running around the little villages. It's fine for my daily trips to Manchester, but if we need to go around Castleton, we tend to use the Aygo.'

'Did you notice anything about the car's interior?'

'Only that both front seats were damp, but I figured Marnie had been doing her good Samaritan deeds and had given someone a lift because of the heavy rain. It wouldn't have been the first time.'

Hannah was making notes, and she glanced up at her boss, waiting for the next question.

'It didn't occur to you that it could have been Orla in that passenger seat?'

'Of course not, she had said she was walking...' his voice trailed away as he realised the implication in Tessa's question.

'So, Andy,' Tessa moved on, giving him no time to process his thoughts, 'what did Orla ring you about earlier that afternoon?'

'She didn't...'

'She did. We have your phone records and we have confirmation from witnesses. Orla told them she was ringing you. So...?'

There was a long silence and he looked at Ursula Pentland, almost begging her to step in to stop him having to answer. He received no support, other than an encouraging smile.

'She told me she was going to talk to her mother before setting off for Hope, unless the weather got any worse. If it did, she would put it off until the day after, when Marnie and Orla had planned a day at the shops. I asked her what she was going to talk about, and she said there had been developments in her life. That was exactly how she phrased it. We now know she meant the pregnancy, but then I thought she meant this person at the church, the one she'd used as a reason for seducing me. The weather did get worse, so I just assumed from Marnie's lack of conversation, that Orla had put off the great reveal until the following day.'

'Thank you, Andy. Now let me give you a different scenario. We believe that Orla wasn't talking about the man at church, we believe she was talking about the pregnancy, and because of the detailed scan she had that morning, she already knew who the father was. It could only have been you. I think she realised what this would do to your marriage, and she needed to try to explain to her mum how it had happened.'

Harrison's eyes were locked onto DI Marsden's face. 'But Marnie was as shocked as I was when she found out how everything had played out. She didn't know in advance.'

'Exactly. She didn't. I don't think Orla managed to tell her everything. I suspect she told her she was pregnant, and how sorry she was, but that you were the father. Marnie was baking that afternoon, and I think in her grief and distress, she picked up the first heavy implement she could lay her hands on, and hit Orla on the head with the rolling pin. Orla's blood's been found on it.'

'No,' Andy Harrison moaned. 'No, not Marnie...'

'Marnie knew she was about to lose you. With that baby on the scene, there was no way your marriage could survive, and I think she put you before her daughter and grandchild.' Tessa was relentless. She could see how close Andy was to collapse. She saw Ursula begin to open her mouth, and she said, 'No!'

'Marnie killed her daughter. She strangled her, then manoeuvred her to that little Aygo. By this time they were both wet through, and although Orla was very petite, it would have been a struggle getting her in that small car. Marnie drove through the village, and up into the hills, a place she knew because she visited with Eileen McIver, a dead end road where there would be nobody to see what she was doing. Unfortunately she was seen driving by the McIver house, and the car was identified. You hadn't even left Manchester at this point, Andy.'

Andy dropped his head onto his arms, now resting on the table, and the room went quiet. He was stifling sobs; his shoulders were shaking, and finally he lifted his head. 'Marnie's confirmed this?'

'No, I'm about to go and interview her. We have proof that Orla was in the Aygo, Andy. Her blood was on the back of the seat where Marnie put her body to make it look as though she was a passenger. We believe she drove past the McIver home until she couldn't go any further, and then tipped Orla's body into the water. We also found Orla's Nike backpack hidden beneath empty carrier bags in your pantry, proving Orla was there that afternoon, and didn't set off for Hope straight after finishing work. Your home is a crime scene, and we have teams in there gathering evidence. I'm going to release you, Andy, and thank you for your cooperation. You won't be able to go home for a few days, but I will need to know where you're going in case we need to speak with you again.'

'Can I see Marnie?' He hesitated for a moment. 'Please.'

'I'm sorry, Andy, you can't. DS Granger will take you to the custody sergeant and see to your release.' Tessa stood, signed the interview out as finished, and left the room.

Marnie jumped when the cell door opened. At last – maybe she could see Andy now. She was escorted down a long corridor to the interview room, and asked to sit at the table. A young police constable was left with her, and Marnie stared around, taking in the bleakness of the room, the thick small-squared glass in the windows, the sound the key had made when she was locked in.

DI Marsden entered, her face showing no emotion.

'Where's Andy?'

'He's been released, Marnie.'

Hannah entered the room carrying a holdall which she placed between the two chairs the police officers would be using, and Tessa recorded the people present.

'I understand you don't want a duty solicitor.'

'That's right,' Marnie confirmed. 'I haven't done anything, so I don't need one.'

Tessa gave her a long stare, then looked down at the file she had carried in with her.

'Marnie, we are looking into the events of the night in November when your daughter, Orla, met her death.'

'It's about time,' Marnie responded. 'You've done very little so far.'

'What time did Orla arrive at your home that day?'

'She didn't. You know she said she was going straight to Hope.'

'Let's take a step back, Marnie. You left Orla's café about one, then went home. What did you do after arriving at your house?'

'I did some baking. I made a lemon drizzle cake, and I made an apple pie for dessert that night.'

'Were you still baking when Orla arrived home?'

'Orla didn't come home.'

Tessa gave a sigh. 'Okay. Although we have this in your statement, I'd like you to repeat for the recording what Orla was wearing when she left for work in the morning.'

There was the first sign of hesitation in Marnie. 'Erm... she had on a red padded full-length coat, my black knee-high boots and her waitress uniform underneath.'

'And her bag? Presumably she took a change of clothing for her sleepover at Emily's.'

'She took her Nike backpack.' Marnie interlaced her fingers.

'So, if she didn't come home, presumably the bag was with her when she was attacked.'

'That's right.' Now she was defiant.

Tessa and Hannah exchanged a brief glance, and Hannah reached down into the holdall and produced an evidence bag. She lifted it onto the table.

'Can you look at this bag, Marnie, and tell me if it is Orla's.'

She shuffled uncomfortably. 'How should I know? There must be thousands of these bags.'

Tessa leaned forward, removed the backpack from the evidence bag and placed it on the table. She opened the front flap and written inside was the name Orla French. 'Can we now agree this is Orla's bag? For the tape, I am showing Harrison the name inside the front flap of the bag. Marnie, is this Orla's?'

Marnie nodded.

'For the tape, please, Marnie.'

'Yes, it is.' It was almost a growl.

Hannah then pulled another evidence bag from the holdall and placed it on the table. It contained a mobile phone, a purse and a photograph.

'This is Orla's phone and purse, and this is a scan photograph of your grandchild. We have another evidence bag with a nightie, a pair of pants and a fresh jumper in, presumably clothes she would have needed for the next day.'

Marnie stared. 'How... where...?' She seemed to recover for a moment. 'Did you find these in the river with her?'

Tessa gave a small laugh. 'They would hardly be in such good condition if we had, Marnie. No, we found them in your pantry, inside a carrier bag that held other scrunched-up carrier bags. We also found this.'

Hannah delved down by her side and produced yet another evidence bag, this one containing a rolling pin.

Tessa placed it on the table, and Marnie reached forward to touch the bag.

'Do you recognise this rolling pin, Marnie?'

'Yes, it was my grandmother's.'

'There is blood evidence on this rolling pin that has been identi-fied as belonging to Orla. We removed this from your kitchen, Marnie. We believe your kitchen was the place that Orla died as a result of you hitting her on the head to immobilise her, then stran-gling her. She was then transferred in your car to the hillside above Castleton and tipped into the Peakshole Water. We have concrete evidence of that as well.'

Marnie remained silent.

'Do you have anything to say, Marnie?'

'Can I see Andy?'

'Marnie, I would heartily recommend that you now avail your-self of a duty solicitor, or get one of your own. It will be some time before you see Andy again.'

. . .

Even with Oliver Waring by her side, Marnie continued to deny having any knowledge of her daughter's death. She made several requests to see Andy, all of which were ignored. Eventually Waring asked to confer with his client.

When Marnie's confession to the murder of her daughter was read back to her, she cried constantly throughout. She cried through the charges part of the process and she cried even harder when she was told there was no chance of her seeing Andy.

When Tessa and Hannah walked into the briefing room, there were cheers and claps from everyone, but Tessa quietened them.

'I can't celebrate this one, it's just been one bloody tragedy morphing into another. Yes we have results on two dead girls, but we leave grieving families, a mother who will probably have to spend the biggest part of her life in prison, and Andy Harrison... who knows what will happen to him.' Tessa placed some money on the table. 'Go for a drink tonight, boys and girls, but if you don't mind, I won't be joining you.'

EPILOGUE

Orla French's funeral was over, and Andy Harrison had left the village, unable to cope with the consequences of his wife's actions. The house would sell very quickly, and Castleton would settle back down to how it had been before two girls were murdered.

Kat stood at the front of the church and inspected the tree. With Christmas only three weeks away, the excitement was starting to build. She walked to the candle stall and lit candles for Mandy Williamson and Orla French, then she knelt at the altar rail and prayed individual prayers for everyone who had passed through her life during the past few weeks. It took a long time.

Eventually she stood and rubbed her knees. 'Old age,' she grumbled to herself, then went outside to her car. In the boot were five Christmas wreaths, all with names and messages attached to them: Craig Adams, Danny McLoughlin, Mandy Williamson, Orla French and one that simply said *Rest in Peace*. She hooked them over her left arm, squealed ouch every time a holly leaf stabbed her, and set off for her walk to all the graves that mattered the most to her. She dropped the garden twine and scissors into her pocket.

At each one, she tied the Christmas wreath to the headstone, said a small prayer and stood for a moment in remembrance of the person they had been. Her final stopping place was the grave desecrated by Jacob Thorne as he buried Mandy Williamson. The mud had been removed, the ground levelled, although it would be spring before the surrounding grass began to recover.

Kat repeated her earlier actions, and then walked back to her car.

Doris was holding Martha up to the office window, both of them looking for Kat returning from her church business.

'Look, Martha, is that Mummy's car coming down the hill? Yeah! It is.' Martha punched her in the nose. 'Ouch, little monkey. Don't you know I'm a black belt?'

They watched as Kat pulled up outside, and Martha let out a little squeal as she spotted Kat. Doris released the door, and Martha lunged to get to her mummy.

'Hey, you,' Kat laughed, and grabbed the wriggling little girl. 'I love you, too.'

Mouse's office door opened and she wandered through, holding her mobile phone to her ear. She spoke, her voice soft. 'I'll be there, I promise. And of course I'll invite my two partners. This is one brilliant amalgamation, and we'll all be happy to share in the celebrations. Bye, Joel.' She listened for a moment longer, then giggled, before disconnecting.

'Something we should know?' Doris asked.

'Oh, that was Joel. He wants the three of us to go to Manchester next week. They're having a big launch to celebrate the amalgamation of Connection with them. He said it looks good if all the partners are there, so that we can spread ourselves around to talk to people. We could potentially pick up more business from this, because it's the top companies who will be attending.'

Doris smiled. 'Can I just point out to you two numbskulls yet again, that I am not a partner, not even an employee.'

Kat and Mouse turned to each other and smiled.

'Okay, Nan, there's something we want to talk to you about,' Mouse said.

'About you not being a partner...' Kat followed on.

THE END

ACKNOWLEDGMENTS

There are many people to thank for being involved in some way with the production of this book. Firstly I have to thank Bloodhound Books, particularly Fred and Betsy Freeman for their continued faith in me, and also for the staff members who never fail to come up with answers to queries: Sumaira Wilson, Alexina Golding, Heather Fitt and Tara Lyons. Thank you one and all.

During the writing lifetime of Murder Unearthed, I ran several competitions where the winners got to be mentioned in the book – my grateful thanks go to Marnie Harrison, Nadine Bond, Mandy Williamson, Alyson Read and – accidentally – Sue Rowe. Sue Rowe didn't win anything, she simply happened to have the same name as a character who has been in all three of the Kat and Mouse books, so I couldn't change the name! I contacted her, explained the situation, and she was more than happy to be in the book. Problem solved!

In addition to competition winners, I also need to thank others who allowed me to use their names: Siân Dawson and Lucie Davison.

The name for Little Mouse Cottage was another competition won by Kim Howell. Thank you, Kim, it was so right.

ARC group members, who read my manuscript before it goes live on Amazon, are such an essential part of my book launch. Thank you so much ladies and gentlemen, your reviews during the first two days are so essential and so amazing.

Sarah Hodgson is my one beta reader. She sees the book before anyone, but with this one it caused some stress, which created laughter in me but not in Sarah. I sent her the book up to the end of chapter thirty-seven, and asked her if she knew who the murderer was. She didn't (which was the point of the exercise) but she also didn't have the rest of the book. Thank you, Sarah, you're a star.

My editor, Morgen Bailey, is more than worthy of my thanks. She takes my manuscript, demolishes it and sticks it back together with consummate ease, sends me reams of notes explaining why she has done it, and then puts little ticks where I get something right, to make me feel better. I love her. Thank you, Morgen with an e.

And finally a massive thank you to everybody who has read Murder Undeniable, Murder Unexpected and now Murder Unearthed. This is the end of my trilogy, but... there will be a fourth and final book for Kat, Mouse and Doris. This is planned for an October 2019 release. Your response to my change in genre has been overwhelming, but I haven't forgotten the psychological thriller aficionados out there – there will be a new book at the beginning of 2020!

Anita Waller
    March 2019

Printed in Great Britain
by Amazon